Gargantuan Gigolo

by

John Davies

Trafford
PUBLISHING®

ISBN: 978-1-4251-9022-4 (Soft)

Our mission is to efficiently provide the world's finest, most comprehensive book publishing service, enabling every author to experience success. To find out how to publish your book, your way, and have it available worldwide, visit us online at www.trafford.com.

Rev. Date 8/7/2009

 www.trafford.com

North America & international
toll-free: 1 888 232 4444 (USA & Canada)
phone: 250 383 6864 ♦ fax: 812 355 4082

FOREWORD

The emancipation of the fair sex is partly responsible for the intriguing increase in the demand for male prostitutes. I make no apology to readers who find the topic obnoxious. My advice to those people is to consign this book to the rubbish-bin-pronto! But as a former hard-nosed newspaper journalist, now a fiction writer, I am essentially a curious being, someone compelled to deal with the facts of life as they unfold. What led me to writing this novel was a news item in Spain's highly respected daily journal 'El Pais' which announced that 'ANELA', an association of Spanish whore-house owners, was helping to establish a brothel exclusively for the use of women clients in Valencia. It was a pioneering step even in Spain, a nation that adopts a liberal stance towards the sex-trade.

'*Today women are free, they have considerable acquisitive power, in some cases more than men, and they have the same needs,*' explained José Luis Roberto, Secretary General of '*ANELA*'. '*It proves that prostitution is about sex and not, as feminists would have it, about exploiting women.*'

That controversial statement was enough to set me off on the research trail and eventually to pen this work in succession to my previous novels '*Lorenzo's Legacy*' and '*Inseperable*'. Remember this is a work of fiction. All the characters are products of the author's imagination. But they are out there in the twilight world of the sex-trade which is moving rapidly to a new innovative level where women can express their natural feelings just like men have always done.

Who is disingenuous enough to cast the first stone?

John Davies

As this novel is located almost entirely in Spain I have included a Spanish-English glossary of certain words and phrases at the rear of the book to assist readers to follow dialogue. JD

DEDICATION

It is a pleasure to dedicate this novel to my long-term friend and colleague, Bristol-based David Foot, one of the finest journalists I ever came across in my career

'Footy' is a great guy who has penned a pithy sports column for the highly respected '*Western Daily Press*' for nigh on thirty years? An awesome word spinner, a talented tale-teller, a sympathetic student of life. A modest man who opted to ply his trade in a small pond, choosing also to nurture his marriage and bring up a lovely family. But make no mistake 'Footy' is a better journalist than many I knew in, what used to be, Fleet Street.

I also place on record my gratitude to three ladies who have coded the colours of my life. Beryl French, who has trial-read all my earlier fiction work before they were despatched to my excellent publishers, *Trafford*. Also my beloved late wife, Rosa, and the lovely Renate who have always been there for me.

Having spent many hours often burning the candle at both ends, researching and writing this novel

'*GARGANTUAN GIGOLO*', I don't know whether to sympathise with, or feel jealous of, the randy guys who sell their sexual skills, or pity the lonely women who yearn for real affection and believe they can find it in the sleazy world of sex-for-sale.

John Davies

CONTENTS

1

Not even one macho male at the crowded tables in the renowned Restaurante Los Caracoles failed to turn his head as the bewitchingly attractive Angela Di Silva glided in to join her husband for a late lunch at the highly rated eaterie *'rustica'* in the throbbing heart of Barcelona's *Barrio Chino.*

Apart from her jet-black hair which rippled half way to the nape of her swan-like neck, vibrant eyes of emerald green, peach-blossom complexion, stunningly coloured nails enhancing tapered fingers, her hour-glass figure was breathtaking. The *caballeros* eyed her hungrily as if they were lustily famished. Their companions, be they e*sposas o amadas,* were either thrown into pangs of jealousy or rapturous envy at her beauty, reputation and wealth.

For this was one of the most notorious women in the teeming capital of Catalonia and was well known throughout the region, and beyond, as *'Adorable Angela from Asuncion'.* She had arrived in Spain from her homeland in Paraquay, at the age of 16, to work as a street-walker. Within a year she was the star attraction in Barcelona's world famous brothel *'La Huerta'.* Three years down the line, with a considerably impressive, and ever-growing, bank balance, she married one of the celebrated whore house's wealthiest clients. Within the year she handed proud husband, Klaus Di Silva a bonny baby boy.

Backed by Di Silva's huge stash of cash, harvested mainly from one of the largest wholesale jewellery firms in Spain, Angela, now in her early thirty's, and at her peak, had established her own escort agency.

Throughout the centuries prostitutes have often sunk to

the lowest level of the social scale because their profession was considered degrading. But Angela was one of the few harlots who historically acquired wealth and power through marriage. Although she had never thought about it that way, she followed the pillow-pattern of the Byzantine Empress, Theodora, who became the wife of Justian 1. Theodora liked to be described as an actress in the grand sense, but everyone in Rome knew that she was a strumpet who first took the Emperor's gold in payment while she lay straddled across the royal couch.

But on this day, as Angela looked down from *Los Caracoles* celebrated minstrel gallery at the perspiring chefs cooking their meal on the blazing *hornillos* and red-hot *parrillas* in the open-plan *cocina* below, her astute brain was working on how to talk her ever-loving *esposo* Klaus to funding the new project she had in mind. Hitherto her escort agency *'Adorable Angela's'* had been dedicated exclusively to offering sexy-looking women for hire.

She presented the agency's male clients the chance to be wined and dined with high style in the company of her attractive girls.

Having paid the hefty restaurant bill, the sexually aroused client would be offered the chance to join his shapely dinner companion between the sheets at either one of *'Adorable Angela's'* luxuriously appointed *apartmentos di amor* or at a hotel of their choice at a cost of 1,000 Euros plus a generous *propina* for the girl. The Agency would recover €600 from the girl for expenses while she could go back the next morning to sleep the day away in the comforting knowledge that her bank account would be richer by another €400 when the monthly cheque arrived from the Agency.

With 25 girls working around the Spanish Peninsula in Madrid, Valencia, Sevilla as well as Barcelona the agency

2

gleaned a staggering €15.000,00 or more on a good night for Angela who arranged all the bookings and arrangements over the phone. Payments to the Agency could only be paid in advance by bank card to avoid defaulters, unless Angela knew the client well enough to allow them credit.

The girls were paid each month by cheque from the Agency while it was up to them how they wheedled a sizeable gratuity from their clients. Woe betide the customer who tried to cheat these attractive, but street-wise, hard-working whores. If he did he would go home not only one thousand euros poorer but bent double in agony from a well-aimed kick in his 'crown jewels' to remind him of his paltry pettiness.

Value for money was the message always preached by Angela to her girls. Any wayward lass who engendered a complaint from a client was quickly informed where the nearest brothel was or forcibly told to go back and walk the streets. It didn't happen very often. Angela's girls got to like the furs, jewels, dresses, shoes and expensive perfumes they could buy with the steady money they earned from the Agency. As the Di Silva's first course of mixed aubergines, peppers, tomatoes, and potatoes, listed on the menu as *tumbet*, followed by delicious *chuletas lechal con ajo*-chops of suckling pig cooked in garlic--was elegantly served accompanied with a bottle of full-bodied *Gran Reserva tinto Rioja* .

Angela chose her moment to broach the topic with her husband Klaus that had been buzzing through her brain all the morning.

'Klaus darling, did you read today's edition of El Pais?' noting, as she posed the query, the nod of approval accompanied by a wry smile from her spouse.

Di Silva's reply was typically to the point. *'Si, si Angela amado,'* he confirmed and then elaborated. *'The news item about the proposal to launch a brothel in Valencia, exclusively for women and serviced by male prostitutes. The first such bawdy house in Spain. You can see a business proposition in that development I am sure.*

'*Adorable Angela*' nodded enthusiastically and said: '*Let the Valencia people launch the cheap end of the business. What I have in mind is a nationwide escort service for lonely women manned by sexy men, who will provide them with a new experience. I have recently been approached by several women who, for one reason or another, have been spurned by their husbands.*

'*They need a remedy for their lonely frustrated, desperate condition and I aim to provide them with that. A first class service for neglected ladies. At a price!*'

Klaus Di Silva, handsome , elegantly dressed, nodded his distinguished head attractively greying at the temples, in approval of his wife's dissertation.

'*Angela liebling,*' he boomed, lapsing into German, one of the six languages he could speak fluently. '*In the ten years we have been married, ten happy years I should have said, and partners in the escort agency business I have never queried or had reason to doubt your acumen as a business woman. A very astute business woman at that. I am not about to do that now.*

'*Although, as I was brought up to honour the strict code of Spanish manhood I could never bring myself to approve of pimps. I call them creatures, who prey on prostitutes. As for men who sell their bodies for sex they are beyond the pale, as far as I am concerned. Neither can I condone a woman that betrays her husband and commits adultery. But I respect and understand your judgement that out there in the world there are women who are sexually starved because their husbands*

4

are frail, sick or too old to satisfy their physical needs.

'Therefore I approve of your idea to set up an escort agency for women willing to pay to be entertained and serviced by male prostitutes. I have so much respect for your skill in the sex business that I know your new agency will have style and dignity, giving privacy to the women who patronise it.

'I will arrange with the bank tomorrow for fifty thousand euros to be transferred to your Adorable Angela's Escort Service account to set up the new business. Now let me ask the sommelier to bring us a bottle of Los Caracoles best French champagne to celebrate the launching of our new business venture.'

As always, when Klaus was in such an expansive mood, Angela was overwhelmed by his support and understanding.

'Gracias, gracias darling,' she said stretching her slender right arm to stroke his hand.

'I married the best man in Spain.'

Klaus roared with laughter. 'Only Spain?', he asked. 'Why not Europe or even the world?'.

That is how the notorious 'Adorable Angela's Escort Agency for Women' was launched and a new macho dimension given to the oldest profession in the world.

* * *

2

Angela arose early next morning, quickly donning breeches, boots and helmet to go for her morning ride on Zephyr, the beautiful white thoroughbred gelding that her generous husband, Klaus, had bought her for a birthday present.

Although muscular and fast this elegantly toned equine athlete, a former Olympic Games cross-country eventer, as its well chosen name suggested, had a character like a brawny breeze. At least he did when Angela was astride the ornately tooled and pommeled Mexican saddle Klaus had also bought her. When she was first given the beautiful animal she was only a novice rider with a few lessons, as a schoolgirl at the local livery stable in her native Paraquay. But Zephyr completed her education as a horsewoman. If she prompted too much pace with her heels as they approached a fence Zephyr, ignoring his mistress's impetuosity, would apply the brakes, gently and unbidden, then clear the obstacle like a stag in full flight.

If the target hurdle was too formidable even for his considerable prowess Zephyr would cleverly veer clear of the fence without unseating Angela. During their years together Zephyr taught his mistress the intricacies of equestrianism. Now she was rated as one of the best amateur female riders in Catalonia and won several prizes at local gymkhanas while the wooden wall of Zephyr's home stall was a klaidoscope of rosettes.

Angela never forgot the help she got from her four-footed friend. In turn Zephyr knew how to nudge and apply sloppy kisses until she put her hand in her riding jacket pocket to find the pack of Polo Mints for which he had an insatiable liking.

On this particular morning she set Zephyr an invigorating gallop and felt a rush of adrenalin when she pointed his nose towards a five barred gate on her husband's estate. The astute gelding adjusted his pace and sailed gracefully over the gate.

It was just the boost she needed on a day when she would begin to organise her new escort agency and also absorb the interest of many sex-starved women in Spain, create revulsion in others, and envious criticism from machismo *caballeros* to whom the thought of women having to pay a man for sexual services was a slur on their own manhood. In the following weeks and months she brushed the criticism aside and would often strongly defend her views.

'Many men are so self-centred that they cannot accept that women have a need to be sexually satisfied,' she would argue. *'Men by nature are polygamist and can make love with many women yet, incongruously, believe they are not being unfaithful to their wives. While women who find the right man prefer not to change. My agency is aimed at meeting the needs of women, who for one reason or another, are neglected and sex-starved.'*

* * *

Angela, always alert and street-wise after her years as a hooker, noticed the handsome young man who loitered at the ferry-terminal end of Barcelona's *Rambla*, overlooked by the statue of Christopher Columbus significantly pointing towards America some several thousand miles away across the Atlantic. The lad was always standing there around lunch time every day obviously trying to pick up an interested lady amongst the thousands of tourists continually parading up and down Barcelona's famous street of flower-sellers. Good looking but down at heel in his faded jeans, tee-shirt and woolly hat Richard Martin was trying to earn a euro or two to pay for his scruffy hovel at the low class pension in the Bario

Chino red-light district. Desperation had transformed this middle-class product of an English public school into a male street-walker, a gigolo, albeit not a very successful one.

Many women looked, pondered and were tempted to take up what he was offering but were too timid in such a public area where it seemed the rest of the world was watching. Occasionally he managed to pull a trick for a measly ten euros but quite often the lady concerned was revolted when she saw the room where he lived with *cucarachas* crawling out of the cracks in the crumbling walls. There was no doubt he was on skid-row with little space to fall any lower down the social scale.

But where prostitution was concerned Angela Di Silva was a shrewd judge of style and marketable sex appeal. Experience made her see his potential in the business which she was an expert. She sensed that this physically attractive boy, scrubbed up and smartly suited, could be a puller. What she needed to find out was did he have enough class and finesse to take a woman out to dine at a top restaurant? Had he got any sexual hang-ups? Had he the patience to woo a woman, flatter her vanity, before taking her to bed, and then show the patience to satisfy her needs between the sheets?

On the books of her new agency she didn't want impetuous beach-boys with swollen penis who jump into bed and bang, crash, wallop finish the job in five minutes leaving the unfortunate client scratching her fanny in frustration.

He was there as usual after she had parked her Porsche near the Balearic Islands ferry terminal and had walked across the crowded square towards the Bario Chino. There leaning on a bollard outside the *tienda* that specialised in the sale of much sought after Lladro ceramic figures straight from the kilns at the famous *fábrica* in Valencia. Richard had chosen that spot to solicit because when he had left England

8

six years previously to become an undergraduate at the University of Valencia he partly paid for his food and lodgings from part time labouring work in the Lladro kilns. But he had fell foul of the straight-laced faculty chiefs when he was discovered in bed with a 17-year-old Spanish girl , a fellow student at the ancient University founded in 1510. He was ignominiously dismissed for breaking University rules.

* * *

It came as a shock when this mink-coated beauty came up to him and said: *'Follow me and I'll buy you lunch at a little tapas bar I know round the corner.'* She strode off without as much as a glance back with the almost arrogant certainty he would follow her. There was in fact no doubt that he would accept the impromptu invitation as, in anticipation, he mentally theorised: *'This could be my lucky day . At least it could be a meal ticket, or even better than that. This is a classy dame. I could elbow her for more than the usual ten euros, perhaps 50 or even a 100 euros. I only hope she has got a hotel room or an apartment . I can't take a chick of her standard to my flea-pit of a room.'*

Still the pipe-dream flowered as he followed Angela finding it difficult to keep up with her designer high-heels nimbly clattering along the ancient street tiles of the Bario Chino to the small *Delfin Tapas Bodega*. She ushered him to a secluded booth table where they were out of sight of the other clients. In an officious voice Angela ordered a bottle of *tinto Rioja Classico* and a huge tray of hot and cold *tapas* accompanied by two plates, cutlery and napkins.

Angela was impressed. Although he must have been hungry he was patient and polite as the *tapas* were prepared in the *cocina*. He manipulated the cutlery skilfully, and as he ate enthusiastically she noted that although his jeans and tee-shirt were threadbare they, like his finger nails were quite

9

clean. Although he was obviously on skid-row he had not quite reached the bottom rung of the ladder.

He described how he came from a respectable family in England where his father was a Church of England vicar. He had attended an exclusive college in Bristol and the future looked pretty good for him when he won a scholarship to the University of Valencia. He now regretted that he had been expelled from the University after that silly affair with a Spanish girl and he hoped that his father would never find out what had happened.

Angela approved the way he patiently ate his food and sipped his wine despite the fact he was probably starving and this was the best meal he had eaten for some time. They were all signs, she observed shrewdly, that he had enjoyed a genteel upbringing.

But first she had to teach him the facts of life if he wanted to cash in on the rich rewards on offer in the business of organised sex.

Having been well fed and wined the fantasy that he had been picked up by such an attractive woman was running amok in his mind. He was about to get a traumatic awakening for his escalating dreams.

'Now we have finished our comida, Senora, where would you like to go?' he asked, emboldened by the satisfaction of a full belly for the first time in weeks. *'I am afraid my room at the pension near here is shabby and I wouldn't want to take an elegant lady like you there. Have you an apartmento or do you prefer to go to a hotel.'*

Angela's bewitching smile belied the savagery with which she volleyed at him his first lesson into the art of becoming a top-earning male escort capable of attracting, frustrated,

10

well-heeled women to bed.

'*Listen buster, let me straighten you up,*' she spat as venomously as a cobra, swaying to the unmelodic wail of the snake charmer's flute. '*You didn't pick me up this morning. I am not lusting for your under-fucking-nourished body. I've fucked better guys than you before desayuno. For your information I am married to one of the richest and most powerful men in Barcelona. As I said you didn't pick me up today. I became your fucking meal ticket because I believe you could be useful to my organisation. In return I could transform you into quite a prosperous young man and set you up for life.*'

'*My name is Senora Angela Di Silva and I am the owner of Adorable Angela's Escort Agency which is the best escort agency in Spain, supplying beautiful escorts for well-heeled businessmen . These men pay one thousand euros for taking one of my attractive girls for dinner. The client pays all the costs. It is up to them what extra money they pay the girl escort if she consents to go to bed with him. Such a deal is a private matter between my girls and their clients. Now I am setting up and Escort Agency to service women's needs.*'

'*If I am going to take you on my book, groom and finance you, you will repay me with respect due to me as your boss. You have one foot in the gutter at the moment. Face facts you are almost on skid row with a poor future ahead.*'

'*Do you want to come on board or not?*'

Richard's reply exploded with the staccato of an automatic pistol.

'*I apologise Senora Di Silva for not recognising you,*' he snapped, overly anxious to convince Angela that he was not fool enough to look a gift horse in the mouth. '*You are right,*

I am in a desperate situation at the moment. I was thinking of appealing to the British Consulate in Barcelona to lend me the money for a flight back to England so that I can return to my family. But I have heard the Consulate do not hand out money for that purpose. In any case I have a lot of pride and I wouldn't want my mother and father to know what dire straits I am in. I will jump at the chance you are offering if you take me on.'

Angela was pleased that her initial judgement of this English boy was on target. He was just the kind of young man she wanted to recruit to the new escort agency. *'OK then Richard it is agreed,'* she smiled. *'The first thing we must do is to get you out of that awful place where you are staying. I have some better accomodation for you. A little apartment on the other side of the City. It is small but clean and respectable. But when you start work you will use one of my agency's luxury apartments to take your women clients back to. If you go and collect your belongings from the pension now I will take you to your own apartment where you can move in straight away. Tomorrow I will buy you some new clothes both for day and for evening wear when you are working.*

'So run along and collect your things from the pension and we will meet in half an hours time at the car park next to the ferry terminal. I'll be waiting in my car there for you. It is a red Porsche-so I wont be hard to find.'

So, excited at the prospect of what lay ahead, Richard sprinted to pack his humble belongings into a plastic supermarket bag, slipped the unshaven porter his last 10 centime coin and sped off to join his new boss.

* * *

12

3

By arrangement made with Richard Martin the previous day when she had installed him into a one-bedroom apartment in one of Barcelona's nicer dormitory areas Angela met him the following morning for a make-over she knew was essential if he was going to provide a sociable and sexy service to her lonely women clients.

She piled him into her Porsche and sped him to one of Barcelona's top mens' outfitters.

'Right Senor Lopez,' Angela addressed the portly manager, who in typical tailor style, greeted them adorned with a canary-yellow measuring tape draped around his neck. *'I want him completely kitted out. Two top quality day suits, lapels hand-stitched. Two evening suits of top quality, one with a black double breasted black jacket and the other with a white tuxedo. Measure him up now but don't cut the cloth until you conduct a final fitting in a month's time. He is going into training for the next four weeks and will hopefully put on muscle weight in the gymnasium.*

'I want shirts and all accessories to match the suits, including stylish shoes. Meanwhile give him a couple of off the peg outfits , with shirts and underwear to stand him in the next four weeks. Oh! Senor Lopez he will need athletic vests, shorts and Nike trainers. He's going to be working his bollocks off in the gym for the next month.'

'Take your clothes off Richard,' she snapped. *'Don't look so fucking shocked. Your snowy skin is not fucking precious and for God's sake drop those tatty jeans in the basura bin before they disintegrate with old age.'*

Richard's goose bumps appeared more from modesty than the chill of the outfitter's shop.

Yet the situation had caused him to embarrassingly experience a semi-erection. Angela, educated and alert to the signs of sexual arousement, noticed the respectable enormity of his manhood. *'Gargantuan, fucking gargantuan,'* she gloated complimentarily. *'You are going to make women's eyes water when they see that heinous hammer. That is after we teach you how to use your titanic tool properly.'*

The next stop, on what was to be a big day in Richard's induction into the seamy avocation of the escort agency world, was for a light lunch. Angela had chosen the venue carefully. An exclusive restaurant in a select area of Barcelona. a rendezvous he would be encouraged to take his clients to in his future career.

It was called *El Papagayo Rosada-The Pink Parrot-a costly establishment specialising in seafood and widely patronised by visiting Americans, English and wealthy Spanish businessmen.*

Angela ordered *Ensaladas Langostas* with a top of the range chilled white wine, without even giving Richard the courtesy of asking what food he would like. For the second time in 24 hours the astute Angela noted how correctly he handled the restaurant's elegant silver cutlery.

'At least I don't have to teach him how to use a knife and fork,' she thought.

* * *

Louis Samuels was the owner of the select *Gimnasio Campeóns* and no one could deny him the right to give his elite gym that distinguished title. The enormously muscled Samuels had been England's undisputed weight-lifting champion of the world before emigrating to Spain five years earlier. Now many of Spain's top weight lifters, body builders, athletes, footballers, Formula 1 drivers, tennis players and indeed, to the abhorrence of animal-loving Brits, star *toreros,* came to his gym to build up their fitness under the tough regime he had worked out for them.

Angela was a close friend of Samuels and frequently arranged for one of her beautiful escort girls to satisfy his rapacious sexual urges. When he greeted her warmly with a Spanish style kiss on each cheek she replied by giving her hardest clenched-fist punch to his corrugated abdomen muscles and then amusingly ringing her bruised hands.

'How are you luv?' he queried in an accent honed during a tough boyhood spent along London's Old Kent Road.

Then, glancing at the young man accompanying her, asked *'What can I do for you?'*

Angela grinned broadly as she replied: *'I'm fine you old bandito. This young man, Richard, is going to work for me in my new project an escort agency for lonely and sex-starved women. I want you to work on him for the next month and get him as fit as possible before he starts doing the business for me. He'll work out with you as many hours a day as you think he needs to get top fitness. There will be an extra thousand euros on top of your usual fee if you can bring him up to scratch in that time.*

'What do you think, Louis, darling?'

Samuel's took a long and analytical look at the young and slender Englishman.

'Strip off young man, let's see what I have got to work on,' said the gymnasium boss, waiting while Richard removed his jacket shirt and shoes. *'Now your strides...there's no room for*

modesty here...we've seen it all before!'

However, there was an audible gasp of admiration from the former weight-lifting champion, followed by a look of dismay.

'You are certainly well-hung, son' said Samuels as his appraisal, inevitably took in Richard's remarkable nether region. *'You could choke a camel with that donker! But as Angela will tell you that it is not just the size but the way you use your joystick that matters.'*

But then came the downside as Samuels cast his eyes over the rest of Richard's undernourished body emaciated by weeks of starvation diet.

'I've seen bigger muscles on a feral cat than you've got son,' he opined. *'We've got to build you up. I'll have failed Angela if I can't put on a stone or two of extra muscle for you inside a month. Remember muscle weighs heavier than fat and you have got very little of either at the moment.'*

Then, turning to the anxious Angela Di Silva, he gave his final diagnosis to the escort agency boss who was going to pay his bill.

'He's going to need stamina as well as strength for the kind of work you have in mind for him,' said Samuels. *'I'll train him to attain both those goals. It will also require the proper food. So you have to leave his meals to me. He will live here at the gym for a month training and eating lots of steak, salads, pasta, high protein-white of egg-omelettes, and protein drinks.'*

Angela agreed with Louis Samuels' professional judgement and confirmed the agreement with the statement: *'I leave him with you. He's all yours, Louis.'*

That settled, Louis gave his final instructions to the

anxious Richard with the warning: *'Report to me here at the gym at 7.am tomorrow morning. You will stay here at the gym for the next four weeks and that will be your daily wake-up time. Bring your gym gear and trainers with you. Any extra training kit you need I will supply you with. You will work , eat and sleep here for a month.*

'Your life is about to change.'

* * *

4

Angela Di Silva reported to her husband, Klaus, detailing the promising start she had already made in the launch of her new escort agency for lonely and deserted women, as they dined at their favourite table in the *Restaurante Los Caracoles* later that evening.

'I know the old English saying that one swallow does not make a summer,' she told her *esposo* enthusiastically as they made serious inroads into a second bottle of Moet Chandon. *'But this young English muchacho is going to be a big earner. Handsome, well endowed tools of the trade and he will have considerable sex appeal after Louis Samuels has worked on him at the gym for a month. He obviously comes from a fine English family, breeding counts you know, and has received a good education.*

'If I can find five or six men of his calibre, of varying ages, it will complete my stable of male escorts in this city of Barcelona. Then I can open similar branches of my new escort agency in Valencia, Seville, Granada, Malaga and eventually the capital, Madrid. In fact my aim is for the agency to be represented in all the areas where rich and famous women from the USA, England, the rest of Europe, South America and, of course, here on the Spanish Peninsular, congregate.

'I aim to have the English mozo, Richard Martin, working and earning money for the agency in just over four weeks time. Apart from recruiting such quality studs as Richard the big task will be to get the agency up and running with an outstanding service it will offer to lonely and sex-starved women.

'Of course we could advertise both in the national and

local press which is already full of offers from prostitutes, masseurs and deviants. There is no law against such lurid and explicit advertising in Spain. But I prefer my new escort agency to become well-known in a more dignified manner. The best way for that is by word of mouth with our women clients spreading the news personally to their friends. We will soon get known, and our contact numbers will quickly circulate amongst potential clients. That is how the quality of the discreet service we are offering will become familiar to lonely and desperate women.'

Klaus, as always admired his *esposa's* perspicacity. But he had a shrewd business acumen himself.

'Excuse me casting a small doubt, my darling Angela, but will you not find some difficulty in finding so many young, virile men like this handsome English boy?' he queried. Angela, however, already had a considered counter to her husband's negative query.

'Hold on Klaus, amado,' she expounded. *'My aim is not to recruit a stable of frisky colts. I want virile studs of all ages under 60 years. The mature wife whose husband has left her for a younger woman, or through death, or whose libido has taken a downturn because of sickness or advancing age, will be looking for companionship equally as much as sexual satisfaction.'*

Angela's explanation seemed plausible enough to the astute Klaus.

'Yes, yes Angela my love,' was his appreciative and candid comment. *'As usual you are the complete professional and have thought everything out. Having said that let me know if there is any way I can help you in what promises to be a daunting task ahead.'*

19

Having said farewell with a passionate kiss for Klaus at the *Restaurante Los Caracoles,* Angela pointed her *Porsche* towards a *peluqueria* situated in an up market estate at the foot of Barcelona's nearby 532 metres high *Tibidabo* mountain, a favourite tourist spot for the city's multi-national visitors.

Angela often used this exclusive ladies hairdressing salon when her attractive tresses needed a shampoo and set or re-styling for a special event. The proprietor of *Bernardo's Pelequeria* , who had given his Christian name to the salon, was once one of Europe's most celebrated ladies hair stylists whose tonsorial talents had graced high-class hair emporiums in Paris, New York and, for ten years, at Beauchamp Place, adjacent to London's distinguished Harrod's department store.

Like many male hairdressers Bernardo Sanchez gave a perception to strangers that he was homosexual. At a lusty age of 54, his long silver hair cascaded in deep waves secured into a ponytail by a solid gold clip above the neck. There was always a whisper of his favourite *Chanel for Men* after shave drifting from a friendly face. His fingernails immaculately manicured and clear varnished. His wrists tastefully adorned with a bracelet on the right and a Rolex Oyster on the left. Both crafted in top grade gold. But Angela knew better than most that Bernardo was all red-blooded man. A macho sex guy despite his effeminate front, who went to bed with a different woman most nights. If he could not persuade one of his clients to leave his hairdressing chair for a place between the royal-blue sheets at his luxury apartment on a particular evening he would telephone his friend Angela Di Silva to fix him up with a beautiful and shapely girl from the Agency.

The result at the end of the evening was inevitable.

'*After you give me a shampoo and set Bernardo darling can you leave the salon in charge of one of your assistants for half an hour or so?*' Angela requested. '*I need to talk to you about a business proposition.*'

Bernardo Sanchez did not know at this point but he was about to be persuaded by his good friend Angela to switch from the role of amateur roué to that of a semi-professional male prostitute or, to give it a more respectable title, a male escort.

Angela was very persuasive as she explained her plans for the launch of a new escort agency for women serviced by men.

'*I am offering you the chance of turning your hobby into a profitable sideline, Bernardo darling,*' she laughed. '*You will be handsomely paid for the nightly fuck you so much enjoy. In fact, at four hundred euros a night as a fee from the agency, plus expenses, and a possible minimum €500 for bedding your client it will be more lucrative than doing a shampoo and set.*

'*In fact your new side-line could even boost your hairdressing business. It might titillate your agency clients to be coiffured in the afternoon by the guy who seduced them the night before.*'

Angela's proposition appealed to Bernardo and it took him only a few seconds to accept it.

'*OK, OK Angela it's a deal. When do I start work?*' he said chuckling at the humour of the unusual situation. '*Oh, don't forget you haven't paid me for the shampoo and set I gave you this afternoon. You have now turned me from being a willing amateur into a professional so I am not doing free fucks or free shampoos anymore.*'

Angela grinned all the way at Bernardo's parting shot as

she tooled the *Porsche* home to tell her beloved Klaus of the latest development.

*   *   *

5

Things were looking good, in Angela Di Silva's opinion, as she unfolded plans for her new escort agency to serve lonely, sex-starved women who, through no fault of their own, were left in a hopelessly, in some cases almost suicidal, depressed state.

Pyschologists and other top medical experts often found it almost impossible to help such unfortunate women who sadly very often did attempt to kill themselves. No 'shrink', licensed or quack, could do more than prescribe mind-bending tranquillising tablets that frequently prompt suicidal tendencies.

Such women had in many cases reached this desperate state because their husbands had suffered a health problem, or advancing years had caused impotency. This left thousands of unhappy wives with their own sexual desires unrequited. The only possible escape from the nightmare was adultery. Many of them decided not to take such a serious step either because of respect, and love, for their equally unfortunate spouse, or for fear of losing their marital security if their indiscretion was made public.

An escort agency for women was the only solution. An escort agency which pledged and guaranteed their precious privacy. An escort agency where their unfulfilled desire for a lusty man could be achieved without commitment apart from payment of a sizeable fee. Angela Di Silva was wise enough in the ways of the sordid sex-trade to know such pitiable women came in all age groups.

'I don't want a stable of male escorts made up of boy-hookers,' she told her husband Klaus over a glass of Mumms

at Barcelona's luxurious Hotel Ambassador, located in La Rambla, less than four minutes away from Plaça de Catalyuna. *'Now inside a week I have signed up the English lad, Richard Martin, not yet in in his twenties and my old hairdressing friend, the handsome Bernardo Sanchez who is 54--the right age to attract any blue-rinsed ladies looking for a romp between the sheets. That's what I am looking for an escort agency with a stable of sexy men with varying ages from early 20's to 60.'*

Klaus Di Silva, the greatest admirer of his wife's business talent, replied cunningly with tongue in cheek, leaving Angela guessing whether he was serious or not.

'Ah, my old poker partner Bernardo,' he said. *'I am sure he fucks with as much skill as he manipulates a deck of cards. You know I can admit now that before we were married I suspected you were having an affair with Bernardo Sanchez.'* Angela laughed heartily.

'It kept you on your toes darling,' she replied. *'Whether or not I had an affair with caballero Bernardo is for me to keep secret and you to contemplate. Whatever, amado, you have my assurance that ever since I stood alongside you at the altar of the Catedral de Santa Eulalia, and took my wedding vows , I have never been unfaithful to you. I loved you then and I still do, passionately. So forget Bernado Sanchez. He is nothing more than my hairdresser and a future employee for the escort agency with a penis for hire to sex-hungry women. Nothing more than an enthusiastic male hooker.'*

Klaus di Silva raised both hands in the air.

'Hold on, hold on Angela novia,' he said firmly. *'I have never doubted your constancy as a wife. Perhaps it was the understandable jealousy that I felt before we were married. Whenever I saw you with another man before I took you to the altar I could feel pangs of envy.'*

Having won the good natured verbal joust with her spouse Angela told Klaus about the next move she intended to take in assembling her squad of sexually orientated male escorts for Barcelona's newest agency.

'I need a guapo hombre midway in years between the English muchacho, Richard Martin, and the peluquero Bernardo Sanchez,' she informed Klaus. 'I think I know just the guy. He is Jose Eugenio Moralés, the former torero, who now keeps a tiny bar in the Bario Chino. He is only 39 and he has gone through much of the money he earned as a bullfighter. I happen to know his bar has not been doing too well recently. He's handsome, virile and was a real pin-up before he had to retire from the corrida after a terrible cornada in the Plaza de Toros.'

Angela had chosen her next candidate carefully. Jose Eugenio had been at the very top of the bullfighting profession when he was gored by his third bull of the afternoon in the cauldron of Madrid's Plaza de Toros, Las Ventas. It was eight years earlier when the animal's right horn went in through his lower stomach and out through his anus. At 31 years of age, desperately near to death, he was incarcerated in the intensive care ward of Madrid's Hospital La Paz for 12 weeks and then for the next eight months in an expensive nursing home 20 kilometres from the Spanish capital. Much of the fortune he had banked from his bullfighting career, plus the cash gleaned from a Testimonial *corrida*, which was well supported by his large following of *aficionados*, evaporated in paying off medical fees and nursing care for the next few years. He managed to retain enough pesetas in his account to buy the bar in Barcelona, where he was the idol at the local bullring.

But the corrida was an expiring ritual in Catalonia where the performances of the famous Barcelona Football Club was now the popular spectator past time. Now the clients of his tiny bar in the Bario Chino were mainly greybeard *taurominos* in their sixties and seventies who were still fans of the corrida in a city which had become the first in Spain to turn its back on the *fiesta brava.*

It was outside *'Jose's Bar'* that the mink-coated Angela parked her Porsche. She was a former *aficionada* of the bullfight herself having watched many corridas when she was a young girl in South America. In fact her father had been a *banderilla* in the *cuadrilla* of Argentino's most famous *torero* for many years. Her beloved *padre*, she never forgot, died in the blood stained sand of the arena of death.

'Senora Di Silva it is my pleasure to see you,' said Jose Eugenio Moralés as Angela entered the bar. *'May I offer you a glass of our best Cava or would another drink be more to your taste? To what do I owe the honour of your visit?'*

The cork was popped on a bottle of *Cava Gran Reserva* and as they toasted each other Jose Eugenio accepted the proposition that Angela Di Silva offered him.

'It is time a little excitement came back into my life,' thought the former idol of the *Plaza de Toros.*

* * *

26

6

Richard Martin did the sensible thing by turning in early at the tiny apartment that his new boss and benefactor, the lovely Angela Di Silva, had provided for him.

He knew as he strode the three kilometres, at the crack of dawn, across downtown Barcelona towards the *Gimnasio Campeóns* that he faced a very tough day. He seriously thought, as a puny 20-year-old, who had never played organised games or exercised in any way since he had left school in England three years ago, that it was unlikely he would ever have to go into serious training.

Louis Samuels, the owner of the gym and former world champion weight lifter, was there to greet him.

'Right lad put on your training gear as quickly as possible,' snapped the burly fitness instructor. *'We are going for a little run before the day gets too hot.'*

Then a few minutes later Samuels, who had once been called onto devise a fitness regime for Britain's elite SAS soldiers at their Hereford headquarters, barked: *'Don't put on those Nike trainers, you will need to wear something heavier on your feet for what you are going to do today.'* Whereupon a pair of army boots were slung across the dressing room towards the astonished Richard Martin.

'We are off on a ten mile run today through rough country climbing all the way up Tibidabo,' explained the gym master. *'Yes Richard, my boy, a ten mile up-hill grind across rugged terrain. I'm going with you and if I can do it at 45, as sure as hell, you, at 20 years of age, are going to do it.'*

The astonished Martin managed to stammer: *'But Tibidabo*

is a mountain...

Sammuels grinned sadistically, and said: *'Bingo first time Richard. Just a little climb to 1,745 feet above sea level and you are going to run every inch of the way. What is more you are going to run down hill on the return journey when you will already be knackered, your quad muscles will feel as if your legs have dropped off, your heart will be pumping overtime and your lungs will be bursting. Coming down might well be more agonising than climbing up the mountain. But rest assured boy I'll be with you all the way.*

'If I catch you slacking lad I'll kick your ass all the way to La Rambla and back. Just do your best and I'll not complain. Then I'll be able to assess just what we have to do get you really fit, which is what your boss, Angela Di Di Silva wants.'

Richard got through the first five miles without too much trouble. The lumbering giant Louis Samuels trundling beside him without hardly losing his breath, and his own pride, spurred him on.

As he began the ascent up Tibidabo, passing an endless queue of tourists ambling and puffing their way up the mountain, he began to hit the wall of pain that all long distance runners experience. His breath came in long searing gasps, he wobbled in his stride, nearly missing his footing several times on the sloping terrain. Could he keep going? His pride kicked in and he decided he just had to continue. But oh, what he would do for a rest at that moment.

'Now son dig deep' gasped Samuels, striding purposefully alongside. *'Run through the pain barrier. If you stop now you will have to be carried home and I ain't going to be the one to give you a piggy back. I promise if you run through the wall the pain will disappear. You only have another kilometre to go before we reach the peak, and then we will begin our descent*

down to Barcelona.'

As they neared the peak of Mount Tibidabo, as far as the millions of *turistas* had ever been allowed to reach since global travel opened up big-time at the end of the Second World War, the heavens opened, a fierce downpour that left the two runners drenched to the skin. As often happens when a violent storm strikes in this part of the Meditterranean the temperature dropped dramatically leaving Louis Samuels and Richard Martin dog-tired, soaking wet and freezing cold.

When they staggered into the *Gimnasio Campeóns* a few hours later Louis was quite pleased with the way Richard had borne the formidable difficulties of the day.

'You'll do kid,' said the former world champion weight lifter. *'You couldn't have faced tougher conditions than what you have just ran through. Now I know you have what it takes. You really cut the mustard today. In four weeks time, after I have put you through your paces, I'll have you honed to perfect fitness. Now get yourself into the steam room over there for half an hour and after that I will arrange for our physiotherapist to give you a really deep massage.'*

Little more than an hour later Richard left the treatment table still glowing from the session in the steam room, with every muscle in his body throbbing after the punishment of the mountain run and the expert pummelling from the physiotherapist.

He was greeted by the gym boss, who said: *'How do you feel ? The training will get easier every day. Just remember the oldest saying in the fitness training world is : No pain, no gain! Now you need a good meal and then I am going to bed you down for the night in one of our single cublicles. You need a good night's sleep because tomorrow you will have to go through a full days work in the gym.'*

The two men sat down together at a table in the gymnasium restaurant. Richard was puzzled at what was on the plate when the first course was placed in front of him.

'What's that?' Richard asked Louis staring at the pudding-looking pale soggy mass on the plate placed in front of him.

Samuels laughingly explained: 'It is an omelette made from the white of ten eggs. White of egg consists of albumen and is almost entirely protein which an athlete in training needs for strength and stamina.'

The second course needed no explanation--a 16 ounce entrecôte steak accompanied by a green salad.

'You will need this kind of quality food every day to push you towards fitness,' explained Samuels. 'Protein helps to build muscle and will assist you as you strive towards your goal in the next few weeks.'

* * *

7

Angela Di Silva was too much of a hard-headed business woman to idly wait for the month that her young recruit, Richard Martin, was undergoing a rigorous regime under fitness coach Louis Samuels, before getting her new escort agency up and running.

Richard would be an important addition to her quickly growing stable of male escorts when the former international weight lifter had trained him up to fitness, but the other two men she had enrolled, the greying 54-year-old hairdresser, playboy and hitherto amateur roué, Bernardo Sanchez, and the darkly suave José Eugenio Moralés, a hugely courageous caballero whose highly-esteemed prowess between the sheets had been honed by a tsunami of testosterone during his glittering career as a star toreo at imperious *Plaza de Toros* in the leading cities of Spain and South America.

Now 39-year-old Moralés, miraculously, had survived a severe goring in Madrid

Madrid's majestic *Plaze de Toros, Las Ventas,* seven years earlier. Although this ghastly *cornada* threatened his life for the next 36 months, amazingly, after recovery, his libido was unimpaired.

'When José sees a woman he fancies, he performs like a fucking stag in rut,' Angela told her husband, Klaus, with a touch of undisguised admiration for the former bullfighter.

Angela had not yet completed her Escort Agency roster for the city of Barcelona. She needed three more escorts to complete her squad but, she shrewdly figured, there was absolutely no reason why Bernardo and José could not go out on the tiles and start earning money for the Agency, and, of course for themselves.

Her next task was to find suitable clients for those two stags as they began their career as semi-professional male prostitutes. Sagaciously she knew just where to look for them!

*   *   *

Astute Angela, deviously, arrived early at the banqueting suite of a top Barcelona hotel the following day where the monthly meeting and lunch of PTAPS (*Profesional Tenderos Asociación Para Senoras)* was held. The fact that she was welcomed as a member of this exclusive organisation of business women illustrated the respectability which she was accorded by the city's broad-minded top people.

Her scheming reason for arriving early at the function was to confer with the hotel's banqueting manager, who was busily laying out the place cards around the individual tables ready for the meeting which would be followed by lunch. A fifty euro note changed hands. Angela's card was placed next to one that bore the legend: Senora Sofia Fosch.

Angela had been close to Sofia Fosch for several years, she knew her friend had serious problems in her private life. Sofia owned an upmarket boutique and jewellery shop in the centre of the Catalan capital. A dazzling beautiful and highly sexed woman , the 40-year-old Sofia's marriage to successful *abogado*, Juan Fosch, had recently taken a disastrous down turn. The Fosch and Di Silva families were closely connected. Sofia bought most of the costly jewellery she sold in the boutique from Klaus Di Silva while Juan Fosch handled all the Di Silva's legal business.

But when Juan was struck down with testicular cancer six months earlier things went terribly wrong on the operating table in the Barcelona clinic where the earlier prognosis from the surgeon and consultants, more or less, promised a complete cure. The failed surgery left him irreversibly impotent. It was nobody's fault such an operation normally carried less than a 20 per cent risk of complete failure. Tragically the impotency that Juan Fosch was unfortunately struck with inevitably disturbed the harmony of his marriage to the lovely Sofia.

Sofia would not think of shaming Juan publicly by engaging in a sordid extra-marital affair. He had been a kind, considerate and generous husband throughout the 20 years of marriage. A meeting the previous week between Juan and Klaus, over a bottle of Rioja Gran Reserva, hinted of a way around the lawyer's distressing dilemma.

Juan had confided to his friend Klaus and explained the cruel result of his recent surgery. *'Testicular cancer, according to the medical profession, is eminently treatable,'* explained Juan. *'In my case I had probably left it just a bit too late before reporting the symptoms to my doctor. Probably my embarassment at the symptoms held me back from seeking help. But at the end of the day when the surgeons went in they discovered the cancer had spread. In fact in the end they said that I was lucky they were able to save my life.*

'But the sad fact is that my beloved Sofia is being punished equally as much as me, probably more so, through no fault of her own. Sofia, throughout our 20 years of marriage, has always been very active sexually. I am not saying she is a nymphomaniac but she revelled in performing four or five times a week. I went along with that only too willingly. When the doctors told her that my impotency was irreversible she took the news bravely and stoically. She insisted that we faced the situation together and told me that I was the only man she had ever loved, and that she still did.

'When I suggested that, if she insisted on remaining as my

wife, she should take a young lover with my permission, to satisfy her physical needs, Sofia dismissed the suggestion out of hand. But it is cutting me up mentally that I should cause her so much anguish.'

It was at this point Klaus paid his *bueno amigo* the compliment of imparting a confidence of as great an import as the one he had just received. Juan was fascinated to hear of the new project that Angela had launch with the very motive of helping unfortunate women like her friend Sofia.

That night the pillow talk between the Di Silva's, Angela and Klaus, took longer, with a far more serious content than usual.

* * *

The formal monthly meeting and lunch of the *Profesional Tenderos Asociación* for the business women of Barcelona was over. The lunch had moved on from the first course of *pimientos padron con jamon jabugo* and the guests were chatting, as women do, while waiting for the main course of *cordero asado* when Angela Di Silva turned to her long-standing friend Sofia Fosch and said: '*I don't know how much your Juan has told you about the talk he had with my husband Klaus last week. But I am only too happy to help you, dear friend.*'

Angela breaking the ice was just what Sofia needed in her misery!

'*Juan told me everything,*' said Sofia, finding it difficult to disguise the excitement in her voice.

Angela was not going to let the topic drop now that she had her troubled friend on the hook.

'*Everything will be done discreetly,*' explained the escort agency boss. '*Nothing, but nothing, will be allowed to leak out* to the public. What is more Juan has offered to pay the cost of your nights out with my new escorts. It shows how much your husband loves you and will do anything to make you happy. What is more it will help to salve the anguish of the physical misfortune that has so cruelly befallen him.'

That is how a new phase of contentment in the Fosch family's life began. Some would frown at such an arrangement. Such people would never understand it. Only narrow-minded people would deny a married man and his beloved wife the chance to live the rest of their life in comparitive contentment.

* * *

8

Angela Di Silva had another happy and interesting pillow talk with her husband Klaus when they lay between the silk sheets discussing what happened to them during the day.

'I received a phone call from the Spanish Foreign office in Madrid,' Klaus disclosed. *'They explained they were ringing on behalf of a member of Saudi Arabia's royal family who came to Barcelona on a diplomatic mission yesterday. The Foreign Office spokesman explained that the Saudi prince had said that he wanted to buy some jewellery while he was in Barcelona and asked for a recommendation to a dealer who could provide quality service.*

'His Royal Highness arrived at my office and spent two hours looking at much of the jewellery I have in stock. In all he spent twenty thousand euros to pay for several diamond rings, precious bracelets and two gold Rolex watches. It was a good day for business and His Royal Highness's seven wives .

'Now tell me your news of the day Angela mi amada.'

Angela was just as ebullient as her *esposo.*

'The meeting with our dear friend Sofia Fosch went well,' she explained. *'After I had told Sofia how my new escort agency would work and assured her of its strict policy of confidentiality, Sofia seemed to think I was her guardian angel. She is still in love with her husband and always has been throughout their marriage.*

'I will do my very best to suit her needs. Not because she will be the very first client of Adorable Angela's Escort Agency for Women but because she has been a close friend of mine for several years. But one can only admire Juan Fosch for his

*unselfish attitude towards Sofia-as someone more eloquent
than me once said: Greater love hath no man'*

* * *

Angela Di Silva was all aglow in the early morning
wind gusting down from Tibidabo's majestic heights her
reddened cheeks, unusually devoid of make-up, as she strode
energetically towards the stables. Her imperious equine pal
snorted with anticipation as he crunched the usual sugar
lumps Angela produced from one of the immense pockets
of her Harris tweed hacking jacket. Zephyr, scratching his
hooves noisily across the stable yard cobbles signalled to
his mistress that he matched her mood and was 'up' for an
exhilarating cross country ride.

No gate was too tall, no hedge too spiky, no muddied
stream too formidable for the scintillating Zephyr on this
sharp morning.

As the ride reached a crescendo, and Angela blended
with Zephyr's high spirit's the friction of the Mexican saddle
almost brought her to a sexual orgasm. A phenomena often
experienced by female show jumpers and cross country event
riders.

The whole experience set her up for what was going to be a
busy day thought Angela as she unsaddled Zephyr and hosed
him down to wash away the perspiration spume that oozed
down his neck and withers. She rewarded him as usual with
several juicy carrots, an affectionate kiss, and a whisper in
his pricked ears: *'Thank you, thank you darling Zephyr. I love
you!'*

* * *

Klaus also noted Angela's happiness as they breakfasted
on American style flapjacks drizzled with maple syrup and

accompanied by scrambled eggs.

'*So what is your programme today darling?*' Klaus queried.

Angela thought for a moment before replying: '*First I am going to call at Louis Samuel's gymnasium to see how my protégé, Richard Martin, is coping with his physical fitness regime. Then I am going to see if I can pair up our friend Sofia Fosch with a suitable escort to entertain her to dinner and hopefully fulfill her urgent needs-that is if she takes a liking to the guy I arrange for her.*

'*After that I am going to see another prospective client. She is a 49-year-old German woman whose sex life was cut short six months ago when her husband, a banker, died after two massive strokes. She is too proud and considers herself to be too old , to go down the road of seeking a lover. Most respectable men of her age are already settled and married , with only their grown-up children and their business to think about.*

'*She is just the sort of unhappy woman I had in mind when I set up the agency. I met her in the cocktail bar after the lunch for the Profesional Tenderos Associación Para Senoras. As a matter of fact Sofia Fosch introduced us and we arranged to have a drink and tapas together today.*'

Klaus guffawed at his wife's enthusiam,

'*As usual Angela you are on the ball as they say at Barcelona Football Club' s Nou camp headquarters a couple of kilometres down the road,*' he said. '*Let's hope you score another goal today.*'

It was just on 10am when Angela skilfully wheeled the Porsche into the parking lot outside the *Gimnasio Campeóns*.

Proprietor Louis Samuels greeted her as soon as she walked through the entrance and courteously invited her into his office.

'*It is nice to see you Senora Di Silva, please take a seat,*' he said indicating a massive black leather arm chair. '*Can I offer you some coffee or maybe a glass of cava might be more to your liking?*' Angela switched on the allure as the former world champion weightlifter kissed the back of her outstretched hand with all the charm of a 19th century *caballero*. '*Thank you Louis,*' she teased. '*You are always a gentleman, a perfect ladies' man. I wonder why you never got married.*'

He had the perfect reply ready as, with a wry grin, he chuckled: '*Because senora I never was lucky enough to meet a woman like you.*'

Angela was equally amused with the exchange and said: '*You are a crafty old charmer Louis. Be careful I don't waft you off to my "cama". In answer to your original question a pot of coffee please, it is too early for cava , even for me. Now can I ask you how my boy is doing?*'

Samuels picked up the phone on his desk and ordered coffee and '*galletas*' to be brought in from the gymnasium's restaurant.

'*He's doing just fine,*' he said. '*He came through the first day well when I took him on a ten mile run up the Tibidabo mountain and we ran into a terrific storm. He stood up to it really well particularly even I was feeling knackered when we got back here to the gymnasium. Since then he has been working four hours a day in the gym. Two hours in the morning and two hours "a la tarde". He ends the day with an hour in the swimming pool, followed by a sauna or steam bath and a massage from our physiotherapist. Then he will join me for a high protein dinner of steak and green salad. In two*' *and half weeks, when I hand him back to you, he'll be fit as a flea. He's a handsome lad and not afraid of hard work. He has never ducked out of doing anything I have asked of him, and I do mean anything.'*

Angela was delighted with Louis Samuels glowing report and before she left the *Gimnasio Campeónes* she sought out Richard, who was working out on the treadmill, and told him how pleased she was with the progress he was making.

* * *

As arranged Angela met Frau Edelgarde Durke in a tiny, but exclusive, tapas bar just off the main La Rambla *via publica*. In true Spanish style they put their arms around each other in an affectionate *abrazo* and *besos* on each cheek.

They instantly warmed to each other, making it easy for Edelgarde Durke to pour out her troubled heart to the sympathetic escort agency boss.

'I had just reached my 49th birthday when my darling husband Heinrich died suddenly after a second major stroke inside a week,' the Frankfurt born Edelgarde explained. *'I had begun to go through the change of life about ten months earlier. I was always under the impression that the dreaded menopause gave women of my age an aversion to making sex. In my case the opposite happened and I could not get enough of Heinrich as the time between periods got longer and longer. From the usual monthly cycle they went to intervals of three months and then spasmodically.*

'I found it strange that as I went through the change of life my desire for sex is unabated and Heinrich's death has left me with a deep physical and mental problem. A widow of my age, with her looks and figure in decline, finds it difficult to find a man willing to engage in a love affair. That is my problem

40

Angela, the loss of Heinrich has hurled me into a mental chasm. All my doctor has offered me is anti-depressants such as the mind-bending Prozac, which reduces the frequency of the hot flushes that go with the menopause, but can also cause mental side effects such as suicidal tendencies.'

Angela Di Silva was, as Spanish people say, *muy simpático*, with Edelgard's dilemma. The problems that women face during the, so called, change of life was something she had researched. It went with the territory of someone who had worked in the sex trade for most of their life.

'*I attended several symposiums at the medical department of the University of Barcelona on the subject of the menopause,*' Angela told her new German friend. '*Also, when I was in the USA five years ago, I attended a series of lectures at the Harvard Medical School, who have studied this topic and the pros and cons of hormone replacement therapy which is often prescribed to help women of a certain age.*'

'But, please Edelgarde, let me correct your misconception that you have developed namely your surprise that your desire for sex has not disappeared while you go through the menopause. Sex can even get better for some women after the menopause. It depends who the person is. This is because in late 40's and early 50's women are more experienced and unafraid to satisfy their bodily needs. Their children are grown-up and have flown the nest leaving their mother with more time to nurture their intimate relationship with their partners. It is quite possible that your sex-drive intensifies during and after the menopause as you experience a surge of oestrogen when your hormone levels undulate. On the other hand there are also women whose hormones work in opposition causing a dramatic dip in sexual desire during the menopause phenomena.

'My advice to you Edelgarde is to follow the urges of your

body as long as you can. You no longer have a man in your life to be faithful to. You are a free agent now. So go for the sexual satisfaction that you are craving for. The alternative is to risk severe depression which could scar you mentally for the rest of your life.

'The decision is up to you but I am here to help. If that is what you want I can find a suitable bed mate to put your problem behind you.'

* * *

9

For a street-wise woman who had spent nearly two decades in, or on the fringes, of the seamy world of the sex-trade, Angela Di Silva, bizarrely, woke up with the proverbial butterflies in her stomach

There would be no triumphal trumpet call, no dazzling pyrotechnics illuminating Barcelona's night sky, no popping the cork of vintage champagne to celebrate the event, at least for her there wouldn't. But Angela was animated that her new escort agency would go full steam ahead that very evening. She had paired up 49-year-old Berlin-born widow Edelgarde Durke with ladies hair stylist Bernardo Sanchez. Now Angela could only wait and hope that nature would take its course. Time would tell whether her judgement, honed in the twilight business of prostitution, was sound.

Although modestly fearing that her looks might be starting to wither, because of the female trauma of menopause, Edelgarde was not doing justice to herself, she was still an attractive woman.

Angela was banking on her own shrewd knowledge of the art of sex as she figured that the svelte Sanchez would help the genteel German widow to restore her confidence and fulfill her physical urges, if only for one night of passion, after the death of her adored husband Heinrich.

Angela had decided from the outset that her new escort agency would be, as it were, 'bespoke'. The client's wishes and preferences would be paramount. Edelgarde had decided that her tryst with Bernardo Sanchez, who she had never previously met, should begin, and possibly, end at the four star Hotel Ambassador, located in Barcelona's historic centre and close to The Rambla in *Calle Pintor Fortuny*. This was Edelgarde's choice rather than using one of the luxurious *apartmentos di amor* that Angela had installed for her agency around the city, Edelgarde had nervously asked Angela how she would be able to recognise Bernardo at the meeting point in the plush cocktail bar in the opulent Hotel Ambassador, which had been built in time for the 1992 Olympic Games.

'*Let me put it this way,* 'replied Angela, tongue in cheek. '*I doubt that there will be more than one man with a pony-tail hairstyle held together with a diamond clip. If there is you will find that Bernardo Sanchez still stands out from the crowd like the NorthStar.*

'*Eldergarde, my love, don't be put off by first sight. Bernardo Sanchez may appear to be homosexual when you first meet. But I'll guarantee that by the end of the night you will discover that he is all man!*'

* * *

The truth was that despite her age, the elegant Edelgarde felt like a 17-year-old virgin out on her first date as she pulled her three-quarter length mink jacket around her shoulders , entered the imposing hotel lobby, confirmed at the reception desk that the suite she had reserved was ready and arranged for her case to be sent up, nervously took a deep breath and slid into the cocktail bar. Angela Di Dsilva had been absolutely correct. She recognised Bernardo Sanchex immediately.

How could anyone miss his majestic 6ft 8inches? The flowing, and highlighted, black hair, the ringlets nipped at the nape of his neck and the ponytail secured by a dazzling diamond clip. The style and perfect tailoring of his royal blue velvet dinner jacket? The sweep of his hand-tied bow setting off a perfectly tailored, silk-frilled, evening shirt? Gold cuff links and limited edition *Cartier* wrist watch? The exciting musky waft of his after-shave cologne which was neither effeminate or garish but essentially manly. Before she could say anything Bernado rose toweringly from the cocktail bar sofa. She was indelibly attracted as he took her right hand and kissed it gently.

'You are Edelgarde Durke?' said Bernardo, his eloquent command of the English language spiced with an intriguing Hispanic accent. 'That is a ridiculous question because our mutual friend Angela described you perfectly. Look for the most refined woman in the bar , Angela told me. So you just have to be Edelgarde Durke.'

Bernardo poised in his gallant salute, and, releasing her hand gave her the traditional Spanish abrazo accompanied by a gentle kiss on each cheek. 'I have taken the liberty of having a bottle of pink French champagne placed on ice,' he said, exuding charm yet avoiding being too gratuitous. 'Can we do away with the formalities and immediately address each other with our Christian names? What do you say Edelgarde?'

She sipped her champagne with a charm that elegant women seem to acquire when imbibing bubbly. Yet once again inside she felt like a teenager on her first date, but she smiled at his courtesy and answered: 'Yes of course Bernardo, that is a good idea. Angela Di Silva told me you are a hairdresser. Where is your salon?

'I am not really conversant with the lay-out of Barcelona , for I only came here with my late husband from Germany just over 12 months ago. But unfortunately he died of a stroke six months ago so I have not yet got to know the city very well.'

Bernardo explained that his exclusive tonsorial emporium was situated at the foot of Barcelona's regal Tibidabo mountain.

45

'I have built up a select clientele over the years,' he exclaimed. 'Many of the top ladies in Barcelona now patronise my salon. Incidentally Edelgarde, as we talk, I have been admiring your hair. I rarely see such a = auburn colour here in Spain, where it is mainly very dark natural brunettes or bottle blondes. Nothing wrong with that, it's my job to deal with all shades and styles . But your auburn is the colourful hue of early morning sunshine on the Mediterranean horizon. The kind of hair I would expect to see on a young Irish colleen with green eyes.

'I would really love to style your hair.'

Edelgarde was delighted with the compliment, and entering into the repartee that Bernardo had so gallantly instigated, she countered coyly: 'That would be lovely Bernardo. I must make a point of making a reservation at your salon as soon as possible.'

They finished the pink champagne and Bernardo, chivalrously, asked if she was ready for dinner. When she acquiesced Bernardo offered his arm to escort her to the hotel restaurant.

*   *   *

Manolo, the masterful *Jefe* of the restaurant greeted Bernardo warmly, as was due to a long and much respected client, gently kissed Edelgarde and bowed when she was introduced and, with a flamboyant wave beckoned one of his waiters to take her mink jacket to the cloak room before ushering them to a secluded table.

It had all the makings of what promised to be a wonderful evening. Both Edelgarde and Bernardo already sensed they would not be disappointed.

*   *   *

10

It is not always the case when client and escort meet for the first time that they gell. The pairing of Eldegarde Durke and Bernardo Sanchez hit the top note from the beginning, to the delight of the orchestrator, Angela di Silva.

Angela explained that theory to her husband while they lay in bed the evening after Eldegarde and Bernardo consummated their new found friendship between the lavender-scented sheets of the Ambassador Hotel.

'You see Klaus, for most men a fuck is just a fuck and it is no problem for him to pass on his libido to a different woman every night,' Angela told Klaus. *'But for a woman, even the first night with a man often means she wants to feel a little in love with the guy. But I am really glad those two seemed to really like each other. Eldegarde, in particular, needs closure of her agonising grief for her dead husband. That is why I am happy for their sake, not just for the reputation of my escort agency.'*

* * *

Eldegarde had been glad that she had allowed Bernardo take over ordering the meal and choosing the wines. The fifty euro note that he had surreptitiously slipped into the hand of the *Jefe* of the hotel restaurant, Manolo, had worked wonders. The table was secluded and out of range of the curious glances of other diners. Significantly the service they were given by an echelon of two senior waiters supported by two junior *camarero's* and the attention of a studious-looking *camarero di vino*, was superb.

A few minutes after the obsequious Manola had ushered them to their table and a whispered discussion between

Bernardo and the wine waiter a bottle of *Jerez Fino* was produced for approval.

'*That will do it is an excellent brand,*' said the stylish hairdresser with an authority that emphasised a wide knowledge of wine. '*Please open the bottle and accompany it with an ice bucket. We would also like large sized schooner glasses.*'

The precise terms of the order produced a smile to the normally melancholy wine waiter's face in appreciation of a customer who obviously knew his wine.

Eldegarde was intrigued with the sherry, sipping it and holding the cut-glass schooner towards the electric chandelier to admire the pale ochreous hue of the fortified wine.

'*You know it's strange to say but this is the first time I have ever tasted sherry,*' Eldegarde exclaimed. '*It's not a very familiar aperitif in Germany despite our reputation for producing quality white wines, in particular. But I really like the flavour of this sherry and I wish I knew more about it.*'

Bernardo felt Eldegarde's interest was a compliment to his choice of aperitif. '*By law,sherry must come from the triangular area of the province of Cádiz, between Jerez, Sanlúca de Barrameda and El Puerto de Santa Maria. Sherry is a fortified wine. As Spaniards we mainly have to thank the British for its popularity. When Sir Francis Drake in the 16th Century sacked Cádiz, one of the most important Spanish sea ports, he took back to England every barrel of sherry he could find in the city. Many of the Jerez cellars have British names having been founded years ago by entrepreneurial Brits.*

'Shakespeare portrayed his character Falstaff as addicted to sherry, known in those days as "sack" and penned this Falstaffian dissertation: "If I had a thousand sons, the first humane principle I would teach them should be, to forswear thin potations and to addict themselves to sack."

'Like all wine there are various types of sherry, for instance you are drinking Fino, the driest and palest of the varieties of Jerez; Manzanilla is also a variety of fino made around the port of Sanlúcar de Barrameda; Amontillado, which is darker; Oloroso a darker and richer wine; and Palo Cortado that is fortified and aged.'

Eldegarde was doubly impressed with Bernardo. Firstly for his wide knowledge of many subjects including food and wine, and secondly with his kindly patience in taking time to explain in depth the intricacies of sherry.

They had between them consumed three quarters of the *Fino*, washing down delicate plates of *acetunas, almejas en vinagre y salmón ahumado.*

After a few minutes Bernardo nodded to , Manolo, the *maitre d'hotel.* It was the signal for the second course to be served. It was snowy white *lenguado Dover,* cooked *a la plancha en mantequilla* and skilfully taken off the bone by the delicate knife skills of the *camarero.*

The accompaniment was plump stalks of fresh asparagus. A delightful dish in its own right but it was the arrival of the wine that brought a gasp of pleasurable surprise from Eldergarde. It was served in a distinctive flat green flagon.

'I am astonished to see this wine presented,' commented the excited Eldergarde. *'Volkacher Windisch is from the Franken region of Germany, the area where I was born and brought up. I come from the baroque city of Wuerzburg which is in the centre of the wine producing Franken region. This wine is traditionally bottled in flat flagons which are called Bocksbeut.'*

Bernardo, delighted with Eldergarde's joy, said: '*I wanted you to feel at home and I am glad that it pleases you. A wine you know should taste all the better for your appreciation of it.*'

The harmonious timbre of the evening was enhanced by the music emanating from the melodious harp, delicately strummed by a beautifully *senorita* in a pink diaphanous gown in the corner of the restaurant.

The main course of *paletilla cordero asado* arrived at the table on a large salver, surrounded by an impressive and colourful battalion of grilled fresh vegetables.

They had previously each consumed a palate-cleansing ramekin of minted sorbet to prepare them for the shoulder of lamb which arrived at the table oozing with succulent juices. Once again Bernardo amazed Edelgarde with his choce of wine *Burg Layer Schlosskpelle Kabinett.*

'*You might also possibly recognise this wine Edelgarde it is a wonderful Kabinet from the Nahe region in Germany,*'he said. '*The Nahe and Moselle regions are close to each other in Germany.*'

Edelgarde lifted her glass and tasted the wine and held up the bottle to admire its blue glass and artfully designed label also in blue.

The wonderful repast concluded with a German cheese, *Livarot,* served with finger slices of freshly toasted croissant and a bottle of *Sekt,* the German sparkling wine, which some people prefer to French champagne or the Spanish *cava.*

* * *

Finally over a pot of coffee there was an embarrassing pause in the conversation as both of them searched for a way to break into a delicate topic. Bernardo signed the restaurant bill, which would be finally sent to Angela Di Silva for settlement by her escort agency.

'Look Edelgarde, we have both enjoyed a wonderful evening,' said Bernardo. 'But I want to spare your embarassment so I will say what has to be said. Would you like me to join you in your suite.? One way or the other I will respect your decision. I understand that it is always difficult for a lady to make such a move at the end of a first date.'

The gentle tones of Bernardo's dissertation had calmed the nerves in Edelgarde's tummy. In fact she felt quite bold, bolstered by the fact she was physically attracted to the hairdresser, when she said: 'Yes, Bernardo, dear, I would like nothing better than you join me in the suite.'

The first asignation in the history of the newly-launched *Adorable Angela's Escort Agency for Women* was literally about to reach climax.

* * *

11

Edelgarde took a taxi from the Ambassador Hotel the following morning and arrived at Bernardo's hairdressing salon at the arranged time of 10-45 am.

He had left her bed only three hours earlier after a night of sexual bliss. As she passionately kissed him goodbye she said: *'Bernado please don't think I am pushy, but you did say last night that you would like to style my hair. I haven't got a regular hairdresser here in Barcelona and as I do need my hair cut, shampooed and styled, and I would love to come to you it you can fit me in some time this morning.'*

Bernardo was quite pleased with her suggestion and replied: *'Well that would be lovely Eldegarde. I'll leave my business card on the dressing table and the taxi driver will know where to take you. If you come to the salon about 15 minutes before 11 o'clock, I will personally attend to you.'*

Eldegarde could hardly contain herself, as she signed the hotel bill and checked out of the Ambassador, for she intended to return that evening to the four bedroom villa at Sitges, just down the Mediterranean coast, which had been left to her in his will by Heinrich , her late husband.

* * *

Bernardo was a passionate, yet considerate and gentle, lover. He knew that patience was the name of the game. Women frequently took longer to climax than men. He sensed he would have to have a lot of patience and show understanding to bring the widowed Eldergarde to a peak.

His foreplay told her that here was a man experienced in love-making. His hand wandered and traced a pattern lower and lower down her body. She trembled as he slowly massaged her Mound of Venus, and she felt her vagina moisten as he found and toyed with her clitoris. It was the action of a man highly experienced in the art of love making. Among the colloquialisms that exist for the Mound of Venus, or in Latin *Mons Pubis*, is the pun created by Cockneys who called it *'fanny hill'*, and in rhyming East End of London slang shortened it to *'fanny'* a Briticism for the female genitals.

His probing fingers left her gasping in unbridled ecstasy.

'Oh! Bernardo darling fuck me,' she whispered urgently. *'Fuck me hard please, darling!'*

He did. Not once but three blissful times in the next hour. Each time the sex was more unbridled and physical. Then a cloud of satisfaction enveloped her as she felt him ejaculate inside her.

'Oh, Bernardo, my love that was marvellous. I didn't want it to stop,' she cooed with all the intensity of a turtle dove recalling its mate to the loft.

It was then they fell asleep in each other's arms.

* * *

She awakened first, all aglow with the passion that had dominated the night. The time was nearly 3-00am. In his sleep, Bernardo, had turned towards her. She encircled her arms around him and her excitement was aroused as she felt the firm muscles of his abdomen. Her fingers closed round his manhood and she felt it pulsate and engorge.

He entered her and they both went into a frenzy that prompted their juices to cascade in a fountain of semen.

Eventually their desire was sated as the need for sleep overcame both of them.

Four hours later she felt him stir, get out of bed, and start dressing. She coughed to let him know she was awake.

'I'll see you later at the salon,' he said. *'I have to get back now to open up for my staff to arrive for work.*

* * *

Bernardo guided her to a private room at the salon equipped with hairdressing chair and an elegant oyster-shaped wash basin. The four young lady hairdressers who worked for him were busy with other clients in the main salon which was fitted out with six chairs and washbasins. Eldegarde shivered when he kissed her on the nape of her neck before busying himself to restyling her hair with utmost professionalism.

When he had finished his work he produced a hand mirror and showed her what her new hairstyle looked like. She was ecstatic with the result.

'You have made me look younger,' she trilled. *'It's the very best hair-do I have ever had.'*

Bernardo accepted the compliment gracefully, and modestly commented: *'All I have done is to enhance the beauty you already have.'*

Eldergarde left Bernardo's salon a very happy woman as she took a taxi across the city of Barcelona and headed for an arranged meeting with Angela Di Silva.

'Goodbye Eldergarde, my love, it has been a pleasure being with you,' said Bernardo as he kissed her farewell. *'I hope I see you again soon.'*

Her final comment was meant to be pertinent: *'Oh, you will, you can be sure of that darling.'*

Angela was waiting at her office when Eldergarde arrived to settle up her account with *'Adorable Angela's Escort Agency for Women'*. The invoice read:

Fee to Agency €1.500,00

Hotel suite & dinner €1.200,00

Propina/Sr.Sanchez €1.000,00

Total €3.700.00

This represented a net profit of €1.320.00 to the Agency.

Made up of fee less €300 paid to Bernado Sanchez plus 10% discount from hotel €120,00.

Bernardo Sanchez's take from his first assignment as an escort amounted to €300 fee from the Agency plus the generous €1.000,00 propina [*gratuity*] from Eldergarde. Clearly Angela Di Silva's new escort agency was destined to be a money-spinner.

For Eldergarde Durke her night of companionship which turned into a torrid sex session cost her three thousand seven hundred euros. Sex for hire at the top end of the business did not come cheap. But to a widow who had been left a luxury villa in Sitges, and apartments in Frankfurt and London plus €18 million in cash and assets by her late multi-millionaire husband it was a drop in the ocean.

Eldergarde was not complaining. In fact she already wanted more, much more of the handsome hairdresser. At the same she had pride and did not want to send a message to Bernardo that she was so enamoured that she could not do without him. But she had her own dream for the future and, at the moment, it certainly included Bernardo.

'Let a couple of weeks go by Angela and then make another appointment for me with Bernardo,' she told the escort agency boss. 'I really liked the guy but I don't want him to think that I am too keen. I know how quickly men can get big-headed.'

Angela thought it was appropriate to issue a word of warning to her friend. 'Look Edelgarde dear, apart from my professional interest with what went on at the Ambassador Hotel last night , I am really happy for you that you enjoyed Bernardo Sanchez's company, and all that went with it, so much.

'You are, by nature, a very affectionate woman. Don't make the mistake of falling in love with Bernardo so quickly. He's rather like an autumn leaf and could be blown away by the slightest wind. Play the field a bit. I can fix you up with other men who are just as sexy as Bernardo. Not that I have anything against Bernardo, after all he was one of the first men I signed up for the agency. I agree with you he is a very attractive man. But he is a loose cannon and might not want to be tied too closely to one woman.

'However I can tell you, after so many years in the business, that men falling in love with hookers has been littered with heart ache, pain and even disaster. With this new escort agency I have switched the male-female roles. I can see the perils for warm-hearted women like you falling in love with a "guapo hombre" like Bernardo. I chose him as a very suitable candidate as an escort for my new agency. He is now doing for money what he had done as an amateur roué for most of his adult life by bedding every woman that attracts him. I have nothing against Bernardo but do not rely too much on his fidelity until you are sure of him. What I am saying is don't let yourself get hurt by exacerbating the pain you have been through since the death of your husband.'

Eldergarde was silent for a few minutes after listening to

Angela's words of wisdom. *'You are right of course darling,'* she replied as she handed over a cheque for €3.700,00.

'But Bernardo came like a ray of sunshine into my life after the deep depression I have been suffering. My husband, Heinrich, was a loving generous, gentle man. I emphasise the word gentle. But in bed he was a passive man. I don't think that, even to his dying day, did he realise how frustrated he always left me. Yet I loved him dearly for his kindness and I knew he loved me.

'The truth is that, throughout our marriage, I always had to keep a dildo in my bedside cabinet because Heinrich always left me dissatisfied. Throughout the years I never experienced a climax when having sex with Heinrich.

'Regular assignations with a red-blooded man like Bernardo would satisfy my cravings and I can now consign my eight inch rubber friend to the garbage bin. I thank you for your well-meant warning Angela and I will bear your advice in mind.

'But please don't forget to fix me up with another night out with Bernardo in two weeks time.'

* * *

12

Klaus Di Silva was in frisky mood that night and Angela, despite the past years when she plied her trade in the *via públicas* and then worked her way up the slippery ladder of the sex trade by working on her back in the best *burdels* of Barcelona, was delighted that her husband for one rapturous evening desired extended sex.

'*You must have been eating* viagra *tortillas ,*' Angela joked but nevertheless failing to disguise her admiration. '*Not just a quickie but you have managed to raise a gallop three times in an hour. If I was still on the game I would have to charge you double.*'

However Angela could see that Klaus was now spent and yawning but she had something she wanted to say to him before he lapsed into a deep sleep.

'*Klaus amado,*' she said endearingly. '*I believe the English have a saying that one swallow does not make a summer. The success of the evening I set up between Eldergarde and Bernado was a good start. But if my new escort agency is going to prosper I have to pull a few more irons out of the fire. Now I have a new client in mind. She is a 40-year-old Irish lady, Kathleen Clooney whose husband Peter, a famous 53-year-old racehorse owner and stock market entrepreneur was diagnosed with prostrate cancer 18 months ago. His malignant tumour was surgically removed but, as frequently happens in theses cases, the tumour has grown again. Further surgery, radiation and hormonal therapy have failed and unfortunately he has been left irreversibly impotent.*

'*But, poor lady, her husband's calamity has left Kathleen Clooney in a desperate state of hypertension through stressful frustration. I know that, following the unfortunate case of Eldergarde Durke, it makes our new escort agency sound like a clinic specialising in mental problems. I suppose, in a way, that is what it is-a therapeutic haven. Although, as time goes on, every client we attract may not necessarily fit into that category.*

'*Kathleen has been my bridge partner for the last six months and approached me at a tournament after hearing about my new escort agency.*'

Klaus Di Silva could only admire Angela's perspicacity.

'*Your shrewdness never fails to impress me,*' he said appreciatively. '*Who have you got in mind to match her with?*'

Angela's guileful grin was triumphant as she replied: '*The great Don Juan of the bullring-ex torero Jose Eugenio Moralés.*'

Klaus Di Silva was aghast with his partner's audacity and could only mutter admiringly: '*You devious bitch! That oversexed Moralés will plant a banderilla inside her that will ignite a flame that could transform her into a nymphomaniac. I am not sure whether you will be doing Senora Clooney a favour or disservice.*'

Although Klaus Di Silva's zealous disquisition was somewhat tongue in cheek it was nevertheless full of esteem for Angela's discerning decision in the choice of Kathleen Cooney's forthcoming sex partner.

* * *

For the first 16 years of her life Kathleen McDonnell, as she was known until she married her boss Peter Clooney, had lived under the oppressive rule of the nuns who taught at the

Roman Catholic school in County Mayo. Like many of her peers, who sat alongside her on the hard wood benches and ancient knotted desks with gaping holes for ink wells, she had suffered the cruel rap across her knuckles from a black-veiled Sister who spotted the merest whisper of lipstick, or slightest dab of rouge. Skirts had to be well below the knee at a time when across the Irish Sea British girls were flouncing down the High Streets of England in mini-skirts that, to the delight of goggle-eyed teenage lads, tightly encompassed their bouncing bottoms.

When she left school at the age of 17, moved with her family to Dublin, and started work as a junior clerk in the Dublin office of Peter Clooney's stock brokering firm, life became a little brighter. Even although her salary was small and she had to hand half of it over to her widowed mother each week. Yet she managed to buy small and attractive pieces of clothing more suited to a modern girl.

Kathleen's shapely legs first attracted the lecherous eyes of her boss, a well known womaniser, who, against the tenet of the Roman Catholic Church, had been divorced twice. Peter Clooney at 35 years of age and with a fortune of three and a half million Irish punts, and mounting every day in his account at the *Irish Banc nah Éireann,* a distinguished member of the Irish Stock Exchange, and an up and coming race-horse owner with a team of equine athletes of both codes, flat and over the sticks, champing costly hay at his trainer's stables and regularly appearing at the Curragh, Fairyhouse, Leopardstown and across the turbulent Irish Sea from Ascot to Aintree.

Clooney, now thought it high time for him to give up chasing the dolly birds and settle down in a lasting marriage with a respectable Irish lass and eventually a bunch of kids romping noisily in the backyard. The desire for respectability did not necessarily mean that he no longer appreciated a good looking piece of skirt and he had noticed that Kathleen had a good figure to go along with those lovely pins and child bearing hips. With a cream complexion and eyes as emerald as the left-sided third of the Irish flag she was dead ringer for the Hollywood legend Maureen O'Hara.

But at 17, with a strict widowed Catholic matriarch chaperoning her as tightly as a chastity belt, Peter knew that it would have to be marriage or nothing if he was going to couple with the bewitching Kathleen. She would have to be patiently groomed and cultivated. Her mother would have to be gently brought to heel also.

Cunning as a fox voraciously stalking a pecking chicken in a cornfield he watched Kathleen's movements closely for a few weeks. Although she had long since moved away from the austere strictures of the convent school the nuns had drilled into her about modesty her skirts were shorter than the Sisters would have approved she never let them encroach above her knees.

Despite her severe education Kathleen McDonnell did her utmost to be a modern girl and knew what she liked and wanted in the way of clothes. The mini-skirt had been developed by Mary Quant at her popular boutique in the Kings Road, Chelsea, London in 1965. The scanty garment got its biggest boost however when beanpole model Jean Shrimpton wore a precariously short white shift dress at the prestigious 1965 Melbourne Cup meeting in Australia.

The world's paparazzi, massed in forced at the teeming Flemington Racecourse to capture images of rich, famous and infamous celebrities, had a field day. The "Shrimp's" choice of daring apparel caused a sensation throughout the fashion world globally. There was a move in the rag trade to re-introduce a longer skirt line but the teenagers and their older sisters, and in some cases their mothers, united in mind and choice. For, in truth, the mini-skirt has never really gone away and nearly every man for the past four decades has worshipped at the shrine of Mary Quant's skimpy skirt.

Kathleen Mc Donnell, demure by upbringing and a strict Convent School education but an Irish rebel at heart, joined her teenage peers of the 1980's who laughed uproariously when they read Jean Shrimpton's explanation of the incident two decades earlier: '*The dress I wore at the Melbourne Cup was only so short because the designer, Colin Rolfe, had run out of material!*'

After Peter Clooney had wooed her for several months with trips to night clubs, theatres and race tracks Kathleen, having celebrated her 18th birthday, had to face her angry mother with the news that she had accepted her boss's proposal of marriage.

'*But he's been married twice,*' screeched the horrified Bridie McDonnell. '*You'll never be able to get married in a Roman Catholic Church you silly little "eejit". I've saved my long lace wedding dress for 35 years for you to wear, it belonged to your grandmother before that. You'll have to tell that cock-happy boss of yours a definite "no". I'll be made a laughing stock at the Catholic Mothers' Union just 'cos you've had a silly rush of blood to your head.*'

Her mother's furious tirade set the Irish bagpipes wailing in Kathleen's rebellious head. Her answer was seditious and spiteful.

'*Look Mother, it's my life we are talking about,*' she yelled angrily, hands on hips. '*I am old enough to make my own decisions . Whether you like it or not I am going to marry Peter. As for your silly old wedding dress you can stick it up your jumper, I wouldn't wear that if you paid me. I am thinking having a mini-dress specially made for Registry Office ceremony.'*

That was how another Irish rebellion ended.

* * *

13

Rebel teen-aged bride, turned model wife and loving stepmother, Kathleen Clooney, looked back on more than two decades of marriage to stockbroker husband Peter and could only recall two really bad days during that long period.

The downside was that they were both two awful days. The first, 18 years back, was when the paediatrician had told her that she would never be able to bear a child. The second and more recent time was the dreadful day after Peter' second prostrate operation when he was given the terrible prognosis that he was irreversibly impotent. Peter had been wonderfully supportive of her when she told him that she would never be able to present him with the baby son, or daughter, he craved for.

'Don't worry Katie me darlin' consoled Peter, his Irish brogue as broad as Dublin's River Liffey. *'We have the money and we'll adopt kids and love them as if they were ours.'*

That is exactly what they did-a boy from Sri Lanka, and an orphan girl from Cuba, both were seven years of age. Anka and Carmen had taken the Clooney surname and loved both their caring parents. They had both basically flown the nest having got their degrees at the world renowned University of Dublin founded in 1592 by Queen Elizabeth 1 of England. Anka was working as an interne doctor at Dublin's Clonkeagh Hospital while his step sister, Carmen, was a junior solicitor at the law practise of Riley, Coulter and Ryan in the City of Cork. A good future career was predicted for both the adopted Clooney kids. When Peter received the dreaded news it was Kathleen's turn to do the consoling.

'Despite the short shrift the old harridan, my mother, gave

you when you proposed to me you have been a wonderful husband and a magnificent father to our two adopted children,' she said with conviction. *'I am not about to turn my back on you just because of this setback. Our marriage will survive darling.'* But they both found it hard. Peter, because the sex life he had enjoyed almost since puberty was over. Kathleen because he was the only man she had ever made love with and she had become addicted to his robust way of making love.

She realised already that she would find it hard to honour the promise she had made to her stricken spouse. She quickly fell into a depression desperately searching for a way to satisfy her own cravings without hurting his feelings.

*   *   *

Peter had flown to England to see his horse *Rojo Belleza* run at Cheltenham that day, and was not due back in Barcelona until after the weekend. That evening, as arranged with Angela Di Silva, Kathleen turned up at the five star €300 a night Hotel Rey Juan Carlos 1, in Barcelona's Avinguda Diagonal.

Don José Eugenio Moralés, former star torero, hero of the *aficionados por de corrida,* nowadays a distinguished bullfight television pundit, Barcelona bar owner and a favourite of Spain's colourful celebrity magazines made an immediate hit with Senora Kathleen Cooney.

There was only one year difference between them. Kathleen would eventually look back and analyse what it was about the handsome Spaniard, of gypsy stock, that attracted her most. The jet black hair which was once adorned with the *torero's coleta* (pig tail), traditionally worn underneath the *montera* (bicorne hat). The sultry dark eyes indicating his Romany background. The fact that this courageous man

65

featured more than 400 times in *la fiesta brava* and in his final appearance flirted perilously close to death in the blood and sand of Madrid's imperious *Plaza de Toros*. Or that testosterone seemed to ooze from every fibre of the taut body of a man who was once compared by knowledgeable critics of *tauromaquia* with immortals of the 'ring' such as Juan Belmonte and El Cordobés. Whatever it was that, perhaps even a mixture of all those attributes, after an hour in his company at the hotel's plush cocktail bar she felt randy in a most immodest way that would have took the starch out of the snow white *guimpe* that the nuns who used to teach her wore around their shoulders.

'*Call me José,*' he told her as he waved a finger signalling the *camerero* to serve the French champagne he ordered to be put on ice. '*May I call you Kathleen?*'

She immediately felt at ease with this flamboyant man who she was to learn always looked as if he needed a shave to remove his permanent dark stubble. She had never encountered his like before in her fairly sheltered life. She told him that he was the first '*toreador*' she had ever met.

'*Oh dear!*' he rebuked her with a smile. '*Never, never use that word to describe a bullfighter-a toreador only appears in the opera Carmen, the correct term in Castillian is torero or matador.*'

Kathleen joined in the good humour with which he had corrected her, and said: '*I consider myself slapped across the wrist for that mistake. But what I was about to say is that although I have never been to a bullfight I have seen the spectacle on Spanish television and have always admired the ornate uniform that the torero wears in the bullring.*'

Jose warmed to her enthusiastic interest and rejoined: '*Correction number two coming up. The torero does not wear* a uniform. His costume is called " traje de luces", in English that means "suit of lights". They each cost many thousands of euros and a top matador needs at least six of them each bullfighting season, which, in Spain, is summer-time.

'The toreros' traje de luces consists of a silk jacket generously embroidered in gold, skin tight pantalónes, all topped by the bi-corne montera which is worn untilted on his head.'

Kathleen was fascinated by the former matador' description of bullfighting as a ritual.

'But isn't it cruel to the bulls? she asked naively, adding. 'You know the Brits are quite frenetic on the topic of cruelty to animals. But the Irish are not as sensitive. Many of us were brought up in farming communities. We know that at the end of the day, so to speak, that the cattle, pigs and sheep we rear will finish up in the abattoir. From there they inevitably finish up on our dinner plates.'

Jose was surprised that this intelligent woman was showing such genuine interest in the corrida.

'The bull that enters the ring has been developed from thoroughbred stock over centuries of selective breeding,' he explained. 'Unlike the domestic bulls raised and fed on your lush rain enriched Irish meadow-lands to fatten them up the fighting bulls are lean and fit and instinctively charge at anything that moves. The instinct bred into them over the years is to charge. They are not starved or tortured to make them savage. The animals selected for the bullring, have been tested for bravery, and allowed to live a year longer than the animals assigned to the slaughter house. When they enter the ring at four years of age, to the roar of the aficionados, it is the first time they have ever faced a matador.

'The torero greets this noble beast with a series of passes

using his large cape to dominate the animal. The bull goes for the large moving target of cloth of the cape , not the colour red. In fact bulls are colour blind and will equally attack the reverse side of the cape which is yellow.

'The second phase of the corrida brings the picadors, riding horses and wielding lances, into the action. The horses are padded and the picador's job is to weaken the bull's neck muscles so the animal lowers its head for the kill later.

'The next phase brings the banderillos into action. At considerable risk to themselves they place their barbed sticks, known as banderillas, in the neck of the bull, again weakening the muscles so that the bull must lower its head.

'The torero's estoque (killing sword) must go between the bull's shoulder blades for the perfect kill which is known as "the moment of truth". It takes raw courage from the torero to plunge the sword into the bull's aorta. Significantly every matador statistically will receive at least one goring a season. That is why bullfighting is known as the fiesta brava.'

Jose turned his left wrist to look at the engraved gold Rolex watch his aficionados had subscribed for and presented at his Testimonial corrida after the awesome *cornada* which threatened his life and ended his career as a bullfighter eight years earlier.

Later that evening after a magnificent, wine enriched, dinner at the hotel Jose and Kathleen lay spent on ornate four poster bed at the escort agency's luxurious apartment put at their disposal by the thoughtful Angela Di Silva, when she noticed the scars of the awful cornada wound on his backside left by the bull that ended his career as a torero.

Tears welled up in Kathleen's eyes as she shrewdly understood the agony he had endured.

'You, poor, poor thing,' she sympathised. *'How you must have suffered.'*

* * *

14

Angela Di Silva immediately acceded to Kathleen Clooney's request for a get-together at The Ladies Bridge Club of Barcelona which met for lunch and a game of cards every Wednesday.

'It was a wonderful, wonderful evening with José,' enthused Kathleen as they sipped their *Jerez Finos* apéritifs. *'Thank you darling for arranging everything. I never knew sex could be like that. Although my husband, Peter, has always been a kind considerate husband in his lovemaking, when he was capable. But his performances could be timed by boiling an egg. A soft boiled egg at that -of the three minute variety. Once over for Peter it was finished for me. He has never suspected and I have never told him it continually left me frustrated. I had too much respect for him in other ways to say so. Yet he had a reputation as a womaniser before we were married. Perhaps he had used up all the lead in his pencil with his previous women. I learned to live with the inadequacies of our sex life until fate hit me with an even crueller blow when he was struck down with prostrate cancer.*

'Making love with José was entirely different. He hardly let up all night. As compared with boiling an egg with Peter it was like enjoying a full-blown beef dinner cooked on a slow roast. Perhaps it is the testosterone, of a courageous man who once killed bulls for a living, surging inside his scrotum. He was insatiable. Regular appointments with José would enable me to cope with Peter's unfortunate impotence and thereby save our marriage, which is still precious to me.

'I leave it to you dear Angela to arrange further meetings with José and to maintain the high degree of secrecy required if my marriage to my beloved Peter is to remain intact.'

Then, delving into her capacious handbag, as women tend to do, she finally retrieved an envelope and said, as she handed it over: *'There Angela, and thank you once again, is my cheque which includes the thousand euros "propina" for José which I know you will pass on. Now let's enjoy our lunch which is on me today then we can enjoy our afternoon and evening playing bridge. I feel lucky today. There is a saying in Ireland, lucky with playing cards lucky with love!'*

The new *Escort Agency for Women* had chalked up yet another success to the delight of livewire business woman, the alluring, Donna Angela Di Silva. The following day, after her tryst with Kathleen Clooney she set about again increasing her growing stable of three studs, the English lad Richard, who was still to be blooded, libidinous hairdresser Bernardo and concupiscent former *torero,* José. This shrewd business woman had a candidate in mind.

Angela was no racist. When she worked in the brothels she made friends with sister *putas* of all colours and nationalities African, Chinese, Asian, Middle Eastern as well as Europeans.

The next recruit she had targeted as a recruit to the agency was black, as dark a shade of ebony as the Negroid race produces throughout the globe. But, the colour of his skin aside, there were other interesting facets about the towering 6ft 6inch Kote Rabtana that made him stand out from the masses. His astuteness, his perspicacity, his educational achievements were, arguably, wasted in his job as a paramedic with the Barcelona ambulance service.

He was 24 years of age when, as a *Falasha*--Ethiopian Jew-he was evacuated with 14,000 of his peers from refugee camps in the Sudan and air lifted to Israel. Although a further 12,000 *Falashas* had been flown to Israel in 1984-85 in a rescue operation codenamed *Operation Moses,* the highly sensitive

Kote felt that the 'white' Israelis, many of them descendants of the gruesome Holocaust, paradoxically turned their back on their coloured brothers-in-religion.

So he left the land of the "Chosen People" for the land of opportunity, the USA. He spent the next four years qualifying for a degree in psychiatry. But unable to get a job in that field, because of his colour he angrily suspected, he decamped to Spain who had little record of racial discrimination. He finally landed up in Barcelona where the only job he could find was as a paramedic in the city ambulance service-an important duty but hardly compatible with his qualifications. Angela Di Silva met Kote Rabtana in the coffee bar at the *Gimnasio Campeóns,* where she had called to get an update fitness report on her protégé, Richard Martin, from the owner of the gym, former champion weightlifter, Louis Samuels.

Kote was sipping a large glass of protein drink after his workout in the weight room. Despite the towel draped over his well-toned shoulders Angela could see the taut arm muscles and six pack abdomen. His handsome looks and dark wavy hair was accentuated by the ebony shine of his honed body. Kote chivalrously invited her to have a coffee when she perched herself on the adjacent bar-stool.

Impressed by his courtesy Angela, matching his politeness, accepted the invitation.

'*Gracias,*' she acceded coyly, '*Café con leche, por favor. Would you prefer to speak English? I notice you have an American accent.*'

Kote's smile was infectious as he carefully weighed up his reply.

'*Spanish-English it is the same to me,*' he said in a matter of fact tone in his anxiety not to appear boastful. '*As a matter fact I can also speak Hebrew, Arabic and passable German. But you were absolutely correct in detecting the American accent for I lived in the USA for some years before coming here to Spain. In answer to your question however let us talk in English.'*

Now the ice had been broken Angela, emphasising her interest in this handsome coloured giant, queried: *'But you are not American are you?'*

Draining the last dregs of his large glass of protein drink Kote launched into a detailed account of his bizarre background, saying: *'You are absolutely correct. I am not an American. I am a Falasha. You might well look puzzled Senora, in other words I am an Ethiopian Jew. Or to use a common description, which I don't like--a black Jew.*

'For many thousands of years my people were stranded in Ethiopia. A country where half the population is Christian and many of the rest are Muslims. A third of the 30,000 Falashas fled Ethiopia to escape famine, war and persecution and were hustled into refugee camps in Sudan. Between 1984 and 1985 the Israeli government secretly air-lifted 12,000 Falashas from the inhuman Sudanese camps. It became known throughout the civilised world as Operation Moses.

'My family were evacuated from Ethiopia to Israel in 1991.'

Angela Di Silva was stunned by Kote's passionate discourse.

'What a strange story,' she said sympathetically. *'Were your people welcomed by the Israelis as fellow Jews?'*

Kote wrinkled his face in painful denial as he answered truthfully: *'Not absolutely. Many of the more orthodox Israelis claimed that the Falasha was only a fringe splinter-group of Judaism. Yet it was a form of the Jewish religion that almost*

73

certainly dated before the 2ⁿᵈ Century BC. '

Angela was amazed and queried curiously: '*So you decided to leave Israel and go to America?'*

Kote grinned and replied: '*Yeah, and there I found there was still a religious barrier with American Jews. The problem that in the eyes of so many American Jews I didn't qualify to be Kosher because of my colour. I can never understand how that great entertainer Sammy Davis Jr was such a cult figure to American Jewry. Sammy was converted to Judaism when another great show business figure, Eddie Cantor, told him about the similarities between the Jewish and black cultures. During a hospital stay after he had lost his left eye in an automobile accident Sammy Davis Jr switched religions after reading a history of the Jewish race.*

'*So many American Jews thought the colour of my skin was a barrier to me being accepted unreservedly into their faith. This despite the spell-binding preaching of the late Martin Luther King.*

'*Although I earned my degree in psychiatry I spent two years unsuccessfully applying for jobs inside the US medical profession. So, all in all, I was happy to land up here in Spain where there are virtually \no colour bars or bias against any form of religion. Being a paramedic is not a job that a man with a degree in psychiatry is expected to land up with, and is not very well paid, but at least I am doing work that helps my fellow human beings. So I am not complaining.'*

Angela was thoughtful for a moment as she mulled over what she had just heard.

'*Look Kote,'* she said. '*I have some business with Louis Samuels, the owner of this gymnasium, so I must leave you in a moment. But I think I might be able to help by putting a proposition your way. When are you free for lunch this week? So we can talk about my proposition.'*

Kote was quite surprised by the suggestion this luxuriously groomed and beautiful woman had made to him. Was he being propositioned in a romantic way? He tried not to show his understandable excitement, and replied: *'Well I am free tomorrow at that time of the day. I am not on duty at the ambulance station until eight o'clock in the evening.'*

Angela showed she was pleased and, with a warm smile, as she said: *'That's fine Kote. Tomorrow it is then. Here is my business card in case you need to get in touch. Please meet me at* 2 o'clock at the Restaurante Los Caracoles in the Bario Chino. Do you know it?'

Kote nodded his head to signify his assent: *'Who doesn't Senora? It is one of the best eating places in Barcelona. I'll be there.'*

* * *

15

Louis Samuels hustled into the coffee bar to meet Angela hurriedly pulling his Adidas fleecy top over his sweat-soaked athletic vest.

'Hi, Donna Di Silva,' the big man boomed. 'Sorry I have kept you waiting but I was finishing a training session with a client.'

Angela waved the gym boss's apology aside. 'Oh, don't worry Louis,' she replied. 'I was bought a cup of coffee and thoroughly entertained by a guy called Kote Rabtana. In fact I was quite intrigued by him.'

Louis Samuels concurred with Angela Di Silva's first impressions of the charismatic Kote Rabtana. 'Yeah, yeah--our Kote is quite a fella, 'ain't he? He told you, of course, how he came to be here in Barcelona? That he is one of thousands of Ethiopian Jews who fled away from oppression in their own country to what they believed would be a warm welcome from the Israeli Jews? How he earned a degree in psychiatry at the University of California , Los Angeles, but failed to get a job in the US medical service, probably because of his colour he suspected?

'But he is in his element as a paramedic with the Barcelona ambulance service helping unfortunate people who are injured or sick. But I am afraid it is not a very well paid job and not commensurate for a man of his qualifications and ability. I let him train here at the gymnasium free because, on his wages, he cannot afford our fees. But he repays us by being a member of our team when we compete in club weight lifting contests against other gymnasiums.

'He is big, as you have already observed and immensely

strong. But what is more important he is a really nice modest guy. A gentleman you might say with the emphasis on the word gentle.

Angela expressed her agreement with Louis Samuels summing up of her new acquaintance, Kote Rabtana.

'Kote is also an extremely attractive man,' she emphasised. 'In fact Louis, after a brief talk with him I am thinking of offering him a job as an escort in my new agency. With his looks, physique and personality he would turn the head of most women.'

Louis Sammuels concurred, and asserted: 'As usual Donna Di Silva your judgement is impeccable and furthermore I am sure Kote could do with the kind of money he will earn working for you. But please tell me what else brings you to my gymnasium at this time of the day.'

Angela immediately switched her mind towards the main purpose of her visit, and replied: 'Louis I really came for a progress report on my protégé, Richard Martin. 'He's been under your wing for almost a month now. How has he shaped up?'

There was an air of confidence, and a touch of pride, in the studied answer that came from the former weight lifting champion. 'Donna Di Silva, I am delighted to tell you that the boy is ready. He has trained hard and has put on five kilos muscle weight. He is, as they say, fit as a fiddle. If you will follow me into the gymnasium I will unveil him for your approval.'

It takes a lot to surprise a worldly wise woman of Angela Di Silva's calibre but she admitted to be taken aback when she saw the excellent shape Richard Martin was in.

'Strip off lad, show the lady just how hard you have worked

in the past month,' Louis rapped in the direction of the bronzed figure of the English lad. Richard, piece by piece discarded his training gear. First the Nike top, then the red vest with swoop logo. Louis then yelled: *'Now your strides boy. The full monty, as they say. Let Donna Di Silva see that she has won the jackpot by backing you.'*

Richard stood as still as a statue. Biceps, quad muscles and abs rippling with bulk and tone. Angela gazed at his half erect manhood as she looked him over from head to foot.

'Fucking gargantuan,' she reiterated the coarse comment she had made over four weeks earlier when she had seen him strip off. *'You'll be the star of my show Richard. As for you Louis you have done a magnificent job on him and, as I promised, there is an extra thousand euros in it for you.'*

Then focussing her attention once more on Richard Martin she said: *'You are almost ready to go to work for the agency. But first I want you to spend a night with my best girl escort--Monica--she is very experienced in the business and she will teach you some of the tricks of the trade and how to please a woman. She will show you how to be patient in your love-making and how to make sure the client you are escorting gets full sexual satisfaction.'*

* * *

If Richard Martin harboured the illusion that he was God's gift to women it was going to be rudely shattered by Monica Kepler, a 39-year-old dark-eyed beauty, who once plied her trade as a street-walker in Montmartre and then the bawdy houses of Madrid before joining *Adorable Angela's Escort Agency.*

* * *

The afternoon following Angela's visit to the *Gimnasio*

Campéons she briefed one of her longest serving women escorts, Monica Kepler, about how she wanted her to put her newest recruit, Richard Martin, through, as it were, a *"dress rehearsal"* that evening

'*Go to dinner with him just as if he is a client,*' Angela gave her instructions. '*The Agency will pay for the night and that includes a €500 propina for you Monica. After dinner hire a taxi to take you from the restaurant to the agency's luxury apartment at the foot of Montjuic, where the Miró Art Foundation is situated.*

'*Make it a night of hot passion. Remember this boy comes from England and the English are noted for being rather restrained in their love making. Strip away all his inhibitions. Teach him that pleasuring a woman is not a sprint but a dusk to dawn marathon.*

'*Incidentally Monica I think you are going to enjoy the evening yourself. This Englander is a very attractive boy and he's got a joystick that would not be out of place on a donkey. In fact I have only two words for it---fucking gargantuan!*'

* * *

They met, as arranged by their boss Angela Di Silva at the excluisive *Restaurante Gaig* arguably rated as one of the best eating places in Barcelona and in the top ten of restaurants in the whole of Spain. A long established restaurant the *Gaig* had recently moved to its new luxurious premises in the *Hotel Cram* Angela, in keeping with her propensity for detail, had not only booked the table for two but arranged for the bill to be sent to her at the agency.

Neither Richard or Monica felt it necessary to go through the nervy, tentative and lengthy ritual of getting to know each other when escort and client first meet on a romantic tryst which would inevitably end up with a romp in bed.

They were both professionals in the sex trade and rated the assignation as just another job. But secretly, perhaps a little arrogantly, Richard questioned why Angela Di Silva had delegated Monica to teach him how to make love. But he was diplomatic enough not to openly question the escort agency chief's decision. She was paying the bill after all. He needed the money his new job promised to provide him with. It would rescue him from Skid Row where he was certainly heading when Angela had first picked him up in *La Rambla* just over a month previous.

'Why the bloody hell does Angela want this Monica to give me a sex lesson?' he asked himself nevertheless. *'I've never had any complaints from the women I have made love to before. Nevertheless this Monica is an attractive woman so the night might be a bit of fun. I doubt that she will be able to teach me anything though. On the other hand I might teach her a thing or two.'*

Monica Kepler was about to put a serious dent in Richard's ego which was nigh as colossal as his outrageous wand, so much admired by Angela Di Silva.

Brought up in a well travelled and reasonably wealthy English family Richard was well versed in his knowledge of good food and fine wine. After joining Monica in an *aperitivo* of *Campari con zumo de naranja* at their table Richard called over the *Maitre d'Hotel* to ask for the menu and wine list.

'Will you leave it to me to chose from the menu?' Richard asked his attractive companion who arrived for the rendezvous dressed in a stylish red leather outfit with white accessories.

Monica, who was already warming to this young Englishman, replied: *'Of course darling, I leave it up to you. I like a masterful man. In any case I am not hard to please where wine and food are concerned. If I hear that you are ordering something that I really don't like I'll give you a shout.'*

Richard's broad smile indicated how pleased he was and he said: *'Fair enough Monica.'*

Recalling the *Maitre d'* to the table he ordered two roasted pepper and aubergine salads as starters and, after a careful perusal of the wine list, he selected a well-chilled bottle of *Palacio de Bornos Rueda Superior* to accompany the salads.

'This is as good a Rueda wine as one can buy--that is if you can afford it,' said Richard with a wry smile. *'My father always ordered it when we came to Spain on our family vacations. It is unique in the respect that it is made with a blend of 90% Verdejo and 10% Viura grapes.'*

Monica endorsed the wine after taking her first sip from the wine that had arrived at their table in a well-filled bucket of ice. *'Oh that wine is really to my taste,'* she said approvingly. *'Obviously your father was a wine connoisseur.'*

Monica's comment pleased Richard and he explained: *'Dad always kept a good cellar and still does , although he is a Church of England cleric.'*

While they consumed their salads and leisurely finished off the excellent Rueda wine, Richard explained how he had come to Spain a few years back to study at the University of Valencia. He also detailed how he was caught in the middle of the night with a young Spanish girl student in his room and expelled from the University.

'I was too ashamed to go back to England and explain my disgrace,' he said ruefully. *'My father is a kind person and would have stood by me in my hour of trouble. But I just would not like to hurt him. So I bummed my way round Spain*

until I got to Barcelona and, in desperation, tried to work as a male hooker---not very successfully I might add. I hadn't got the money to get back to England even if I could have swallowed my pride and ask my family for help.

'In fact when Angela Di Silva found me soliciting in La Rambla I didn't know where my next crust of bread was coming from. But, as you know, Angela financed me to go to Louis Sammuel's gymnasium for a month to get fit and set me up in a nice little apartment so that I could leave the flea-pit room I was renting in the Barrio Chino. Now, as you also know, I am going to work as a male escort in her new agency that will service neglected and frustrated women.'

He broke off the conversation to order two plates of *Marmitako*---Basque tuna and potato casserole--as a main course, accompanied by a bottle of *Muruve Crianza 2002* from the wine-making region of Toro. While they waited for the food to be brought to the table Monica assured him that he was taking a sensible step in linking up with Angela Di Silva.

'Like me Angela spent several years as a street girl and then working on her back in the bordellos of Barcelona before landing on her feet to make a successful marriage with Klaus,' she said. *'But Angela is a shrewd businesswoman who cares and protects the people who work for her. If you are genuine with her she will look after you and in a year or so you could put away enough money to return to your family in England with your head held high.'*

Richard was assured with Monica's comforting words and they both settled down to enjoy their casseroles which were placed on top of an electric table-heater.

'That was an excellent meal,' said Monica. *'Congratulations Richard, I am sure you will do as one of Angela's escorts if*

you can order a meal and wine like that for the clients. But remember it is what you put on the menu in bed later in the evening that is the most important duty for an escort. I hope you are not offended that Angela has asked me to teach you a few tricks of the trade?'

Richard, forgetting his earlier inhibitions about the evening, said: *'I am really looking forward to it. But first let me order our last course.'*

As he had done throughout the meal, Richard chose the final course carefully. Spurning the long list of desserts, for which tourists often opted for, he selected a more traditional *queso Espanol.*

The discerning Head Waiter nodded his approval when Richard elected a combination of *Queso Manchego Anciano* on a platter with razor sliced *Jamon Serrano,* plus a a local Catalunian delicacy called *Tupi de Sort*--soft cheese served in a ceramic pot.

'May I be so bold, Ustedes, as to offer you a bottle of suitable wine to complement your queso?' asked the Head Waiter bowing respectfully towards Richard, who accepted the offer with equal grace.

A bottle of *Las Reñas Monastrell 2002* soon appeared with the cheese. Holding the bottle towards the light the Head Waiter said: *'I hope the Senora and you enjoy this fantastic red wine, with the compliments of the house, which comes from the Bullas bodega in the Murcian region.'*

Both Monica and Richard gave the wine, the cheese and the wine a vote of approval as they finished their meal with steaming *café con leches.*

'Come on Richard cherié, let's grab the taxi and head for the escort agency apartment in Montjuic,' said Monica taking

hold of Richard's arm as the Head Waiter courteously guided them to the restaurant foyer, *'The best is yet to come!'*

By dawn the following morning Richard had to concede that Monica Kepler was totally right in that assertion.

* * *

16

Angela Di Silva, happy in the knowledge that she had set up Richard Martin, so to speak, for a trial run with former brothel girl Monica Kepler the previous evening, began organising her own day including the lunch appointment she had arranged with the Ethiopian Jew refugee, Kote Rabtana.

She felt good as she put her beloved *Zephyr* through his equine paces during a brisk gallop at dawn. Angela followed that up with an energetic stint in the heated Di Silva swimming pool churning up her usual 20 lengths. Over their breakfast of choice Scottish smoked salmon and scrambled eggs Angela told her husband, Klaus, about Kote, the man she was meeting for lunch, who she believed would make an excellent addition to her growing stable of male escorts.

'A Falasha, an Ethiopian Jew eh!,' said Klaus. *'I remember that very strange story about the black Jews who were taken in as refugees by Israel. They had lived amongst Christian and Muslims in Ethiopia, and were persecuted and tortured for centuries long before the birth of Jesus Christ. At the time the newspapers named the evacuation airlift, the exodus of the Black Jews from Addis Ababba to Tel Aviv, Operation Moses.*

'Your man Kote sounds quite a guy and, as usual, I'll back your judgement that he will prove to be a valuable asset to your team of male escorts.'

* * *

Angela arrived at *Restaurante Los Caracoles* ten minutes before the time she had set to meet Kote. As an aperitif she ordered an American-style *Martini* spiked with a large measure of gin, clinking with slivers of ice, to be brought to her table. Kote Rabtana arrived on the dot and quickly spotted her upstairs seated in the restaurant's minstrel gallery. With style and gallantry he kissed her right hand as he bid her a warm *buenos dia*. She ordered *medio hecho* entrecote steak and salad for both of them after asking if that would suit him.

Over the food Angela told Kote how well her escort agency was doing. She explained that she thought he would be a suitable candidate to become one of her team of escorts and detailed the sizeable amount of money he would be able to earn.

Kote hesitated or a moment before replying: *'I accepted your invitation for lunch because you are a very attractive woman. I have to admit I have always had a penchant for beautiful women.'*

Angela decided to make the situation clear from the outset.

'Look Kote my offer to you is purely business--and my business is running an escort agency. The job I have in mind for you caters for frustrated women. If you want to come aboard you will be made welcome as all my employees are. But let me make it clear I do not personally come into the equation . I am happily married to a very good man and I mean to keep it that way. I like you Kote otherwise I would not be offering you a job. If you are not interested please tell me so straight. But don't let it spoil your lunch because it certainly will not affect my appetite, one way or the other.'

Kote was impressed with the brutal honesty of her hard-hitting diatribe, and said: *'You certainly know how to put a guy in his place. I admire that. Now you have made the position clear I will accept your offer of a job on the understanding that the arrangement is purely a business matter, and, of course,*

I will keep it that way. Nevertheless Senora Di Silva I will not apologise for acknowledging that you are an exceedingly good looking woman.'

Angela extended her right hand. *'That's a deal then Kote now that we understand each other. You can call me Angela, all my other employees do. You have my business card please call at my office at 11 o'clock tomorrow morning-if that time suits you. I'll put you on the payroll straight away and also at the same time fill you in with all the details of how my agency works.'*

So Angela Di Silva's organisation now had a line-up of four sexy men. As she had originally planned she needed a couple more candidates to complete her Barcelona set-up before moving on to the next important step to turn the agency into a national business with branches in the other major Spanish cities , such as Valencia, Seville, Bilbao and, of course, in the fascinating metropolis of Madrid. An important event in the recent and speedy evolution of *Adorable Angela's Escort Agency for Women* had taken place the previous evening when her first recruit had received a final briefing on the intricacies of the sex trade from a former Montmartre whore. She was now eager to learn how that liaison had fared.

*   *   *

Monica and Richard had different thoughts as, well fed and wined, they sped across the city by taxi from the plush *Restaurante Gaig* to one of the luxurious *apartmentos di amor* owned by Angela's escort agency.

'She's certainly a good looker and a sexy bitch,' mused Richard. *'There could be worse ways of spending a Friday night than a frolic in the hay with Monica. I wonder how old she is? I guess from what she has told me of her background in Paris, Madrid and Barcelona she's, at least, 35-so there's*

an eleven year difference between us--not that it matters.'

Monica, who in fact had passed her 39th birthday, meanwhile cogitated: *'I like him, which is more than I can say for most my clients when I worked in the brothels. He's got a quiet English charm about him. But what will he be like in bed?'*

*   *   *

Monica heard him turn the shower off as she lay, legs stretched out along the satin bedspread waiting for Richard. When he appeared, his damp hair falling on to the shoulders of the Paisley dressing gown, which Angela had bought when she kitted him out.

'Unveil the goodies buster,' she said, determined to initiate him the hard way. Then opening her long legs, invitingly a little wider, added: *'Come over here and kiss the honey pot.'*

There was a rustle of silk as he let the dressing gown drop to the floor and stood proudly before in all his glory.

She could only gasp at what she saw and drew on a slice of her home country, France's, glorious history, when she told him admiringly: *'As French general Pierre Bosquet said when he admired the bravery of the English cavalrymen in the Charge of the Light Brigade at the Battle of Balaclava--C'est magnifique, mais ce n'est pas la guerre--That is magnificent but it has not won the war. Now climb into the saddle soldier, let's see if that formidable weapon of yours can win the battle.'*

*   *   *

Both of them summed up the night of passion in glowing terms when, weary after a six hour romp between the sheets, they yawned their way through a breakfast of warm buttered croissants and creamy hot chocolate.

'That is the first time in years that I have truly experienced an orgasm,' Monica ruminated. 'For once I did not to have to fake the grunts and sighs of satisfaction at his lovemaking like I do with many of my clients. What's more he's got the stamina to last the whole night through--he'll drive women crazy.'

While Richard Martin reflected, rather coarsely: 'She was an absolutely wonderful grind. I could get to like her too much. I must not forget the things she taught me about making love.'

Later that day Angela Di Silva received a terse but lucid phone call from Monica who simply said down the line: 'Angela darling the young man will do! I promise you there will be a lot of happy and satisfied women after a night with him.'

17

There were no bounds to Angela Di Silva's energy. Apart from the arduous task of running the most successful escort agency in Spain with it's new spin-off for frustrated women; her passion for equestrianism, involving regular appearance at local and national gymkhanas; her two afternoons and evenings playing bridge; and the duties performed so seriously of being a good wife to her beloved Klaus and devoted mother to their darling son, Tobajas, she set aside precious time for her favourite charity.

Her dedication to help the growing ranks of unfortunate Spanish victims of domestic violence prompted the benevolent members of Barcelona's *Sociedad Orantes* to unanimously elect her as their founder President. During her four years in office the Society had raised more than €4 million, mainly through concerts, golf tournaments, gymkhanas, bridge drives and personal donations, which mainly went to setting up shelters in various Spanish cities staffed by doctors and nurses, counsellors and social service workers, for the ill-starred victims of domestic violence.

Madrid journalist Jerome Socolovsky highlighted the growing problem of domestic violence in Spain, when in *Womens.eNews* he wrote: *It is largely thanks to Ana Orantes-- to her death by burning to be precise--that gender violence in Spain finally burst into the public's awareness. It was 1997 and, at the age of 60, Senora Orantes mustered the courage to appear on a TV show and testify to the decades of brutal beatings by her husband. She had been unable to get a restraining order despite dozens of complaints to the police.*

'*Several days after the show was aired Orantes was dead. Her husband had beaten her badly one last time. Then he doused her with gasoline and lit a match. Now, six years later, the Spanish parliament had unanimously passed legislation that just might have saved Orantes' life had it been in force then. The "Order for the Protection of Victims of Domestic Violence" gives battered women the option of getting a fast-track restraining order on a violent partner within a maximum of 72 hours.'*

Despite the Spanish parliament's legislation and writer Socolovsky's article in 2003, between January and October of that year, 74 women were killed in Spain recalling the dictatorship of General Franco between 1939-75 when wife-beating was technically allowed.

*   *   *

One unfortunate victim in the Barcelona shelter for these deplorable women was a badly battered girl from Kenya named Somy Múlder, who was particularly befriended by the warm-hearted Angela Di Silva. She was born 24 years previously in Nairobi, one of the largest and fastest growing cities in Africa, from a Bantu mother and a tough entrepreneurial businessman who had made a fortune from slaughtering elephants before the civilised world made the international trade in ivory illegal. However Harry Múlder never lost his love for big game hunting right up until the time he was mortally savaged by a lion. He was carried on a litter, dying from his horrific wounds, by Kikuyo porters several miles and then by converted Land Rover ambulance over rough bush terrain to Nairobi.

On his deathbed he told his wife he had left her enough money in trust for her to rejoin her relatives in her native village near the Mathari Valley. It amounted to little more than five thousand English pounds. Nevertheless it was a sum that represented a small fortune to the impoverished Bantu people in south Kenya. He then called his seven year

91

old daughter Somy to his bedside and thrust a large manila envelope into the child's hands.

'*Guard this envelope with your life my girl,*' he whispered, in the knowledge that his time was nearly up. '*When you attain the ripe old age of 25 take it to the bank in Nairobi. What the envelope contains will keep you in comfort for the rest of your life. Meanwhile the bank, on my instructions, will fund your time at school, and hopefully at the University of Nairobi from an annuity. Have a good life child and always think kindly of your old Dad who loved you.*'

Harry Múlder, formerly of Amsterdam, gave up the ghost two hours later. Only his widow, Samantha Obu, grasping the hand of her daughter Somy, a handful of Kikuyu servants and the clergyman conducting the funeral ceremony, were at the graveside. In death as in life bluff Harry had few friends.

Somy, quietly spoken, seriously shy, sailed through school and later University. She grew up to be an attractive young woman. Her appealing colour, midway between the bony skin of her mother and the rubicund visage of her late father. Her hair was a wiry auburn that required an attractive Audrey Hepburn cut for the rest of her life. Adding to her charm she was a born linguist having mastered Swahili, Portugese, Spanish, English and Arabic.

She was a boarder both at school and later at University only occasionally visiting her mother in her village. But she had little in common with the Bantu way of life and by the time her mother died when Somy was 18 they had grown apart and another funeral was held with few tears being shed.

After three years at the University of Nairobi, founded in 1956, Somy collected her Batchelor of Arts degree. But before she put in the further period of residence to qualify as a full blown M.A she had met, fallen in love, and married a handsome Arab.

Abdul Bin Shakim never ever got around to telling Somy how he earned a living while she, probably because of the love dust in her eyes, never asked.

'I am a Muslim and we do not consider business is a suitable topic to discuss with a woman, even if she is your wife,' he said arrogantly. Within a year of the civil ceremony in Nairobi she had received a first painful beating from the sadistic Shakim. Her 'crime' was failing to have his evening meal ready when he arrived home several hours later than promised. The thrashings and humiliation continued at ever more frequent intervals. She never blew the whistle on him firstly she was still in love with the guy and secondly she did not know who to turn to for help. Two of the most prevalent reasons why battered wives so often allowed themselves to be so badly treated.

Abdul cloaked all his movements in mystery witholding the fact that he was clandestinely working for a Muslim fundamentalist organisation linked with terrorism. He was being chased by Mossad, Israel's Secret Service, and in the style of a fugitive dragged his unfortunate wife around Europe to Germany, France, Italy and finally Spain.

Obviously running short of money he cruelly bullied her in an effort to squeeze any cash that she had. He just did not believe that she could not legally touch the legacy her father had left her until she had passed her 25th birthday as stipulated in her late father's will.

After landing up in Barcelona he flew into a maniacal rage and beat her nearly to death.

* * *

Angela Di Silva first cast her eyes on the pitiful, battered,

Somy, little more than 48 hours after she had been admitted to the *Sociedad Orantes* shelter in Barcelona. She had a broken nose, shattered jaw and several cracked ribs. Her face was a mass of bruises and one eye was sunken out of view amongst an horrific maelstrom of gruesome bruising.

'*You poor, poor child,*' said Angela, putting her arms around the shivering Somy's shoulders. '*You are safe now. No one is going to hurt you here.*'

Angela found it difficult to assess what Somy' reaction would be to the first taste of human kindness she had been shown in years.

Her mashed up, discoloured face was devoid of any emotion below the barbarous riot of black, blue, red and yellow bruising. Her left eye was completely taken over by swelling. Her right eye continually weeping with the trauma of her condition or sorrow for what the man she loved had done to her.

Angela made her mind up there and then that she would be back the next day to see this badly damaged coloured girl, one of the worst cases of domestic violence she had ever seen. Not only the following day but every day during the next nightmarish few weeks when the cruelly treated Somy lapsed in and out of coma.

'*She is so churned up inside that she really does not want to regain consciousness and return to the real world,*' was the considered prognosis of Dr. Diego Fernandes, the shelter's medical officer. '*We'll be lucky if she pulls out of this. Not only physically but with her mind intact, poor girl.*'

* * *

18

Although Angela Di Silva was, as the Spaniards say, *muy simpatico,* toward the unfortunate women who, like the badly injured Kenyan girl Somy Mulder, become victims of domestic violence she found it hard to understand the wives or partners who stayed loyally with despicable womanisers known for treating their down trodden spouses like dishrags.

Angela could understand that in some cases it was finance, future security, and the worry of rising cost of living, that tied such kowtowed women to a life of misery.

'But I would never let any man dominate me like that,' Angela vowed to herself. *'I would go back to whoring on the streets rather than let a man humiliate me. Marriage, living together, call it what you like, is a partnership with both man and woman on an equal footing. Of course they have a duty to each other. As long as married men want sex and some wives withdraw their favour, whatever the reason, then there will always be prostitutes.'*

Yet the escort agency boss, hardened by her years on the game, found compassion when 43-year-old English divorcée Margaret Maitland told her about the 25 years of stressful marriage which had just been terminated in a London marital court.

Margaret's husband, 46-year-old, Stan Maitland first cheated on her at their honeymoon hotel in Torquay, the other party being a busty lass who worked in the cocktail bar. His extramural affairs continued, non-stop, through the entire quarter of a century of their marriage. It took Margaret years of oblivious naiviéte before she could accept what was happening. She just did not want to believe. But the painful realisation of what was going on became obvious when, as the year progressed, hubby Stanley's visits to the marital bed became rarer until once a month became the norm--if she was lucky!

The situation was hard for Margaret, who, from the age of 17 had been a conscientious wife. She kept their home meticulously clean and tidy for there was never a problem of money. Stanley, a highly skilled engineer, owned a tool-making firm in Birmingham, England. Because of a liaison with a precision instrument manufacturing firm in Barcelona, which gave his company profitable work, he bought a four bedroom villa at Mongat, a coastal village 12 kilometres north of Catalunia's capital city.

'It is a lovely fishing village and when we were staying at the villa we would breakfast each morning on fresh sardines, caught overnight, butterflyed and grilled with limon-mantequilla.' Margaret told Angela Di Silva.

They were lunching together at the Restaurante Botafumerio in Barcelona's Gracia neighbourhood. 'We spent about five months each year at the Mongat villa although my husband Stanley would often fly home to England without me for a few days. By then I had became aware his trips home were often linked to affairs with other women. It hurt, particularly as for 24 years I overlooked his philandering.

'I am by nature a very highly sexed woman and was very frustrated that he was depriving me by giving his services to other women. Yet I tried hard to keep the marriage together. The straw that broke the camel's back was the day I returned to the Mongat villa and found him in bed, our fucking bed for God's sake, with a bimbo who worked in the village hairdressing salon.

'I returned to England, broken-hearted, and filed for divorce

96

. Perhaps it was guilt gnawing at him but Stanley did not put a fight in court to excuse his disloyalty over the years.'

In the divorce settlement the judge acknowledged her 25 years as a faithful wife by awarding her £8 million from her husband' considerable fortune, a sum computed as roughly four fifths of his annual income, with no argument from Stanley a sizeable annuity and the sole ownership of the villa in Mongat. After the hearing Stanley walked across the court, shook her hand, apparently holding no malice at the court's rulings, and said: *'Best of luck in the future, Maggie,'* his pet name for her during their 25 year marriage. *'Look after yourself.'*

It was all over. Now Margaret Maitland was looking to Angela Di Silva for help to ease the pain of loneliness and sexual deprivation.

'I am realistic enough to know that, at my age, the chances of me having a true loving relationship with another man are slender,' Margaret confided to Angela. *'Oh I realise there will be plenty of men after my money. But I don't want to get hurt again--once bitten, twice shy, as they say. I would rather pick and chose the men I go out with now that I am independent. I am hoping that your organisation can help me in that respect.*

'Oh, I want my fair share of sex which my husband so cruelly kept me short of. But I just don't want men who take me out for a meal and then dive straight into bed for a quickie. I want to meet interesting males who will squire me to some of the most entertaining events held in the wonderful city of Barcelona. As the years went on in our marriage Stanley rarely took me out, I was always just the little woman waiting for him at home.'

Angela Di Silva warmed to Margaret Maitland who, she

could see, was a most honest woman who had deserved better treatment in her marriage.

'As my new escort agency for women begins to operate fully I can offer you most of the attractions you are yearning for.

'Plus a team of handsome men of all ages and cultures,' Angela assured her prospective new client. *'For instance I have a very cultured man on my books who is a good conversationalist with many interests. He is an Ethiopian Jew and coloured if you have no objections to either of these two attributes. I can organise a meeting if you are interested. He is multi-lingual and I know he loves opera. I could arrange a box for two, next week, at the Gran Teatre de Liceu, on La Rambla, where José Carreras is appearing in a benefit gala in aid of his own International Leukemia Foundation.'*

Margaret Maitland immediately warmed to the suggestion saying: *'That would be wonderful Angela. I love opera and José Carreras has been one of the world's greatest tenors for many years.'*

Angela Di Silva was pleased with Margaret Maitland's response and commented: *'The evening will be special in that José was born in Barcelona and, apart from his fabulous voice, is known for his humanitarian work as the President of the José Carreras International Leukemia Foundation which he established following his own recovery from the dreaded disease in 1988.'*

* * *

19

Having resigned from his job as a paramedic with the City of Barcelona ambulance service the 34-year-old Ethiopian Jew, Kote Rabtana, was awaiting his first professional assignment with Angela Di Silva's escort agency.

Angela had already signed him up and given him an advance of wages to tide him over until she matched him with a suitable client. But Kote had not wasted his time since being put on the Agency's payroll two weeks previously. When Angela had told him about the badly bruised Kenyan girl fighting for her life in a semi-comatose state in the *Sociedad Orantes* shelter for battered women, of which she was founder President, Kote immediately offered his help.

'*I'll call round at the shelter and see if I can help this unfortunate girl,*' said the 6ft 6in Kote. '*Maybe I can help her to come out of the coma if she hears someone talking in her own Swahili language which I speak fluently.*'

In fact the kind-hearted Kote had spent four hours at Somy Múlder's bedside. His kindly intervention astonished the shelter's nursing and medical staff as Somy immediately responded hour by hour and day by day, to the softly spoken words of her fellow African in her own tongue.

'*Come on Somy,*' said Kote as he held a plastic cup of water to her swollen lips. '*The worst is over. Put the nightmare behind you. There is every reason for you to pick up your life again. You are young, and I can see by your passport photograph that you will be an attractive young woman again once the bruises have subsided-as they certainly will in a couple of weeks or so. Don't forget you are amongst good friends here at this shelter.*'

Language was not a problem between them as Somy began to slowly snap out of her comatose state. Both of them were multi-lingual and, after some discussion, they realised they could converse in two of the tongues they were familiar with--Swahili and Arabic.

He told her he was a *Falasha* and described how his nation fled from Ethiopia to join up with other Jews in the State of Israel.

'But it would not be true to say we were welcomed with open arms by all the Israelis,' Kote explained ruefully.

This despite the fact we worshipped a form of Judaism many centuries prior to what is practised in their own schuls or synagogues.'

On his third daily visit he coaxed her to get out of bed. With help from the nurses he managed to lift her into a wheelchair. They placed a blanket around her shoulders and Kote wheeled her through the corridors to the shelter canteen where he bought her a milky coffee and doughnut. Although she only sipped the hot drink and nibbled round the edges of the sugary doughnut it was a start. Somy Mulder was on her way back to the world that recently had treated her so cruelly.

By the end of the week they discarded the wheelchair and she was able to slowly walk on Kote's strong arms to the shelter's garden when they sat for an hour or two each day as she soaked up the healing rays of the sun. Meanwhile the bruises on her battered face were starting to fade changing from a blood streaked montage to her natural milk chocolate brown hue. As his visits went into the second week there was only a slight sign of the once ugly contusions prompting Kote to reach into her bedside locker and hand over her make-up bag.

'Now love, as I told you before, the nightmare is over,' the kind-hearted Kote. 'You can now make yourself pretty again.'

The following day Angela Di Silva sent one of the nurses to ask Kote to come to the President's office where she put in an appearance nearly every day for an hour or so to deal with the ongoing problems of running the *Orantes Shelter* charity.

'Thank you Kote,' said Angela gratefully. 'You have done a magnificent job in helping that unfortunate girl recover from her awful injuries. That is why I have not bothered with giving you work for the escort agency during the past few weeks. But I see no reason why you should be out of pocket for those three weeks and I have had five hundred euros credited to your bank account.

'But now I have a suitable client for you to escort next week. She is 43 years of age, recently divorced, English, by the name of Margaret Maitland.

'Margaret was badly treated by her husband for the entire 25 year span of their marriage. Not in a violent way like poor Somy Mulder, who you have done so much to help on the way back to health, both physically and mentally. To be spurned and continually deceived by an habitual philandering husband over such a long period is debilitating and could leave personality scars on a woman who fulfilled her wifely duties to the letter.

'In the end finding her husband in their own marital bed with a floozy was his ultimate downfall and she divorced him and, deservedly, was awarded a very sizeable settlement from the court. She not only wants to resurrect her sex life but yearns to be squired by an attractive man as she, hopefully, spends the remainder of her life in contentment that had been denied her by a cheating spouse.

'I know you are an opera buff Kote and I have booked a box for the two of you at the Gran Teatre de Liceui in the Rambla, for José Carrera's benefit gala concert, in aid of his own International Leukemia Foundation next Friday.

'Senora Maitland would like you to collect her at 7-00pm at her home in Mongat--the Villa Espliego. She prefers that to a meeting in a hotel.. She says you will be able to leave your car there while you are both at the theatre and you can drive her Bentley up to Barcelona for the show. The fishing village of Mongat is only about 20 minutes drive from Barcelona.

'She is a lady in need of a little tender loving care from a caballero who will take a kindly interest and treat her the way a gentleman should behave with a woman.

'Having met Margaret several times I like her very much and I think she deserved a much better deal than she got from her husband. Although she was awarded a sizeable financial settlement from her divorce sometimes money is poor recompense for a woman who has been stripped of her pride.'

* * *

20

Kote Rabtana was in idyllic mood as he steered his Fiat northwards along the coastal road linking Barcelona with the picturesque fishing village of Mongat.

The sun was setting on the Mediterranean horizon, as the tiny Italian car ratcheted up the kilometres on the thirty minute drive to the villa which was his destination. He had spent most of the day at Angela Di Silva's shelter for battered women comforting his new friend, the unfortunate Kenyan girl, Somy Mulder, who was making a miraculous recovery from her frightful injuries. So miraculous that Angela, and the medical staff, had been discussing that very day the possibility of discharging Somy from the shelter.

Now Kote was anticipating a charming evening in the company of wealthy divorcée Margaret Maitland. There were several bonuses awaiting him before the night was out. Firstly the unique opportunity of hearing once again the dulcet tones of José Carreras, one of the greatest tenors in the world. Then, secondly, the chance of driving a top of the range Bentley the 48 kilometre round journey to Barcelona and back, never dreaming that he would ever get behind the steering wheel of such an iconic motorcar. Finally, if things went well, he would be bedding the woman his boss, Angela Di Silva, had described as: '....*a very attractive middle-aged woman, who will not disappoint you despite the fact she is nine years older than you Kote.*'

* * *

There was a driveway half a kilometre long to negotiate before he reached the imposing entrance to the four bedroom *Villa Espliego*---which translated into English meant 'Lavender

Villa', and explained the fragrant scent that wafted across his open Fiat as he wheeled up that long driveway.

He was courteously greeted by a housemaid who, in fractured 'Spanglais' said: *'Buenos tardes senor. Senora Maitland is "expecteen" you. Por favor, senor, follow me.'* Kote was conducted to an elegant marble-floored lounge where Margaret Maitland, elegantly dressed in a long blue velvet gown was waiting for him. She stretched out her right arm in greeting, which he accepted gallantly, brushing his lips across the back of a beautifully manicured hand.

'Welcome to my home, Kote,' Margaret said warmly. *'Angela has told me a lot about you. Can I offer you a drink?'*

Kote thought carefully for a few seconds before replying: *'Thank you Margaret. As I understand it you would like me to drive your car so I think it would be advisable for me to stick to orange juice at this stage of the evening. '*

Margaret looked across at the maid who was hovering at the end of the room and ordered: *'Zumo de naranja con hielo, para Senor, y vaso de jerez, para mi, por favor Consuela.'*

Having consumed their drinks they donned top coats and made ready for the short journey to Barcelona. *'Rather than going to a restaurant for dinner after the show I have arranged for a meal to be prepared for us when we return here,'* Margaret said, before asking: *'I hope that arrangement suits you?'*

Kote was very much in agreement. *'Of course Margaret that is an excellent idea,'* he concurred enthusiastically.

* * *

By the time they had completed the brief journey to the theatre in Barcelona, Margaret was already starting to be captivated by Kote's charm as he talked about the remarkable singer they were about to hear.

'I last heard José Carreras in 1994, singing live at the Three Tenors concert in Los Angeles,' said Kote, being extremely careful not to let the talking affect his driving--a fact that also endeared him further to Margaret Maitland. 'It was estimated that more than billion people watched the television broadcast of that concert. Fans all across the world had their taste buds for operatic music sharpened by the Three Tenors concert in the Baths of Caracalla in Rome on the eve of the 1990 World Cup Finals. In the next nine years more than 13 million copies of the CD of that concert were sold making it the best selling classical record of all time.

'Carrera's career has now almost completely moved into singing Neapolitan songs, light classical and easy listening. His final operatic performance at the Gran Teatre de Liceu, where his career began and where we are going tonight, was in Samson et Delila in 2001.'

Kote skilfully brought the beige coloured Bentley to a halt outside the theatre where there was a string of red-coated 'parking jockeys' waiting to ferry patrons' cars away to the car park.

After the Parking Jockey gave him a numbered coloured disc, for security purposes, Kote handed the young man a €20 note and the car was slowly driven away for storage until after the show.

He bought Margaret a glass of champagne and ordered an orange juice for himself at the theatre bar as they had about 15 minutes to spare before curtain up.

'Of course José Carreras at 60 years of age is a walking miracle,' Kote told the fascinated lady he was escorting as they waited for the show to begin. 'It was in 1987, when he

105

was only 40 and in the middle of filming La Bohème directed by Luigi Comencini in Paris, that he was diagnosed with acute lumphoblastic leukaemia and given only a one in ten chance of survival. But after harrowing chemotherapy, radiation therapy and an autologous bone marrow transplant in Seattle, miraculously he recovered from the disease and returned to the operatic and concert stage.

'*Listen Margaret, the orchestra is warming up. The show is about to start.*'

For the next two unforgettable hours Margaret Maitland, and her handsome escort, were transported to musical paradise as the melodius voice of José Carreras enveloped the hushed cauldron of the *Gran Teatre de Liceu.*

The biggest standing ovation of more than half a dozen during Carreras' dazzling performance came after the signature aria, *La Donna è Mobile.* His repetoire from Verdi operas *Il Corsaro, I due Foscari, La Battaglia di Legnano, Un Giorno si Regno* and *Stiffelio* also brought the house down.

But the *pièce de résistance* of a remarkable consumation of musical genius was when he accompanied great soprano, and Catalan compatriot, Montserrat Caballé to sing *Gennaro* from Donizetti's *Lucretia Borgia.* The final salute from the Barcelona audience to their favourite son lasted an unbelievable 20 minutes and eight curtain calls.

As they climbed from the chilly night air blowing across the harbour into the warming comfort of the Bentley's state-of-the-art heating system, Margaret turned and kissed Kote on the cheek and said: '*Thank you for making a wonderful night even more interesting with your knowledgeable discourse. After a performance like that one could die happily.*'

A gentle breeze off the nearby ocean fluttered the diaphanous net drapes at the balcony window.

Margaret: *I am not so much nervous but a little embarrassed. Apart from my ex-husband you are the only man I have ever lain with.*

Kote: *Stop fretting Margaret you look so beautiful laying there under the Mediterranean moonlight*

Margaret: *I can gratuitously return that compliment. You look devastatingly sexy with lovely body, dark skin and handsome features.*

Kote: *Thank you Margaret. Now let me help you forget the past. What is gone, is gone. Now I hope a much happier life is ahead for you.*

Margaret: *It is just that I have never been to bed with a man like you before.*

Kote: *I can't help touching your lovely breasts. I have been thinking that ever since we left the theatre.*

Margaret: *Oh, Oh, yes, yes Kote. Rub my nipples harder--you won't hurt me.*

Kote; *Like this darling?*

Margaret: *Yes that is wonderful, you are making me feel wild. I want to hold you too.*

Kote: *That is really fabulous Margaret. I'm flying!*

Margaret: *But that's not all-- I want to do something to you I have never done to any man before-even to my ex'.*

Kote: *That would be really wonderful Margaret. Yes*

please.

Margaret: *It's so hard. I want you to fly even higher.*

Kote: *It's an incredible feeling. You are so beautiful. Now I am going to please you.*

Margaret: *Oh heaven absolute heaven. Your tongue feels like silk. Can you play with my nipples while you do it again darling?*

Kote: *Now is the moment I want to enter you.*

Margaret; *Yes, yes. Now darling, now.*

Kote: *Oh my God. I think I am going to come darling. I can't hold it!*

Margaret: *Hold on my love. Turn over on your back and let me finish you off.*

*   *   *

Kote did as she asked, gasping with the stratospheric sensation as she took hold of him and steered him towards paradise. She didn't want him to rush towards fruition although his groin was aching to complete the sublime act. She was, however, beginning to lose her own control as she mounted him from above rubbing her nipples against his chest as she thrust down on him and within seconds felt his warm fluids ejaculate within her. Wave after wave of sheer uncontrollable lust swept over. She dismounted, rolled over, kissed his now flaccid member that had given her so much pleasure and joined him in the deep sleep that lovers enjoy. But that was only the overture. The fantasy orchestra was to play twice more before dawn broke and the local fishing boats heading for the nearby shore after their night's hunt for sardines. As the golden globe of the rising sun began to emerge on the Costa Brava horizon he turned inwards and entered her again. This time he was responsible for promoting her first orgasm for more than 20 years.

The world hadn't stopped. But for that magic moment the besotted Margaret Maitland felt that it had!

* * *

21

Kote Rabtana and Margaret Maitland found, as they ravenously consumed *Huevos Benedict* for breakfast on the morning after their night of passion, that life can sometimes take a spontaneous change of direction.

It all started when Margaret asked Kote what he would be doing that day. Kote explained that he would be visiting Somy Mulder, the badly battered Kenyan girl who was now almost fully recovered from the injuries inflicted by her brute of a husband. He also disclosed that the Shelter for women victims of domestic violence, headed by Angela Di Silva, were trying to figure out the best thing to arrange for Somy when she would shortly be discharged from the Shelter.

Margaret was tearfully empathetic when Kote explained how the unfortunate girl had been beaten and punched near to death by her Arab husband, a suspected fundamentalist Muslim terrorist who was on the run from Mossad, the Israeli Secret Service.

'Now this tragic girl is at another critical stage of her life,' Kote said. *'Angela and the medical staff consider Somy is fit enough to be discharged from the Shelter. But discharged to where? When her husband beat her up, after dragging her halfway around Europe as he tried to escape from the Israeli agents, they were reduced to living in a medium class hotel in a poor area of Barcelona. But now he had scampered off on his own leaving poor Somy on her own after taking all the money she had. However Angela will not allow the Shelter to discharge her without arranging somewhere safe for her to stay. It is vital she continues to improve so that she is not left with mental scars after the terrible treatment she received from their husband.'*

Margaret was so upset at the story she had just heard that she could not finish her breakfast and she said, with heartfelt sympathy: *'Oh Kote, darling, what a truly awful story. It almost makes me feel ashamed after the happy time we had with each other last night. That poor, poor girl.*

I can relate to what she has gone through because of what I suffered. Not only has she had to put up with an uncaring husband like I did but she has also had the trauma of cruel physical harm.

'She needs help to follow up the treatment that the Shelter for battered women has given her. Tell Angela Di Silva, when you return to Barcelona this morning, that she can send the girl here to this villa and she can stay until she is completely recovered to face the real world again. My housekeeper, Consuela, and I will take care of her, as long as it takes. There should be a sisterhood between us women who have been maltreated by their men. This kind of domestic violence is a worldwide problem almost as serious as the spread of the HIV virus. It is really up to governments and politicians to do something about it.'

* * *

Kote telephoned Angela Di Silva on his mobile phone after kissing Margaret Maitland farewell and heading his Fiat down the long driveway from the *Villa Espliego* and on to the coastal road from Mongat to Barcelona.

'How did the evening with Margaret go?' Angela, always the one for business first, queried.

Kote reassured his boss, saying: *'Oh! Absolutely fine, Angela. José Carreras gave a magnificent performance, as he always has done. Margaret and I got on fine and had a lovely evening. I am just starting out on the way back from Mongat, as I speak.'*

Kote then told Angela about the offer Margaret Maitland had made to take Somy at the villa while she convalesced and completely recovered from the horrendous injuries she had received from her sadistic husband.

Angela was delighted with the news.

'Kote that really is most generous of Margaret and from Somy's point of view the offer comes at a most opportune time,' asserted the Founder President of Barcelona's *Sociedad Orantes Shelter* for the pitiful victims of domestic violence. *'Kote can you make your way straight here to the Shelter when you arrive back in Barcelona. I am presiding at a meeting of directors here this morning and Somy Mulder's case is top of the Agenda. As I told you the other day the doctors and nurses believe they have done as much as they can for this unfortunate girl and it would be better for her future if she learned how to face the world again. Kote I would really like you to be at that meeting.'* Kote immediately agreed to Angela Di Silva's request and said: *'Of course Angela I'll be with you well inside the hour.'*

*   *   *

Angela opened the meeting after introducing Kote.

'Ladies and gentlemen most of you already know Senor Rabtana from his recent visits to the Shelter where he has done such a good job of helping the Kenyan girl to recover from the shocking violence handed out to her by her brute of a husband,' she explained. *'He comes here today with an offer from a very generous and wealthy friend of mine by the name of Margaret Maitland. I know there was a consensus at our meeting last week that it would be in Somy's best interest if she is discharged from the Shelter as soon as possible. She*

112

needs to get away from other luckless women who have been victims of domestic violence.

'Well Senora Maitland has offered to take the Kenyan girl as a guest in her luxury villa at the fishing village of Mongat to convalesce as long as it is necessary for her to be mentally ready to go out into the wider world again. Of course the problem, as we know from previous similar cases, might be that Somy could be scared of leaving the haven of the Shelter.

'But that is where Kote will certainly be able to help. If he is willing. He has built such a rapport with the unfortunate girl that I think it is quite possible he may be able to persuade her that a few weeks in the villa at Mongat might be therapeutic and also very enjoyable.'

The meeting was unanimous that the invitation from Margaret Maitland for Somy to convalesce at the villa in Mongat should be accepted. They also agreed that Kote should be the one to persuade the Kenyam girl that the move would be in her best interest.

*   *   *

Somy broke down in tears when Kote first broached the subject of her leaving the Shelter where she had bonded to him and had felt so secure after her horrific ordeal. Now that security, she feared, would be breached. She was scared. Frightened more than she had ever been during her life. It was even more alarming than when her husband had frequently attacked her. Oddly enough she had learned to tolerate and deal with that.

'Somy, love, you must trust me when I say I won't let anything bad happen to you,' Kote said, putting a comforting arm around her shoulders which were heaving as she sobbed her heart out. 'You will staying at a lovely villa on the Mediterranean coast, with its own swimming pool, sun terrace, and a garden with fruit bearing oranges, lemons , and grapefruit trees. There is a hot Jacuzzi in the garden and several horses in the stables if you like to ride. You will like the owner of the villa, Margaret Maitland who is a friend of mine. In any event you won't entirely be on your own because I will try and get down to see you every day.'

The last assurance prompted Somy to dab the tears from her eyes and she said in a timid voice: 'Oh Kote, if you really promise to come and see me every day perhaps I could give it a try.

Several hours later Kote telephoned Margaret Maitland and told her what had been settled and Somy had agreed to stay at the villa while she convalesced.

'That is marvellous news Kote,' said Margaret. 'I will arrange everything at this end if you can bring her down tomorrow.' An hour later Angela was on the line thanking Margaret for her generous gesture.

'There is no need to thank me Angela,' said Margaret. 'My own experience with an unkind and thoughtless husband makes me sympathise with this sad girl. Believe me I will try and bring a little happiness back into Somy's life.'

It turned out that is exactly what happened.

22

Mercedes was only 21 years of age when her husband, Colonel Tobias Gomez, 15 years her senior, trod on a land mine, while leading a patrol in Afghanistan, which had been planted by Taliban insurgents.

In that traumatic moment she became the youngest ever military widow the Spanish Army had ever known since the end of Spain's three-year-old Civil War in 1939.

A guard of honour representing Spain's armed services was waiting for the coffin draped in the red and yellow tribanded national flag. Six soldiers in dress uniform shouldered the coffin from the huge transporter plane as the guard of honour triggered their automatic rifles, loaded with blank amunition, to volley a salute to a fallen comrade. Waiting on the tarmac, there was also a three star general accompanied by his aide alongside the young widow and her parents who had flown in from Barcelona. Three days later the well-attended funeral was held in Barcelona's *Temple Sagrat Cor*, a church that has been compared many times with the famous *Sacre Coeur*, in Paris. Uniquely it is situated at the peak of the 512 metre high Tibidabo mountain and offers fantastic views over Barcelona.

Nine months after that poignant funeral Angela Di Silva met the wilting widow Mercedes, pale, almost sickly wan, pathetically thin after the sudden trauma of her bereavement. Not that there were any financial problems because the Colonel belonged to a wealthy Catalan family and his fairly high rank in the army meant that the military insurance collected after his death was very sizeable. All in all Mercedes Gomez was now worth four million euros, plus a sizeable widow's pension from the army, and a, mortgage free, four bed roomed house in an up market estate in Barcelona.

But the loss of her dear Tobias, the man she had loved since her schoolgirl days, had hit her hard. That was clear when Angela had a long and sincere talk with Mercedes during a coffee morning and bazaar in aid of the *Sociadad Orantes Shelter* for the battered victims of domestic violence--a growing problem in Spain at the start of the 21st Century

'Of course it has come as a terrible shock to lose your husband so suddenly,' Angela sympathised. *'But that is a risk every soldier takes, whatever his nationality, when they put on the uniform. But Mercedes you are still young. Your life is all ahead of you.'*

'You cannot spend the next sixty years or so in mourning. Retain the love you had for the man you have lost but start to live again. Tobias has left you quite well off. You are a relatively rich young lady.

'If you will allow me I think I can help you put a little sunshine back into your life.'

Mercedes, a girl from proud Catalan stock, whose grandparents were amongst the last in Spain to hold out against the former dictator Franco in the Spanish Civil War, then told the escort agency boss about the pangs of loneliness she was feeling since the loss of her husband.

'Angela I don't think I will ever love any other man,' she said poignantly. *'That is how precious Tobias was to me. To be honest I have spoke to Father Jaime, the parish priest at the Eglésia Sagrat Cor, about the possibility of joining the Order of Santa Benedict as a religosa. But the Reverend Father advised me to make such a move cautiously. It would be a mistake for me, he said, to become a nun on the rebound from a painful bereavement.'*

Angela agreed.

'Father Jaime gave you very shrewd advice Mercedes,' she said. *'A decision made in haste often leads to regrets for the rest of your life.'*

Angela Di Silva then explained about her new escort agency which was helping distraught and lonely women like herself enjoy life again. With her young English protégé, Richard Martin in mind, Angela added: *'I have just the young man who could brighten your life. Forget falling in love. Just play the field, have fun, and it might surprise you how quickly you can shake off your depression. Perhaps later on you will find someone you want to set up a permanent arrangement with.'*

Angela's passionate dissertation made an impression and Mercedes' reluctant fears of starting a relationship with another man began to dilute.

'Let me arrange a date with Richard Martin, ' said Angela persuasively. *'He's in your age bracket, which will give you another slant on things after two years of marriage to a man you no doubt loved very much but was nevertheless 15 years older than you. You have nothing to lose you are comfortably off and will never need to go out and work for your living.'*

Mercedes Gomez was persuaded and allowed Angela to arrange a tryst with Richard the following week.

* * *

On the way back to her office Angela mused: *'Well that looks like solving the problem of getting young Richard off the starting blocks as an escort. He came through, with flying colours, the trial assignation I had arranged for him with Monica Kepler. I think Richard Martin has the quality and personality to shake Mercedes Gomez out of the doldrums.'*

Richard had been wondering when Angela Di Silva was going to find him work for he had now been on the escort agency's for nearly two months, including the four weeks he had spent at Louis Sammuel's gymnasium getting fit.

On Angela's side of the coin she had come to the conclusion that it would be more difficult to match Richard with a suitable client than most of her other escorts. At his age he would have to be a speciality for women needing a much younger man. To pair a lad in his 20's with a 50-year-old plus female, which was the age group that most of her clients came from probably presented difficulties. The reason was fairly simple. Women whose sex life had gone pear shaped mainly could not afford the service she was offering at her agency unless they were in reciept of a fairly hefty financial settlement because of the infidelity, mistreatment or brutality of their spouse.

So it was going to be a challenging project to find a suitable client to pair up with the young English lad. It was going to be interesting to see how Mercedes Gomez reacted to the enthusiastic lovemaking of Richard Martin.

While it would possibly be a culture shock for Richard to be in the driving seat and discard the 'L' for learner badge which was symbolically pinned to his skin-tight y-fronts on the night of educative passion with former Parisian hooker Monica Kepler.

The gargantuan gigolo was about to fly solo!

23

Kote Rabtana, having persuaded Somy Mulder to accept Margaret Maitland's invitation to convalesce at her villa in Mongat, two days after the board meeting, with Angela Di Silva helped the, mentally damaged, Kenyan girl into his tiny Fiat and sped the half-hour journey down the coastal road from Barcelona to the sun-drenched fishing village at the edge of the crystal clear Mediterranean.

Despite the assuring presence of Kote, who had done so much to help her recover from the macabre physical injuries inflicted by her bestial husband, Somy was nervous at leaving the Sociedad Orantes Shelter for battered women where she had felt safe and recovered some confidence and dignity.

'*Don't worry Somy, I am sure you will really like Margaret Maitland, who is a very kind person,*' said Kote reassuringly. '*Margaret knows what you have been through because she was mentally maltreated by her former womaniser husband although she never had to endure cruel physical abuse like you suffered.*'

They were both greeted warmly at the front door of the villa by the housekeeper-maid, Consuela, who said in a fractured Spanglais: '*Senora Maitland ees waitin' in the sun lounge. Pleeze seguir mi.*'

As requested Somy and Kote followed the housekeeper-maid. Margaret greeted them as they entered the room. She gave Kote an affectionate *besar* on each cheek and put her arms around Somy steering her to a comfortable seat on the luxuriously cushioned sofa.

'*Here child, come and sit by me,*' said Margaret. '*As the Spaniards say "mi casa es tu casa" - my house is your house.*

Please make yourself at home. After we have had a little talk I will get my maid, Consuela, to show you to your room.'

Kote, with sympathetic understanding that this was a pregnant moment for Somy, took the opportunity to return and allow the two women to talk and get to know each other.

Looking at the Kenyan girl Kote said: *'Look Somy I'll be down to see you in the morning. Enjoy yourself.'*

Somy pouted. Her lips trembling. She fought hard to stem the tears as her mentor departed. At this moment she felt insecure and vulnerable despite Margaret Maitland's caring attention and kindly intention.

How would she manage without Kote's compassion to which she had bonded? She feared she had made a drastic error in agreeing to stay at Mongat and leave the Shelter where she had felt so safe. What did this stranger, Margaret Maitland, have in mind by inviting her to stay as a guest at this lovely villa by the sea?

Oh well, pondered Somy, her good friend Kote had promised to return to Mongat the following day and check how she was doing. She would wait until then and if she didn't like it in Mongat she would return with Kote to Barcelona where eventually she had found a little happiness again after the horrendous ordeal her husband had inflicted on her.

* * *

They breakfasted the next morning on freshly caught sardines delivered by one of the village fishermen and handed over to Consuela at the villa just after dawn. The housekeeper-maid cooked them Spanish style, scoring them down the middle to butterfly them and basted them with *zumo di limon y aceite de oliva* before cooking them *a la parrila*.

Somy and Margaret continued the talk they had begun the previous evening. Despite her own traumatic experience Somy's inherent sensitivity came to the fore when Margaret described the mental cruelty inflicted on her by a womanising husband who chose to endow his rampant sexual prowess with a number of strumpets, harlots and good-time bimbos. She felt genuine empathy as she realised the agonising pain of frustration the older woman had to suffer for nearly quarter of a century.

Tears welled into Somy's eyes as Margaret said: *'Yet I never stopped loving Stanley throughout all those awful times when in my lonely bed I cried myself to sleep on many nights. I was in mental turmoil because I did everything for him that a good wife is supposed to do for her man. In fact I thoroughly spoiled him--perhaps that was my big mistake. Cooked him food I knew he liked, washed pressed his clothes, even cleaned his shoes, yet at the end of the day he would finish up in the arms of another woman. Even in the court room, when the divorce was finalised, I still loved him although he had committed the unforgivable when I caught him in bed with another woman.*

'In our bed--the filthy bastard. It was that awful moment that finally killed my love for him. Yet, perversely, I still wish him no harm.'

It was confession time. A chance to exorcise the tormented souls of both maltreated women. Somy, in turn, explained how she had been brought up in Kenya by her Bantu mother, who had married Dutch ivory poacher and gold smuggler, Harry Múlder. After a good education which included a University degree Somy told Margaret how she fell in love with a handsome Abdul Ben Shakim, a handsome Arab. She wept when she described what it was like when, within weeks of her marriage to the brutal Muslim, she was savagely beaten and whipped. How Abdul took all of her money after the last

121

beating left her for dead at a ramshackle hotel in Barcelona.

She also told Margaret of the wonderful treatment she received at Angela Di Silva's Shelter and how Kote had persuaded her that life could still offer her something despite the barbarous way her husband had treated her.

Margaret said confidentially: *'I have sworn to myself that I will never fall in love with another man. I don't want all that hurt again. That is why I was grateful when Angela Di Silva told me about her new escort agency for women like us and introduced me to Kote. It was strange to share sex with such a kind, knowledgeable, understanding man as Kote. He is everything that a woman would want in a man. But I am determined I will never give my heart to any other man again and that means Kote, who is an adorable person. I would rather leave my relationship with him on a professional basis. I want to conduct the orchestra in any future liaisons with men.'*

Margaret Maitland's frank disclosure of her assignation with Kote came as a jolt to Somy. In her weak state recovering from the battering she had received from her sadistic Arab spouse she had bonded to the sympathetic Ethiopian Jew who had helped her recover. She had never bracketed him in the role of male prostitute. She felt a tinge of jealousy blended with affection for the former Barcelona paramedic.

In fact Somy could hardly contain her impatience as she waited for Koty's arrival at the villa later that morning. She wanted to tell him how much she really liked Margaret Maitland. She knew Kote would be pleased that she now wanted to accept Margaret's hospitality and convalesce at this lovely villa where she knew she could be happy.

For Somy Mulder the sun was beginning to shine again!

24

Angela Di Silva was shrewd enough to decide that to send the recently widowed Mercedes Gomez and escort Richard Martin out for a conventional dinner in a formal restaurant before despatching them to their love couch would not be terribly exciting for two kids in their early twenties.

Instead, with her usual impeccable intuition, Angela selected one of the most notorious discos for young people in Barcelona-*The Macarena Club* in the Nou de Sant Francese district for the tryst between Mercedes and Richard. Originally a typical Spanish flamenco '*tablao*' the Macarena Club had been modernised to the taste of youngsters in the 21st Century. As a result the club was now one of the most underground places in Barcelona's electronic scene to either rave or chill out.

Frequented in numbers by young ex-pat Argentinians, the Macarena Club is open 24 hours a day. The unique feature is that the resident DJ is situated in the middle of the dance floor and is responsible for the astonishing sound that pervades this popular entertainment spot for youngsters.

It was the ideal rendezvous for Mercedes, as the child-bride of a serving officer in the Spanish army, who had been approved by her strict father and mother, she had been robbed of the disco, club scene which modern teenagers revel in. Perhaps the upside of what she had missed was that she had not been lured into the drug scene that bedevils so many youngsters worldwide.

Mercedes looked decidedly ravishing when Richard Martin took a taxi and collected her at the huge mansion on the outskirts of the city which had been left to her by her late husband. She answered the door herself , having given her maid the evening off, and invited him to have a drink.

He thoughtfully chose to have a glass of red wine as he spotted that she already had a bottle of *Marqués de Cáceres Gran Reserva* already open. Although this meeting with the lovely Mercedes was his baptism as an escort-gigolo, Richard was the first to admit he was certainly not a cock virgin. *'I have probably dipped my wick more times than this young chick has had hot dinners,'* he crudely contemplated. *'Nevertheless her old man must have left a well stocked cellar--that wine she is pouring is first class.'*

The Macarena Club was really hopping when Mercedes and Richard took the floor for their first dance together. With the D.J. stationed in the middle of the dance floor, really close to the punters, the sound was at such a high decibel that the kids were orbited into space and induced into a state of reverie. The action never really started in earnest until 2am, which was called locally *'la hora de bruja'* --the witch's hour--when girls were given free entrance and the boys had to pay five euros and the place became bedlam. By then, after two hours of hip-hop and jigging together beneath the coloured lights both Mercedes and her escort were sagging, almost asleep on their feet.

'Take me home please Richard,' Mercedes pleaded. *'I've really enjoyed the night but I have had enough now. I'll open a bottle of champagne when we get home and we can relax.'*

* * ‘

Richard hailed a taxi crusing down the *Nou de Sant Fresc* outside the club. They dallied over the bottle of French champagne--*Dom Perignon* no less--as they necked on the satin-lined sofa at her elegant home. The kisses had got hungrier, their tongues more exploratory when Mercedes said,

124

impatiently: *'Come on Richard amado, let's go upstairs.'*

Mercedes gasped with a mixture of pleasant surprise and pensive awe when she saw his engorged flagstaff at full mast, as he left the bathroom and moved towards the bed where she was waiting expectantly.. She was hungry with anticipation as she eagerly waited the pleasures that lay ahead for her.

She climbed on top of him, her fingers spread firmly on his bare chest which was well muscled from the weight training he still continued four times a week at Louis Sammuel's gymnasium. Wriggling her bottom she manoeuvred to bestride him. He felt as if he would explode in the effort to prevent premature ejaculation. She levered herself as high as possible, shivering with ecstasy as she dropped on to his enormous erection. Richard groaned as he felt her thrust forward with her hips. Her weight squeezed his testicles. He responded pumping into her with the urgency of a road mender's pneumatic hammer.

He stretched his neck and took her left nipple in his mouth and as he teased it with his tongue they both reached the sublime experience of a simultaneous orgasm. In fact it was the first time in her life she had ever shared that experience for her husband had never been one to play the waiting game until his wife was sexually satisfied. In fact Richard's sexual prowess and stamina took her to a dizzy peak four times during that blissful night .

'I have really enjoyed the night,' trilled the sated Mercedes, as they sipped their *café con leche* in bed at 10 o'clock the following morning. *'I come from a very strict Catalan family who never allowed me to take part in the disco scene like other kids of my age. They were only interested that I made a good marriage. I had only left my finishing school in Switzerland two months, where I had been since the age of ten, when I was introduced to my future husband, Tobias a captain in the*

Spanish army, at a concert. I was only 17 and impressionable. My parents pressed me hard with their approval that Tobias was a good match for me. Only a few months later he met me at the altar of the Sagrat Cor Church in Barcelona. Only four years after we were married I had to put on my widow's weeds and attend his funeral at the same church.

'*So I missed out on a lot of fun young girls experience in the time between when they leave school and have to take on the responsibilities of married life. Tobias never treated me cruelly. Don't forget he had taken the military oath to behave as an officer and gentleman. But he did not believe in employing a servant while he had a wife. He used me as his batman, to polish his boots, iron his shirts, shine the buttons on his uniform, have his meals ready when he returned from the barracks and then take me to bed at his whim and convenience. I was an extra trophy for his collection to go along with his Military Merit Medal before he was killed in Afghanistan.*

'*Thanks to you Richard I got a taste of the life I missed as a teenager. What is more you were so kind, gentle and considerate of my feelings in bed, for which I thank you. You are the only man I have ever made love with except my late husband. I will have a word with Angela Di Silva and ask her if she can arrange for us to meet again.*

'*Also I will enclose an extra €500 as a gratuity for you in the cheque I send to Angela.*'

Richard thanked Mercedes and assured her that he had thoroughly enjoyed the evening also. His assignment as a gigolo had been a huge success for both client and escort.

That is the way Angela Di Silva, a pioneer of the escort business, intended it to be.

* * *

25

Angela Di Silva was delighted with the way her escort agency, was coining thousands of euros each month keeping her team of attractive male escorts busily occupied with a variety of clients often several times a week.

She had even spread her wings by opening, equally successfully, money-spinning branches of the escort agency in Seville, Valencia, and the biggest prize of all, the Spanish capital Madrid.

There was only one downside and that was in her private life which, since she was married had been happily serene between her wealthy, wholesale and manufacturing jeweler, husband Klaus, their young son, and herself.

Klaus had not only generously funded her ventures into the Escort Agency business but encouraged and praised her shrewdness and business acumen. But in the past few weeks Klaus had been uncharacteristically quiet, even a shade sulky. That applied particularly at the breakfast table their main time for discussing business, private and family matters.

What Angela did not know or could envisage that the problem bothering Klaus was triggered by greed. Totally unnecessary greed. For, she believed, he was already one of the wealthiest business men in Spain. Then, having been tempted by his own voracity, Klaus was entrapped by fear. Blind fear for the safety of his beloved wife Angela and their adored little son, Tobajas.

* * *

Unbelievably the drama had started quarter of a century earlier, on 26 November 1983, when the infamous Brinks

127

Mat robbery took place at Heathrow. It was a massive caper. When the outcome was tallied, it was announced that 6,800 gold ingots worth nearly £26 million were taken from the Brinks Mat vault near the airport. Only a fraction of the gold was ever recovered and only one crooked "fence", arrested and imprisoned, a relatively small time manufacturing jeweller in the West of England with a tiny capacity for smelting gold at his workshop.

With gold valued at US $650 an ounce in 2007 as against $380 an ounce in 1983 it was estimated that the precious missing precious metal from that notorious robbery 25 years earlier had soared to something over £50 million. A breathtaking sum of money, a share of which would tempt the conscience of even a reputed millionaire like Klaus Di Silva.

At first, he was tempted when approached by the unscrupulous sons of the evil French hoodlum who had stolen the gold and cleverly shipped it out of England and nefariously stashed it for 25 years in an isolated cave in the Pyrenees. It was a weird story how that fortune in bullion was allowed to lay dormant for 25 years, the secret where it had been stashed, locked in the warped mind of the crook who masterminded one of the biggest and most audacious crimes ever perpetrated.

His name was Papa Dupres, the Godfather of a French-Spanish Mafioso mob-known as the '*Los Cucarachas*' to the world's law enforcement agencies-who had pulled off a number of sensational bank, jewel and bullion heists across Europe since the end of World War II.

Even the debauched Dupres mob had never anticipated the enormity of the bullion haul from the Brinks Mat caper. Neither could they have visualised the intensity of the hunt set up by Scotland Yard and Interpol. It was red-hot loot. It inevitably set up the most intense worldwide investigation ever by police and insurance investigators.

Papa Dupres was not a fool. He knew when he set up the heist at Heathrow that it would be big. As it turned out it was gigantic. With the exception of a relatively small amount of the bullion handed out to a gang of crooks operating from the East end of London to pay for their assistance in the robbery the rest of the enormous haul was quickly ferried out of England through a number of ports. The planning was almost flawlessly brilliant. The security contained within small groups of people on a need-to-know basis.

Temporarily the bullion was stored in a farm house owned by Dupres a few kilometres from Paris. Within hours it was on the move again heading south via Versailles .

Dupres, a married man with two sons, Emille and Maurice, eight and ten years of age, decided that he would quickly have to shift the golden hoard and secrete it somewhere with ultimate security until the search and the heat had cooled. Within weeks , with the help of five of the roughest hoodlums from Montmartre, he had the precious metal piled on to a specially converted pantechnicon and transported to the Pyrenees an area he had known since childhood. Having seen the ingots manually humped, one by one into a deep cave and the entrance cemented over and then covered by natural Pyrenees rocks Dupres promptly instigated one of the most cunning security ploys ever devised. While his five hoodlums sweated and strained carrying the last few ingots into the cave the devious Papa Dupres stealthily attached a magnetic time bomb under the pantechnicon . Artfully having thanked the perspiring men for their help, he then instructed them to take a circuitous route back to Paris and not to stop for food or drink until they were at least two hours journey away from the Pyrenees. He gave them €200 to buy food and booze on the road.

The gigantic vehicle, with the five Montmartre crooks inside, steadily making inroads en route into a half a dozen cases of *San Miguel*, was cruising at a steady 60 kph along the A6 motorway towards Versailles when the magnetic bomb exploded. The whole set-up was blown to smithereens. The explosion was of such an intensity even skilled DNA experts from the Sûrête, Interpol and the French gendarmarie found no identifying traces of the five assassinated gangsters to lead them towards gangster boss Papa Dupres who had arrived back at his farm in his top of the range Mercedes several hours earlier.

For the next 25 years the designing Papa Dupres was never tempted to disturb the golden treasure incarcerated into a Pyrenees mountainside which he humorously always referred to as his *'pension fund'*. This decision was made all the easier by the fact that his notorious mob were making illicit fortunes anyway from peddling hard drugs, pulling off bank heists, burglary and prostitution in the prosperous areas of France, Spain and Belguim.

* * *

It was nearly quarter of a century later Papa Dupres summoned his two sons, Maurice now 34 years of age and Emille, two years younger., to his bedside at the *Hôpital Bichat-Calude-Bernard* situated in the *Rue Henri-Huchard* which serves the colourful characters who populate the Parisian districts of *Montmartre, Pigalle* and *Trinitê*

Papa Dupres did not need his medico, Dr Phillipe Dany to tell him that he was dying. He was under no illusion that the prognosis *'cancer of the kidneys'* meant that his condition was anything other than terminal. The wicked old rogue knew his time had come!

He told his sons, Maurice and Emille, both seasoned drug

runners bank robbers and murderers, how he had hidden the bullion from the sensational Brinks Mat robbery which he had master-minded at London's Heathrow airport in 1983.

'That is the legacy I have left you my boys,' said the rapidly declining Papa. *'But you will have to be as clever as I was 25 years ago when I hid the stash of bullion. If you are going to cash in on this haul, which I reckon nowadays is worth the thick end of seventy million euros. Yes my sons €70,000,000 !'*

He handed his elder son a parcel encased in yellow oilskin. *'There, my lads, is a map which will take you straight to where the gold is hidden, You will need a large vehicle, six strong men, including yourselves, and a pneumatic drill to shift it.*

'There remains the problem of legitimising the haul. That means the complicated process of smelting to disguise the chemical footprint of the gold stolen all those years ago. Mixing it with legitimate gold in the smelting process, adding small amounts of mother metal, even minute amounts of silver. That done competently then the finished product would be totally unidentifiable as the Brinks Mat gold. There are not more than two or three smelting plants in the whole of Europe with the capacity to process the enormous quantity of gold involved.

'One of those is in England and for obvious reasons out of the question. A second is near Paris which is too close for comfort and would bring the flics and the Sûréte round your ears like a swarm of hornets. The best prospect is in Barcelona, which would be a handy place to transport the gold from the hideout in the Pyrenees and is owned by a wealthy wholesale manufacturing jeweller by the name of Klaus Di Silva. In the words spoken by Marlon Brando in the film called "The Godfather" you may have to make that guy an offer he can't refuse!'

Dupres Senior emphasised, with almost his last breath, that it would be different, very difficult in fact, "laundering" stolen bullion , so that it could not be traced to legitimising "hot" money. It had to be professionally smelted to completely blur its metallurgical footprint.

It was one helluva a legacy that Papa Dupres left his corrupt offspring.

* * *

26

Angela Di Silva dismissed her concern about her husband, Klaus', moodiness down to business worries which, although unusual, she assumed would go away.

Already she was planning the next step to boost her ever expanding escort agency catering for sex-starved, neglected and mentally abused women and at that particular moment was considering how best to cater for a prospective new client she had been introduced to at the bridge club.

Maria Torres was an extremely attractive 42-year-old Catalana, who had recently returned to her native Barcelona after a 15 year spell living in Calfornia where she had worked as the hard-nosed Hollywood gossip writer for the top selling "Lat*i*na" magazine which boldly proclaimed itself as *perfecto* reading for the modern Hispanic woman. It was a publication that focussed on Spanish ladies' lifestyle and values. Each issue featuring the latest information on beauty, health, fitness and career opportunities. Maria's speciality was high-lighting the most outrageous celebrities in tinsel town from Robert Di Niro to Catherine Zeta Jones.

But there was more to Maria Torres than harvesting the spicy tittle-tattle from Los Angeles and Emailing it to the editorial offices of "Lat*i*na" under her well-known by-line.

She was one of a rare breed of buxom women equally at home in the role of "dildo-dike" or "carnal courtesan". She had just ended a sensual lesbian affair with a Hollywood starlet which followed her ten year marriage and a bitter divorce from film director Abe Sherman.

She had used the same cruel words to Gloria as she had spat at the doddery Abe Sherman three years previously.

'*I am fucking bored with you,*' she had waspishly volleyed at both partners uncaring at the personal pain she was inflicting on her partner. '*I just don't love you any more. Sex with you is not fun anymore. It's like watching paint dry.*'

Romantic liaisons do not terminate any crueller than that.

Even her 'chance' meeting with Angela Di Silva at the bridge club was sinisterly contrived. She had unceremoniously resigned from "Lat*i*na" after being head-hunted by a sleazy publication called "Chismografia"-which translated into English significantly meant 'Gossip'.

'*Get the real low down on the woman Di Silva who runs this escort agency which supposedly services frustrated women,*' snapped her new boss the tough investigative owner-editor of "Chismografia'. '*Produce a lurid exposé of male prostitutes with interviews and pictures and I'll not only give you a by-line in bigger letters than the fucking title of the magazine, doubling your starting salary but I'll contract you to write a full page gossip column every month. Do a good job on this and I'll make you the biggest star in women's journalism.*'

Such was the predatory priority in the devious mind of Maria Torres as she tried to hook Angela Di Silva with the skills of a fisherman casting his rod in a turblent Scottish river swirling with a turmoil of salmon.

'*I had three years in Los Angeles living and fucking as a lesbian and to be honest I got bored with the silly cow I was shacking up with,*' Maria explained as she shared a bottle of pink Cava with the escort agency boss. '*I am ready to feel the strong biceps of a man wrapped around me and the throb of an enlarged penis trying to enter me again. Call me A.C - D.C if you like but I have tried both and at the moment it's the thought of a macho guy ravaging me that appeals. So fix me*

*up with one of your most rampant bucks that will press the
right buttons. As soon as you can Angela darling.'*

Having accepted a card with Maria's contact details and
phone numbers Angela assured her new client that she would
be hearing from her within 48 hours. She then explained to
Maria how the escort agency worked and what it would cost
for a night out with one of her stable of male escorts. *'Oh
don't worry about the cost, Angela, love,'* she said. *'I received
a generous severance pay-out from from 'Latina' that will
comfortably keep me for the rest of my life even if I don't work
again.'*

* * *

Angela Di Silva contemplatively boasted to herself that she
did not make too many mistakes in business. After carefully
perusing her portfolio of escorts employed by her she decided
that, despite 12 years difference between them, that roué
Bernardo Sanchez would arouse the mixed-up sexual urges
in her agency's newest client, Maria Torres.'

There was a chance that Maria might disapprove if she
was told that ladies hairdresser Bernardo Sanchez was 54
years of age. But Angela shrewdly guessed that the licentious
tonsorial artiste would cast a lascivious spell over the
decamped lesbian.

Angela was bang on the button, for despite years of
debauchery in Hollywood with both male and female partners
Maria Torres was entranced with Bernardo Sanchez's long,
carefully groomed and perfumed long silver hair. The deep
waves of his coiffure sweeping imperiously from the gold clip
that secured his ponytail.

Maria felt a surge in her vaginal quarters as she caught
the delicate whiff of *Chanel for Men* aftershave, noted the

elegance of his bracelet and bejeweled Rolex wristwatch. He exuded the mustiness of a hugely sexed man.

She was not to be disappointed when he bedded her in their luxury suite at the exclusive Hotel Barcelona Princess, where earlier they had enjoyed an exotic sea-food dinner.

* * *

They started to explore each other as they looked around the heavily mirrored bedroom. Bernado was pleased to discover she had a sweet tasting mouth when he kissed her. They turned up the volume on the hotel's Hi Fi system a little higher as they danced and necked.

Slowly, almost sensually, she unbuttoned his linen shirt. He, gallantly responding, helped her to discard her snowy white silk blouse. Paradoxically, for a woman who had explored the neo parameters of sexual depravity she wore a simple silver crucifix around her slender neck. She stretched towards his waistband and unbuckled his ostrich-skin Christian Dior belt and, with a slick flick of the wrist, unzipped his slacks.

He was aroused. There was no mistake about that. He helped her out of the raunchy skin-tight leather trousers that hugged her waist and cocooned her lovely legs.

'*You are a gentleman, or caballero as we say in Spanish,*' she purred expectantly.

They kicked off their shoes and danced their way round the king-sized bed, as the music reached a crescendo. He kissed the top of her shoulder and let his lips lasciviously trail to the hollow of her neck, and down to her cleavage.

'*Do that again,*' she pleaded.

He could feel her breasts pulsating against his chest. He undid her bra' with one hand behind her back. She pulled the garish Y-fronts down and noted how proud his manhood stood.

'Disappointed?' he asked with a wry smile.

'Why should I be?' she counted with matching coyness.

They tumbled into bed and she lowered herself on to him. He helped to ease himself into her. They both revelled with the experience.

The second time they did it was even better than the first. The third time-bingo-it was simply stratospheric.

* * *

Bernardo was so pent-up with the unbridled intensity of their love-making that he did not notice the minute digital camera she had secreted with tape to the crystal chandelier above the bed while he was in the en suite bathroom. Neither did he spot the mini casette recorder incorporated into her mobile phone on the bedside table.

Although it had been just another assignment as an investigating journalist she nevertheless admitted to herself: 'I have to admit that, despite this being just another professional job, Bernardo was a first class fuck.'

* * *

27

Despite the fact that he had been France's most evil gang boss since the end of World War II, Papa Dupres was buried in the prestigious Paris *Cimittiére de Montmartre* where the earthly remains of such celebrities as novelist Emile Zola, painter Edgar Degas, author Alexandre Dumas the Younger and ballet dancer Nijinsky had been laid to rest in adjacent plots and vaults.

He was mourned by his grotesque wart-faced, moustached, wife, Eva, and their two mobster sons Emille and Maurice, 32 years and 34 years old respectively. There was a motley contingent of underworld characters, cauliflower eared, broken nosed, tattooed, knife scarred, colleagues from the Parisian gutters. Yet amongst this plethora of corrupt criminality only Papa's two sons were aware of the staggering legacy in gold bullion secretly cemented quarter of a century before into the side of a Pyrenees' mountain. If this gruesome montage from the dregs of Paris and Marseilles had heard even a whisper of such a haul of gold the funeral would have ended in riotous mayhem, blood, unbridled violence and murder.

Having despatched their mother back to the family farm on the outskirts of the city the two notorious brothers, already on the files of the crime-busting *Surete* and *Interpol* as suspected drug runners, bank robbers and murderers, adjourned to a Montmartre tavern and got systematically drunk consuming the best part of a case of excellent vintage *Chateau Neuf du Pape* as they planned how they were going to recover their nefarious but nevertheless fabulous golden heritage.

The Rolls Royce, a top of the range *Silver Ghost,* purred into the huge parking lot at the jewellery warehouse and workshop owned by Klaus Di Silva. It had made the journey from Paris down the spine of France, via Versailles, stopping for several hours in the midi-Pyrenees to allow the two sinister Dupres brothers to ensure they could locate the stash of bullion, secreted by their depraved father quarter of a century earlier.

The imposing flunkey, smartly attired in green milititary-style livery, a former sergeant in Spain's elite Guardia Civil, strictly controlling those who entered the high-security sales suite where some of the world's highest priced jewellery was brought out from the formidable strong rooms for scrutiny by well-heeled clients, conducted them to a luxuriously furnished reception area.

He greeted the two Dupres hoodlums politely saying: '*Mi patrón, Senor Di Silva, is expecting you, ustedes. He will join you shortly, but, just at the moment he is busy on an internet conference call with business colleagues in the USA. I will have coffee and drinks brought to you while you are waiting.*'

The elegant silver Georgian coffee pot with matching jugs of cream, milk and sugar bowl was accompanied with a frosted silver bucket containing a bottle of perfectly chilled *Cliquot* Champagne bedded in *hielo* with two delicate fluted glasses.

Emille and Maurice glanced greedily what was on offer and opted for the bubbly. The waiter showed his expertise as he folded a starched serviette around the chilled bottle and popped the cork ostentatiously.

There was none of the champagne left when Klaus Di Silva joined the two French mobsters quarter of an hour later apologising for keeping them waiting. The wealthy wholesale jeweller was street-wise and was well aware of the seamy reputation of his two guests as he politely requested them to state the business that had promoted their visit.

Maurice Dupres, red-faced and ebullient after the wine, came straight to the point answering on behalf of his younger brother and himself.

'We have a quantity of gold bullion that we want smelted,' said the elder Dupres brother staring Di Silva straight in the eye looking for a reaction. 'We have chosen you for two important reasons. Firstly we know you are one of the few wholesale jewellers in Europe capable of handling the amount of gold we have in mind. Secondly we know that 30 years ago you provided a similar service for our late father, who was known as Papa Dupres. You were well rewarded for that job and our father was pleased that you knew how to be discreet and keep a secret.'

Klaus Di Silva, silently, had to agree that Maurice Dupres was telling the truth. In the old days when he was trying to make headway in his profession he had smelted a large quantity of stolen gold and laundered it through his retail jewellery outlets for the nefarious French gangster boss. It was a successful caper all round and provided a basis for his present huge fortune. But he was wise and decided that it would be his last venture on the wrong side of the law. Now that lapse, three decades past, had come back to haunt him. He had never intentionally broken the law since. But in the jewellery business, the world over, from Birmingham, England, to Bangkok, Brisbane, Berlin or Budapest, wherever gold is smelted there is always a danger that some of the precious metal being melted down is stolen.

There are other problems to smelting. The furnace has to generate 1062 degrees Celsius-the temperature that must be reached for the precious metal to melt. Iron melts at 1800 degrees Celsius, hence the terrible conditions that men in the steel mills have to work under; while lead melts at only 328 degrees Celsius so is easily separated from gold. Smelting

140

requires a special furnace and a sophisticated system of bellows if the molten metal that finishes up in the crucible is going to be of the purest gold.

'What quantity of gold do you have in mind for smelting?' queried Klaus tentatively.

Maurice Dupres' instant reply sent strident alarm bells ringing through Klaus Di Silva's turbulent mind.

'Let's put it this way,' snapped Papa Dupres' evil heir. *'We are prepared to pay you ten million euros for this job and remember you don't ask fucking questions like that again.'*

Klaus Di Silva was gob-smacked!

A back hander of that staggering proportion meant that only one crooked caper in the history of bullion theft would fit the bill--the sensational Brinks Mat robbery at London's Heathrow Airport.

But that was 25 years back.

Where in the world had that King's ransom in bullion been cached for quarter of a century? Could he, dare he, as Spain's most respected and wealthiest wholesale manufacturing jeweller risk getting involved in such a dangerous affair? Even with the dazzling carrot of ten million euros dangling in front of him?

Klaus needed time to unscramble his brain. The risks he faced if he accepted the hoodlums' offer would be immense. On the other hand the chance of pocketing a tax-free ten million euros was to use his wife, Angela's, favourite descriptive word 'gargantuan'. Yet Angela and he already owned successful businesses..

But it was a tempting enough to create the dream of taking his beloved Angela away from the slightly tawdry business of the escort agency racket and, unknown to her, easing a pressing burden of debt he had secretly incurred.

Away to a fantasy retirement in a luxury villa in Acapulco, the Riviera of Mexico, with their own private yacht bobbing lazily, below the cliffs, at anchor in the *azul celeste Océano Pacifico.*

'*I must have a little time to consider your proposition,*' said Klaus filibusting for breathing space to extricate himself from the underlying threat from the two malicious mobsters.

'*By all means Monsieur Di Silva,*' growled Maurice Dupres. '*You have 48 fucking hours to confirm you will do the job. No fucking longer. We have already compromised ourselves in what we have told you. Things would not go well with you or your family if you fail us.*'

Klaus Di Silva knew, in mob terms, he had received an offer he could not refuse. There was a chill in his heart with the dreaded conviction that he had no option!

* * *

28

Angela Di Silva pushed aside the disturbing thoughts about the puzzling moodiness of her husband Klaus and kept her mind focussed on improving her highly successful escort agency for women which had taken Barcelona by storm.

The last thing she wanted was that either her agency, or her team of male escorts should become stereotyped. She felt the need to ring the changes of her escort-client pairings politely irrespective of differing ages and preferences of the particular couples concerned. She aimed to devise some surprise couplings to emphasise her determination to keep the agency on the boil. To do that she had to ensure that only herself conducted the orchestra--so to speak.

Husband Klaus could go and fuck himself until he snapped out of the doldrums and told her what his problem was.

Angela's next ploy was to turn to Richard Martin, the young lad who was her first recruit into the murky world of male prostitution under its camouflage of respectability as a male escort, to tempt the sexual taste buds of older frustrated women.

So far Angela had only professionally paired Richard with Mercedes Gomez, the former child bride, and young widow of a Spanish Army colonel tragically killed on duty in Afghanistan. Mercedes, like Richard, was in her twenties. Now Angela planned that Richard's next assignation would be with the mature 40-year-old Irish woman, Kathleen Clooney, whose marital sexual activity ended after her husband was left impotent through cancer.

It would be an interesting experiment. Could the English lad cut the mustard with a woman nearly 20 years senior and old enough to be his mother?

Richard came through his initiation with Mercedes Gomez in storming style. But they were two 'rarin-to-go' twenty year olds. Satisfying the 40-year-old matron Kathleen Clooney might prove to be a more difficult task. But the street-wise Angela knew that to be a successful male escort Richard would have to learn how to pleasure clients of all age-groups.

The other important facet of the business from the Agency boss's point of view that there was danger if she paired her male escorts with the same client too frequently . Clients would either be bored or fall in love with the same partner.

'But Angela I enjoyed my date with José Moralés so much that I was yearning for a repeat,' Kathleen pleaded poignantly when she heard what was being arranged.

Angela di Silva smiled confidently and smoothly explained: *'I am sorry Kathleen but you cannot expect to monopolise José. He is one of my most popular escorts and he is booked up for the next three weeks or so. Of course you will have the chance to meet up with José again in the future. But meanwhile I have booked you up with Richard Martin, a most promising lad I signed up as soon as I launched my new escort agency. A change of partner will be good for you in rehabilitating your sex life after your marital trauma.*

'I can promise, with Richard, an experience you will never forget.'

That transpired to be one of the most prophetic understatements ever to be uttered by the notorious boss of *Adorable Angela's Escort for Women.*

* * *

However Angela knew she had to brief Richard Martin

before his liaison with a woman old enough to be his mother.

'You need to know the guidelines on how to impress a woman of a certain age,' Angela coached her young protégé. 'She may not just want to rush into bed. You will first have to place her at ease over a drink. Above all else engage her in sensible and entertaining conversation. It may not be a bit like dating a girl of your own age. You will need patience. Whatever you do don't remind her in any way of her age. You will have to woo her with patience and then come up to scratch when you get her between the sheets.

'If you follow those guide lines you will have an enjoyable and educative experience that you will remember for a long time to come.'

So an intriguing rendezvous, featuring a 20-year-age gap between man and woman was set-up.

* * *

29

Klaus Di Silva descended into a deep depression for the next 48 hours as, agonisingly, he pondered over the ominous offer that the evil French gangster chiefs had presented him with.

He slowly drank a bottle of the best Metaxa brandy each evening as he mulled over the sinister ultimatum that the pernicious Gallic siblings had made him. An offer the macabre mobsters believed he could not refuse--under threat to his life.

Almost from the outset he realised he had to turn the mind-boggling proposition of a ten million euros bribe, to melt down an awesome cache that, he felt sure, was the missing haul from the opprobrious Brinks Mat robbery at Heathrow quarter of a century back.

In short he was on a loser to nothing whatever answer he gave to these barbarous mobsters.

He had two disturbed nights when he moved to the guest room, which drove yet another wedge between Angela and himself. In fact Angela was beginning to suspect another woman might be the cause of his unusual behaviour. Throughout the happy years of their marriage Klaus had never previously failed to talk over his business problems with her.

But, nevertheless on second thoughts, Angela found it difficult to believe that he was philandering. Their sex-life had always been vibrant throughout their twenty year marriage. This was, mainly, because of the tricks of love-making that she had perfected when she was a street tart and afterwards as one of the most sought after brothel whores in Barcelona.

Klaus rose from his restless and virtually sleepless second night in torment over the grim threat that hung over him, his beloved wife Angela, and their son. The 48 hours of mental torment brought him to an inevitable decision on how to deal with the depraved Dupres brothers. There still would be a huge risk to his family and himself but he knew, as they say, there would be no free lunch if he was to prevail against the two malevolent mobsters from across the Franco-Espana border who were trying to lure him into their nefarious net.

He went to the *en suite* bathroom attached to the guest bedroom, showered and shaved with ultimate care before applying *Davidoff* cologne, Angela's favourite, to his smooth cheeks. Downstairs he looked at the kitchen clock and discovered there was still another half an hour to go before Carmella, their live-in cook-housekeeper, came down from her room to begin her day's work looking after the Di Silva family.

He busied himself in the kitchen preparing a breakfast tray of smoked salmon and scrambled eggs, with toast, butter fresh fruit and an assortment of jams, which he carried up to Angela who, by some sixth sense awakened from her deep sleep as he tip toed into her bedroom.

She knew, with the intuition of a woman who desperately loves her man, that whatever had been worrying him for the past few days was no longer such a big problem. In his inimitable way he had shrewdly worked out a solution. She still did not know what that problem had been but she was confident he would tell her all, in good time.

As she gave him a passionate kiss and stroked his face to thank him for her breakfast she tried seductively to will him to climb alongside into her bed. He sensed her feelings and said: '*Later, later amada. First I have to make some phone calls. Then I will join you afterwards and take you to lunch.*'

* * *

In his office an hour later Klaus thumbed through his personal, leather-bound, phone directory and found the Madrid number he was looking for. The business-like greeting at the end of the line he was calling produced a courteous response: '*Centro Nacional Intelgencia de to servicio*'. There was no doubting the respect the telephone operator at Spain's National Intelligence Centre (CNI) accorded him as he asked for the person who was the senior of two personal assistants to the high-flying lady who had been appointed the Secretary General of Spain's secret service.

The respect soared ten-fold when the operator was instructed to put Senor Klaus Di Silva through immediately.

'*Hola, Klaus amigo,*' said the man at the other end of the line. '*It's been a long, long time . Too long in fact my old amigo. We have a lot of "conversación" to catch up with. Now please tell me what I can do for you. Let me switch you over to my secure line and then tell me all.*'

Klaus Di Silva's high-ranked secret service *compañero* listened attentively to what the jeweller had to say and stridently whistled down the line when the notorious Dupres mob were mentioned.

'*Klaus that information really interests my organisation,*' he enthused. '*We have a file as tall as the Eiffel Tower on those evil bastards linking them with every crime in the list from murder, drug running, procuring prostitutes, armed robbery and counterfeiting euros, US dollars and sterling on Spanish territory. But suspicion is one thing and compiling strong enough evidence to prosecute them is another. They*

148

rarely cross the border into Espana--when they do they fly in by helipcopter without filing a flight plan, which is illegal in itself, or speed over the Pyrénées in their armour plated limousine and into the Spanish Pensinular by the back door, through Catalonia and quickly across the Spanish-French border using another route. Above all we would like to get them behind bars for gun-running and supplying ETA, the Basque terrorist group with arms and explosives.

'We had Papa Dupres on our wanted list for more than twenty years and now, since his demise, his sons have replaced him.

'I fully agree with your theory that the amount of bullion they want you to process is almost certainly from the sensational Brinks Mat heist at London Airport twenty years ago. That caper is one of the biggest unsolved robberies the world has ever known.

'I will have to ask for cooperation from the French Sûreté and contact Interpol at their headquarters in Lyon, France. For your information Interpol maintains the world's largest and most comprehensive database of unsolved global crimes and an extensive list of both convicted and "alleged" International crooks.

'I will insist, for security reasons, that your name is kept out of the enquiries because I am aware of the danger you and your family face until the Dupres brothers are securely behind bars.'

Having recruited the aid of Spain's prestigious CNI, secret service, Klaus di Silva believed he had negated the threat to himself and family. However, with the naivety of a curious schoolboy poking a stick into a hole in the rotting trunk of an ageing tree Klaus had stirred up a hornets' nest.

But hornets can sting viciously. Sometimes fatally.

* * *

30

Klaus Di Silva had inadvertently lulled himself into a false sense of security with an assurance, made in good faith, from a high-powered friend in Spain's prestigious secret service , the CNI, that his name would not be linked with any legal action taken by Europe's law enforcement agencies against the infamous French mobsters, the Dupres brothers.

The depression that had weighed him down recently, he believed, was a thing of the past Klaus now paid more attention to his wife, Angela, who had been puzzled by his uncharacteristic moodiness.

They made passionate love that night and Angela responded by pulling out all the tricks she had learned from several years at the sharp end of the sex trade as a hooker, call girl and escort agency madam.

Later they lunched at a table reserved for them at their favourite Los Caracoles Restaurant situated in Barcelona's sleazy Bario Chino district. With harmony between herself and her beloved Klaus partly restored, Angela was able to turn her attention towards the further advancement of her escort agency which serviced lonely and neglected women.

Immediately her next project was to organise the proposed liaison between 40-year-old Irish woman Kathleen Clooney, whose marital sex-life had been cruelly shattered after her husband had been unfortunately left impotent through prostrate cancer, with the agency's youngest escort. A relatively new client of *Adorable Angela's Escort Agency for Women* , Kathleen, had already experienced one steamy tryst with Jose Moralés , a virile former bullfighting virtuoso who had starred in every major bull ring in Spain and south

America. Kathleen really would have liked a repeat *'corrida'* between the sheets with the sexy ex-torero.

But the shrewd escort agency boss had another idea. She next paired Kathleen Clooney with Richard Martin , whose crown jewels, when he stripped off, were always lewdly and admiringly described by Angela as *'fucking gargantuan'.* There was a 20 year gap between Kathleen and Richard but instinct told Angela that this liasion would be yet another success for the agency.

'I am sorry Kathleen but you cannot expect to monopolise Jose Moralés,' Angela had told Kathleen. *'You will have the chance to meet up with Jose again in the future. But meanwhile I have booked you up with Richard Martin, the young star in my team of escorts. I can assure you of an experience you will never forget.'*

Angela wanted to avoid the danger of her clients mentally bonding with the escorts she employed. It was much better if he could train her customers to treat each of the escorts she paired them with as *'passing ships in the night.'*

Before the couple set off on their date Angela briefed Richard Martin on how to handle an older woman.

'You will need patience' the escort agency entrepreneur warned. *'Never remind her of her age. You will need to woo her with patient affection. Then it will be up to you to do your stuff when you get her between the sheets.'*

* * *

Richard Martin looked the part which the city's sultry senoritas described as *'muy guapo'* as they hungrily eyed the young caballeros, during the evening *paseo,* along Barcelona's teeming *Ramblas.*

His muscled upper torso, toned by his energetic two hour daily stints at Louis Samuels' *Gimnasio Campeóns*, and the deep tan of his chiselled face, was accentuated by the superb tailoring of his snowy white linen suit.

All of this did not go unnoticed by a nervous Kathleen Cooney as her young escort, 20 years her junior, strode confidently into the elegant cocktail bar of Barcelona's four star *Granada 83 Hotel* to keep the appointment Escort Agency chief, Angela Di Silva, had set up.

Richard was put on his mettle to meet the challenge Angela had thrust at him in her own inimitable words: *'If you cut the mustard with this 40 year old woman you will be the sensation of the escort agency world. You will have my clients queuing up for your services just for a look at the eighth wonder of the world--your gargantuan wand.*

After giving Kathleen an *abrazo*, Spanish style, with a kiss on each cheek and enquiring about her preference Richard ordered a bottle of *Dom Pérignon* accompanied by a frosted silver jug of *zumo de naranja* for a leisurely *aperitivo* before they moved on to the hotel's internationally renowned restaurant. They were already booked to stay overnight in one of the hotel's luxury suites which Angela Di Silva, as requested by Kathleen Clooney, had reserved for them.

She fell immediately under the spell of the young Englishman and, within a few minutes, she thought: *'He's a lovely lad and, as we say in Ireland, has the gift of the blarney.'* Also she was flattered when he asked admiringly: *'Do you always wear your hair pinned up? I think it is quite attractive when brunette's sweep their hair up at the back.'*

Kathleen answered coyly, strangely with almost the virginal shyness of a besotted teenager: *'Oh, it is kind of you to say that Richard,'* she trilled. *' I have nearly always worn it like that since I was a schoolgirl. The nuns, who taught us at convent school in Ireland, insisted girls pinned-up their hair. They did not approve of pupils who let their locks flow loose thinking it would attract the boys. Any girl who arrived for school with their hair tumbling over their shoulders were sent home with a note for their parent's explaining the school's disapproval of a free-flowing hair style--in the interest of modesty.'*

* * *

Richard let Kathleen chose from the menu and he was not just being polite when he approved her choice of a three-course meal: *'Chiporones-baby squid, dipped in harina-flour-and pan fried to crispiness in virgin olive oil; traditional paella, followed by Crema Catalana a speciality of the area and similar to the French classic--Créme Brûlée.*

She left the choice of wines to him. He ordered a bottle of very chilled *Palacio de Bornos Superior* a white crianza wine from Rueda to go with the chiporones: *Muruve Crianza 2002,* a warm deep wine from the often overlooked Toro region, to accompany the paella, and a bottle of *Las Reñas Monastrel 2002* a fantastic red wine from the Murcian region whose full flavour was a perfect partner to the well-stocked cheese board. It was the perfect meal leaving Kathleen Clooney already entranced with her young escort.

* * *

All lingering thoughts of her encounter with her previous escort, the debonair former torero José Moralés were dispelled in their hotel bedroom when Richard strode in confidently from the bathroom after showering. His *'gargantuan'* member, as Angela so often called it, though not fully erect was certainly not flaccid by normal male standards.

It was a sight that brought a gasp of mixed awe and

154

anticipation from the 40-year-old Irish woman as she waited in trepidation between the crisp linen sheets.

The next four hours, although a little frightening at first as she learned to cope with Richard's prodigious physique, was the longest stint of sex she had experienced since her womanising ex-husband Peter had broken her virginity more than two decades earlier.

The only other man she had known sexually had been the previous escort Angela Di Silva had arranged for her, suave ex-bullfighter José Moralés, who brought subtle Latin libido and know-how to bed.

What Richard Martin offered was the raw lust of youth as he made love to her several times, teasing her love juices to cascade on each occasion. By the end of the evening she was as brazen in their love pit as he was, when between sessions they explored each other with darting tongues.

'My God,' she looked across at Richard's head, his flowing curls lazily spread across the pillow as dawn was beginning to break outside the open balcony window. 'I can't get enough of this lad.' As if to emphasise her erotic thoughts she gently eased her around his taut and slender waist and felt that magnificent baton respond and engorge to her touch.

She smiled in the knowledge that there was more to come.

* * *

31

Klaus Di Silva, had made his decision to denounce the infamous French hoodlums by informing a close friend, who held a top position in Spain's CNI, secret service organisation, that the sadistic Du Pres brothers were trying to coerce him to smelt a massive amount of stolen bullion at his Barcelona jewellery emporium.

His contact at CNI's National Intelligence Centre in Madrid agreed with Di Silva's assessment that the gold in question could be the missing haul from the sensational Brinks Mat heist at London's Heathrow Airport two decades earlier. Apart from a relatively minute amount of bullion, worth a fabulous fortune, the vast bulk of the stolen gold had never been recovered, or the perpetrators of this breathtaking robbery apprehended. This despite the keen interest and efforts of the world's law enforcement agencies.

Klaus, over ambitiously, believed that his name would not be revealed as the 'whistle-blower' when the CNI advised France's criminal investigation department, Sureté, and the international crime detection organisation, Interpol, of the possibility that the heinous Du Pres brothers were sitting on a massive cache of stolen bullion.

Klaus now figured he only had to dot the I's and cross the T's to sever his contact with the malevolent French hoodlums. He sent them a message to the Email address they had given him.

It read simply : 'Sorry. I am not able to accept the offer you made me. My smelting machine is out of order and it will not be ready after repair for several weeks. In confidence. Klaus Di Silva.'

There was unbridled anger in the farmhouse kitchen, on the outskirts of Paris, when the Du Pres brothers read the Email from the Klaus Di Silva.

'*The yellow-livered mother-fucker has chickened out,*' the elder brother Maurice said as they drank their first *Pernod* and coughed on their first *Gaulliose* of the day. '*It is all bullshit about the fuckin' smelter being on the fuckin' blink. We have to teach Mr 'asshole' Di Silva, and that whore he calls his wife a fuckin' lesson that will scare the fuckin' shit out of them.*'

It was then Maurice and Emille Du Pres siblings hatched their vile plot. A week later their spiteful intent against Klaus Di Silva would be transformed from sheer malignity to gory homicide.

* * *

Two days after her lusty orgy with Richard Martin, the buxom Kathleen Clooney turned up as normal for the weekly meeting of Barcelona's Ladies Bridge Club only to be told by the secretary that her usual partner, escort agency boss Angela Di Silva, had cried off and sent her apologies.

Instead she was paired up with sleazy journalist Maria Torres someone she had never met, let alone had a conversation with, previously. She got on well with the attractive 42-year-old Catalan born bi-sexual Torres who had recently returned to her home city of Barcelona after a 15 year spell in California as Hollywood gossip writer for the top selling "Lat*i*na" magazine.

Kathleen found herself unusually outgoing with the ruthless journo', who had a reputation in the magazine world as a relentless reporter willing to sell her soul in pursuit of a good story. Maria listened intently as Kathleen enthusiastically described her night of licentious romp with former University student Richard Martin who was twenty years younger than herself.

The loose-tongued 40-year-old Irish woman did not realise at the time, and was to regret it later, but her indiscretion was to be another arrow aimed at the Di Silva empire whose principals, Klaus and Angela, seemed to be facing mounting problems.

* * *

Angela Di Silva was abruptly aroused soon after dawn that morning by Enrique Ramirez, the groom who managed the stables and the horses for the Di Silva's. He had rapped frantically at Angela's bedroom door and, hearing her sleepy response, he shouted: *'Senora, senora can you come quickly to the stable? Something terrible has happened to Zephyr.'*

Angela, saw Klaus was still fast asleep, quickly jumped out of bed, threw a raincoat around her shoulders, slipped on a pair of *adidas* trainers and hurriedly followed the groom down the huge *finca's* winding double staircase through the beautifully panelled front door to the stables. She immediately spotted, with cringing horror, the monstrosity hanging on the stall's half door. It was Zephyr's beautiful white tail, caked with coagulated blood, nailed to the frame. While inside her beloved gelding was rearing with pain, roaring in agony with blood seeping from his rump.

Angela, tears rolling down her cheeks, had thoughtfully put her mobile phone in her raincoat pocket when she was so suddenly called from her bedroom. She knew the number of the local vet off by heart and within seconds had called him, stressing the urgency.

Tomas Mesquida, one of Spain's most respected veterinary surgeons, was horrified at the atrocity committed against Angela Di Silva's elegant gelding 'Zephyr'.

'If I knew the name of the sadistic bastard who has done this to a lovely animal I would kill him with my own hands,' ranted the enraged vet. *'I have bad news, the worst possible prognosis to give you Doña Di Silva. You can see that Zephyr is in torment his left leg is paralysed and he is dragging it. Even if he survived he would never be able to gallop and certainly*

158

not jump again because his balance is wrecked forever. In fact he would find it almost impossible on only three sound legs. The butcher who did this in roughly hacking off the animal's tail touched the spinal nerves. There is only one thing I can do to end your horse's terrible suffering.'

Then turning towards the stable groom, Enrique Ramirez, the animal medic said: *'Take Senora Di Silva back to the house Enrique while I deal with this dreadful matter.'*

Ten minutes later the spirit of the much-loved Zephyr had been despatched to the ethereal grazing pastures reserved for demised equines.

Angela Di Silva was inconsolable and was left pondering who had perpetrated this outrage on her beloved four-footed pal. Her husband, on the other hand, was in no doubt when he scanned the in-box on his laptop.

The Email read: 'Our next gift will be the ears of your 17-year-old son if you still refuse our offer. Now you know we mean business confirm immediately when we can deliver our goods for processing. THE FRENCH CONNECTION'

Although Klaus was understandably scared following the atrocity inflicted on Angela's horse he nevertheless felt consoled that by informing Spain's Intelligence Centre, the prestigious CNI, about the Du Pres gang's nefarious plans to force him to smelt their huge cache of stolen bullion, he thought he had taken out insurance for himself and his family. The CNI had promised to keep his name out of any action that the French Sûreté and Interpol might take against the Du Pres brothers.

32

Klaus Di Silva created the biggest stir in the Madrid offices of the Spanish secret service organisation, CNI, when he faxed a copy of his Email which informed the depraved Du Pres siblings that he could not accept their offer to smelt the bullion that their late father had stolen in the notorious Brinks Mat heist two decades previously.

He also sent them a copy of the French mobsters threatening Emailed reply. What particularly interested the CNI spooks was the accompanying return fax from the French hoodlums which warned they would cut the ears of his 15-year-old son and send them in a horrific parcel to Klaus and his wife Angela who was already grieving at the sadistic, and what turned out to be fatal, atrocity done to her beloved horse Zephyr.

Although the two Emails would not be considered as conclusive evidence in themselves to guarantee putting the two French mobsters behind bars it could lead to the recovery of the breathtaking cache of gold that, remarkably, had lain in hiding for twenty years. It virtually confirmed that the bullion in question must, almost certainly, be the Brinks Mat haul.

*   *   *

The lines between the CNI headquarters in Madrid, Interpol at their offices in Lyon and the Paris office of the renowned Sûreté were red hot as top brass from these respected law enforcement agencies conducted a telephonic conference thoughtfully discussing the tactics to be used against the Du Pres brothers.

There was a consensus amongst the three esteemed law enforcement organisations that if they were to catch the Dupres brothers napping that a joint and dynamic action should be taken by a SWAT team of elite officers from the Paris police force which would be deployed to raid the French mobsters at their farmhouse hideout just outside the city. Representatives of Spain's CNI, Interpol and France's Sûreté would attend the armed raid as observers. It was also unanimously agreed that the UK's Scotland Yard should be informed of the action to be taken and advised that there could be a possibility of the long-lost Brinks Mat stolen bullion being recovered.

Seven days later a team of 100 specially selected police commandos were mustered in the spacious yard of the Paris police headquarters at Place Louis Lépine, Rue de Lutèce.

Heavily equipped with body armour, shields, battering rams, automatic rifles and tear gas, they were addressed by their commander, Michel Gaudin, *Préfet de Police,* who emphasised the importance of the raid they were about to mount against two of the world's worst hoodlums, known drug dealers, pedlars of pornography and suspected multi murderers.

This mini-army in blue would be backed up by qualified paramedics from the French National Police, fingerprint and DNA experts, sniffer dogs trained in searching for drugs and even bullion which was to be the main target of this formidable attack force. Standing by was a fleet of police coaches, two ambulances and a van equipped to supply coffee and sandwiches to the officers concerned.

They rolled out from *Place Louis Lépine* at 3am and arrived at the target Du Pres farm, on the outskirts, at the vulnerable hour of 4am with the aim of catching the perverse Gallic gangsters off their guard.

'*Good luck men,*' barked the *Préfet de Police.* '*Look after each other's backs. The Du Pres brothers are evil treacherous*

161

monsters. France looks forward to you all doing your duty. Good luck.'

Thus the most formidable police task force since the Paris massacre of 1961 was assembled. Although, it has to be said, that the two events were not entirely comparable. But it was clear that in the minds of police chiefs the recovery of stolen gold was deemed, at least, as important as dealing with a mob of street demonstrators. It was on 17 October 1961, during the Algerian War of 1954-62 that the Paris police under the orders of the head of the Parisian police, Maurice Papon, attacked an unarmed demonstration of some 30,000 Algerians. The French government, at the time, acknowledged 40 deaths, but other estimates put the fatality figures at around 200.

* * *

33

Just as the infamous Maurice Papon had done in 1961 the latest in his line of successors as Paris police chief, Michel Gaudin, who had decided personally to command the raid on the Dupres farm, ordered his men to be subversive in their encounter against the two vicious French mobsters.

'They are very violent men,' said Gaudin at the final briefing *'It would not be the first time they have killed one of "Les flics" although we have never been able to prove it in court. So don't be afraid to rough them up if they show signs of putting up any resistance. I will protect you from prosecution for any action you take in your line of duty. We expect to find hard drugs like cocaine at the Dupres farm but also we are looking for a huge quantity of gold that we suspect them of hiding. But whatever you do don't let these sadistic shits know that we are searching for stolen gold. This is to protect the identity of our informer, and his family, who are based in Spain, from the barbarous Dupres bastards.'*

* * *

It was two hours before dawn, always the darkest part of the night, when the armed convoy arrived at the target. To maintain the element of surprise the task force moved straight into action.

An armour plated police juggernaut burst straight through the large wooden gates embedded in the cemented enclave that surrounded the farm. The Paris police SWAT force and their uniformed colleagues from various stations piled out of the official buses and, in accordance with the pre-raid plans drawn up by the operation's commander Michel Gaudin, split into teams of four men each and made for every corner of the

163

huge farmhouse.

The raid was so instant and well organised that the two malicious French hoodlums were asleep as eight heavily armed SWAT officers led by a sergeant and Inspector burst into their bedroom. They awakened from their baleful pernod-laced-with-cocaine induced slumber to find themselves facing the muzzles of four automatic pistols, four poised police batons and a burly sergeant and inspector.

'Get out of bed you lazy bastards, now,' shouted the inspector. *Don't even think about trying to fuck with us or my boys will teach you a painful lesson that you will not forget in a hurry.'*

Of the two depraved Dupres hoodlums the elder brother, Maurice, was the first to shake off his hangover and recover his equilibrium as he yelled angrily: *'What the fuck are you assholes doing here? This is private property and I sincerely hope you have a search warrant otherwise our lawyer will have your lousy guts for fuckin' garters.*

'..and what about our mother--she's a very old lady--on the wrong side of 90 years of age--what have you done to her?

Inspector Robét Giscard was unfazed. In 26 years service with the Paris police force he had interviewed, charged and arrested some of the most desperate criminals in the French underworld.

'Hold your horses Maurice Dupres,' he replied calmly. *'Yes! We have a search warrant and, starting from now my men are going to probe every nook of this farmhouse. I suspect you have a huge stash of hard drugs secreted somewhere on the premises. We know you and your brother are big dealers, the biggest in France, of cocaine. As for your mother one of our policewomen awakened her gently and has taken her to the*

kitchen where she is making the old lady a pot of coffee as we speak.'

As Inspector Giscard engaged in heated conversation with the profane Maurice little attention was given by the police officer to the younger Dupres brother, Emille, who was surreptitiously easing his hand into his beside cabinet in an effort to grab his trusty .45 automatic pistol secreted there.

But a keen-eyed SWAT policeman, his commando training engaging with impressive speed, spotted the younger Dupres brother's stealthy movement. In an instant reaction he whipped his side handled baton from its sheath and brought it down with one vicious swoop on top of the French crook's right shoulder.

The yell of pain from Emille Dupres was deafening. The police posse crowded inside the Dupres' bedroom sprang to readiness. But a possible bloody massacre had no doubt been averted. As the groaning Emille was handcuffed the pain he was going through from that violent baton blow induced floods of tears.

On investigation a fully cocked M1911A1 .45 calibre US. Infantry automatic pistol was found nestling inside the drawer of the bedside cabinet.

'I am conversant with this type of weapon,' said Inspector Robét Giscard.

'They were originally manufactured in 1926 by John M.Browning's company in response to the US Army's need for a pistol with greater stopping power following the military's experience of close-in combat during the Philippine Insurrection of 1889-1901. Although it was mothballed by the Americans in 1984 and replaced by the modern M9 9mm pistol it is still a deadly piece with its seven round magazine

and range of 1,500 metres.'

Then turning towards one of his sergeants he ordered: *'See that pistol is wrapped in a plastic bag and sent to our forensic department in Paris to be checked out. We have been trying to nail these two Dupres mother-fuckers for several murders over a number of years. Get the weapon matched against the bullets used in every killing we have suspected the Dupres brothers to be involved but have been unable to gather enough evidence against them to secure a conviction, and put them where they belong--behind bars*

'Oh, and sergeant call one of the medics who came with us as part of this task force to check out the French hoodlum's injury the yellow-livered bastard is making as much noise as a piglet being taken to the abattoir to have it's throat cut.'

Inspector Giscard then ordered the Dupres brothers to change from their pyjamas into their jeans and tee shirts which were slung untidily across the chair after their pernod-cocaine orgy the previous evening. The lamentable Emille had to be assisted by one of the policeman to pull his tee shirt over his badly bruised arm. A few minutes later a police doctor who had accompanied the task force examined the wailing younger Dupres.

'His clavicle is broken,' the police medic diagnosed. *'What exacerbates the injury is the fact that his shoulder is also dislocated. He is in excruciating pain at the moment but he is likely to go through the roof when I manipulate the shoulder back into its socket. It will take several men to hold him still while I rotate his shoulder until it clicks back into its socket.'*

Emille Dupres, restrained by three burly cops, one gripping his good shoulder and one on each threshing leg, squealed like a scalded cat as the police medic slowly turned his right arm through a full 90 degree circle until, as if by magic, the shoulder slotted into place.

The Dupres brothers having changed into the jeans and denim shirts, they normally wore around the farm, were taken to an empty milking shed in the cobbled yard and handcuffed to a metal stanchion under the supervision of a policeman while his colleagues turned the premises in the search for the missing gold they hoped was being concealed there. The 100 man task force toiled for 14 hours until nightfall helped by sniffer dogs and metal detectors as wearily they explored almost every square metre of the notorious farm.

Under the eagle-eyed scrutiny of Michel Gaudin, the *Préfet de Police,* they were given no respite from their labours except periodic visits to the motorised canteen, staffed by three policewomen, who dispensed a seemingly never-ending deluge of strong coffee, hunks of cheese and ham baguettes, plus a mound of hard-boiled eggs.

Several square meters of the cobbled farmyard were dug up with the help of pneumatic drills at sites where sniffer dogs, trained in metal and hard drugs detection, displayed unusual interest with a chorus of barks, and growls from fangs dripping with saliva.

Throughout all this turmoil Maurice Dupres whined continually, vociferously demanding that the police chief should allow him to call his lawyer.

'You have damaged our fucking property, kept our 90-year-old mother under guard, seriously injured my brother, Emille, and generally messed up our lovely farm,' complained the elder Dupres brother. *'You are in serious trouble when I complain to the fucking government about the fucking high-handed treatment you have handed out to us.'*

The angry pleas of Maurice were completely ignored until

later in the day, still manacled to the metal stanchion, he received a visit from Inspector Robét Giscard, who was second in command of this massive police raid.

'It is you and your brother who are in the shit,' said Giscard. *'Our dogs and men have already unearthed nearly 100 kilos of cocaine and other drugs so whatever happens you can look forward to a lengthy spell in gaol.'*

But after 14 hours of concentration in controlling the police raid, under the instructions of his chief Michel Gaudin, the conscientious Giscard was frustrated that they were no nearer to finding what they were looking for despite the discovery of the drugs which should put the Dupres brothers behind bars.

A mixture of weariness caused by losing a night's sleep followed by the long and arduous stint at the Dupres farm lulled Giscard into an uncharacteristic indiscretion.

Digging Maurice Dupress in the ribs with his baton the frustrated police inspector growled: *'Now tell us where you have hidden the bloody gold and we'll make it easy for you.'*

It was an incautious, and under the circumstances heedless, contravention of the assurance given to wealthy jewellery tycoon Klaus Di Silva by the Spanish secret service to keep his name out of any action taken by the French authorities against the opprobrious Dupres mobsters.

An inadvertent slip of the tongue that would lead to gruesome consequences.

* * *

34

A lively free press in Spain resulted as a result of democratising the country in the mid-1970's following the autocratic regime of General Francisco Franco which had kept a tight grip on the nation's media for a sizeable part of the 20ᵗʰ Century.

Although not as vibrant as the tabloid press in England, who count their daily readership by the million, Spain's leading media companies are mainly sited in the capital, Madrid. Nevertheless there are more than 100 daily newspapers published in Spain, although only a few have a circulation above 100,000 copies a day.

But there was a surge of morbid interest, sadistic scandal and nauseated condemnation when the main newspapers from the Madrid based *El Pais, ABC, El Mundo,* Barcelona's two respected dailies *La Vanguardia* and *El Periodico de Catalunya,* and the three influential Basque periodicos, *El Correo, Gara and El Diaro Vasco,* printed respectively in Bilbao and San Sebastian blazed almost the identical gruesome *titular* one grim Monday morning. Translated into English from their original Castllian and Catalan languages they relayed the same grisly message:

TYCOON JEWELLER MURDERED

BY GARROTTE

Decent and respectable Spanish citizens, readers who had turned their backs on bullfighting the ancient ritual of the Peninsular by switching their fanatical sporting fanaticism to the nation's renowned Soccer teams like Real Madrid, Valencia, Seville and Barcelona, known affectionately throughout Catalunia as '*Barca*' were horrified..

Spain's other age old ritual of capital punishment by garrotte was only referred to with disgust for it was the standard method of execution in the country from 1812 to replace a crude form of hanging used previously. Garrotting was last used on the 2nd March 1974 when two men were put to death in this gruesome way on the same day for the shooting of a police officer and a member of the *Guardia Civil*. Spain fell in line with the rest of Europe when it abolished capital punishment in 1978.

Spain had inflicted capital punishment with a grisly, continually updated, garrotte machine. It comprised a wooden chair or stool nailed to a post.

The condemned prisoner was strapped at the wrists, arms, waist and legs to the post to which a heavy screw, operated by a handle or weighted lever connected to a spike or small star shaped blade which ran through the post. When the screw/lever mechanism was operated , the blade entered the victim's neck and severed the spinal column ensuring the prisoner did not slowly strangle but died quickly with a broken neck.

But the garrotte that despatched Klaus Di Silva to eternity was the *móvil* type used by the vicious hit men who operated in Spain's criminal underworld. It was simply a length of piano-wire with toggles on each end. The killer simply wrapped the wire around the victim's neck and pulled on the toggles, strangling and sometimes decapitating the poor man within minutes.

The media began speculating that Klaus Di Silva had been murdered by a jewel thief for his headless body had been found in a pool of blood on the floor outside the door of his warehouse strong room. The severed head lay several metres away on the other side of the room.

It was minus its *lengua (tongue)* which had been cruelly

yanked out by its roots. A symbolic sign used by both Spanish and Italian *mafiosi* that the victim was a detested '*infamia*' (traitor and informer.

* * *

The next 48 hours were the most traumatic in her life for Angela Di Silva. First there was the visit to Barcelona's *depósito de cádavers*, where she was asked by the *Guardia Civil* to go through the nightmarish ritual of identifying the pathetic remains of her husband. The image she would recall in nightmares for the rest of her life was the wide-open mouth of her beloved Klaus's tongue-less head and the horrific way his eyeballs were turned into their sockets.

That and the awful atrocity recently committed against her adored gelding Zephyr was just too much for Angela to take in all at once. On returning home her doctor immediately ordered her to be admitted for rest and repose to a medical nursing home run by the nuns until she had recovered from shock.

* * *

But Angela Di Silva's tortuous trek to Calvary was not to end in the sanitized ward of a convent nursing home. There was more agony, much more pain, heart ache and suffering in store for a woman whose world was collapsing around her.

* * *

35

Doctor Rafael Jiminez called in at the nursing home run by the *Sisters of Charity* on the outskirts of Barcelona within hours of his patient, the distraught and grieving Angela Di Silva, being admitted as a patient.

'I want Donna Di Silva heavily sedated for the next 72 hours,' he gave explicit instructions to the Mother Superior. *'There will, hopefully, be times when she will awaken during those three days and nights. Get some nourishing soup in to her and then administer another of the tablets I have prescribed. After 72 hours in a near comatose state hopefully she should be on the way to somewhat recovering from the awful trauma of her husband's murder.'*

* * *

The sinister web spun by the sadistic Du Pres brothers was now becoming glaringly apparent even though the malevolent mobster siblings were currently incarcerated in holding cells at the imposing headquarters of the Paris *Préfecture de Police* located in *Île de la Cité.*

There they would stay under high security until they appeared before the city's investigating magistrates facing, at the very least, charges of possessing quantities of drugs, including cocaine, hashish and opium. Having been charged and held summarily they were allowed to wear their own clothes, order their food and wine to be brought in from nearby restaurants and use their own cell phones.

On retrieving his mobile phone after being installed in his cell at the *Île de la Cité* Maurice Dupres sent a text message winging on its way to a Corsican gangster known throughout Europe as one of the most sadistic murderers in the underworld. His deadly expertise was the use of the gory mobile *garrotte* featuring a length of piano wire with a wooden toggle at each end.

'CONTRACT-terminate Barca jeweller Klaus Di Silva pronto. Make sure the piano wire completes a 180 degree circle. Ten thousand euros will reach you by normal route within 24 hours. '

The sending of that emphatic text and the eventual atrocity that followed was a direct result of the inexcusable breach of security by Paris Police Inspector Robét Giscard just as if he himself had yanked the gruesome toggles of the garrotte that was to decapitate Klaus Di Silva.

The barbarous Corsica-born hit-man, Henri Guerra, just loved despatching luckless victims with his gruesome garrotte. Bordering on the edge of madness he had murdered more than 20 men in the previous ten years by this savage method.

When in his cups at the counter of the Yelllow Parrot Café in Marseilles he often falsely boasted that he was the bastard offspring of A.López Guerra the last public executioner of Spain. López Guerra executed murderer Puig Antich in Barcelona, in March 1974. It was the last time the gory garrotte was used by the Spanish government, who effectively abolished capital punishment in 1978. But there was not a shred of evidence, despite his macabre alias, to substantiate Henri Guerra's ludicrous claim that he was the illegitimate son of executioner A.Lopez Guerra.

* * *

The Spanish media had decided erroneously that Klaus Di Silva's murder had been perpetrated by an international gang of jewel thieves. That the Barcelona tycoon had paid the price

173

of refusing to 'fence' the stolen jewellery from a huge heist on the French Riviera.

For the next two weeks or so the Spanish *periodistas* had a field day expounding their sensational but ill-founded theories on why Klaus Di Silva had been so brutally murdered. But slowly the Klaus Di Silva garrotting began to slip from the front pages to the obscurity that is the inevitable fate of every lurid and sensational story in the media.

As they used to say, with brutal frankness, in London's newspaper centre, Fleet Street, where the world's most sleaziest newspapers like the lurid Sun, Daily Mirror and The Star, were once published: '*Today's headlines are tomorrow's fish and chip wrapping.*' A tart truism guaranteed to deflate the ego of any 'Street of Ink' scribe who believe they are a legend in their own life-time and in love with their own by-line.

* * *

At the nursing home where Doctor Rafael Jiminez had supervised Angela Di Silva's admittance for the treatment of traumatic grief dementia the nursing *Sisters of Charity* kept up around the clock bedside vigil as the escort agency boss slept away the demons that were plaguing her mind during a 72 hour sedative-induced state of coma.

She had awakened four times during that crucial time and sipped the chicken soup that the *Sister* on duty gently spooned towards her mouth. On other occasions the *Sister* tenderly wiped her parched lips and sponged the perspiration from her brow.

After three days the *Sisters*, as instructed by Dr Jiminez, stopped administering the sedatives and allowed Angela to slowly recover from her comatose state. She felt weak, desperately debilitated, but clearer in mind as if she had been brainwashed to put her grief over the loss of her husband behind her.

'*Life must go on,*' she told herself, the toughness of spirit that had supported her years earlier as she plied her trade as a street '*puta*' now stood her in good stead when she most needed strength.

Within a week she was on her feet, discarding her nightwear and donning her own clothes, helping the *Sisters* to serve *zumo de naranja* to the other patients. She was impatient for the next visit of Dr Rafael Jiminez, who she hoped could be persuaded to discharge her from the nursing home.

There was so much to do she thought to get her escort agency business up and running again, to wind up her husband Klaus's affairs, to make arrangements for the future of her son who was now at at an important stage of his education at an English public school, and resume her life again.

'*Yes, yes,*' she mused, wiping away a tear as she thought about Klaus. '*There is so much for me to do!*'

On her first day at work she called all her girl escorts together and assured them business would resume immediately now that she felt better.

'*Let's all carry one where we left off and make a lot of money for each other.*' Angela told her glamorous employees.

The following days she opened four bottles of Dom Perignon Champagne to welcome her team of male escorts including her young '*Gargantuan Gigolo*' the former University student Richard Martin, 55-year-old hairdresser Bernardo Sanchez, former star of the bullring, Jose Eugenio Moralés and the sexy black Ethopian Jew, Kote Rabtana.

'*Business as usual,*' Angela beamed as she lavishly poured the expensive French 'bubbly' for her stable of studs for hire. '*Thank you all for your get well messages while I was in the nursing home. I have been through a nasty time. But that is all over and life goes on. So does the escort agency we have all worked so hard to build up.*'

36

It was the nature of a very gutsy woman, who had learned the hard way how to cut the mustard when she was a teen-aged street walker dealing boldly with perverts, sex-starved married men, deviants and other weird characters of the night, that inside a week she had her escort agency running smoothly again.

As usual the pairing of her escorts with the agency's clients was crucial to the success of the business. The pain engendered by the brutal murder of her beloved husband, Klaus, still bedevilled her, particularly in the darkest hours of the night.

Angela handed over the winding-up of her husband's affairs, particularly his reputedly prosperous wholesale jewellery business, to his *abogado*, Alfonso Torres, one of the best lawyers in Barcelona.

She was utterly shocked to be informed by Don Torres that Klaus Di Silva had died heavily in debt. A blow acerbated by the fact that her husband had always been so gallantly supportive and generous towards her.

The *abogado* had called in a prestigious firm of *contables*, López, Amer y Rada, Accountants, to compute the exact financial position of Klaus Di Silva at his death. The figures were unbelievable to Angela with all Klaus debts, to fellow members of the jewellery trade, bankers, loan companies, the City of Barcelona and the Spanish Inland Revenue Department taken into account, as well as €50.000,00 mortgage on their magnificent home, there was little more than €10.000,00 left in the family kitty.

In fact if it was not for the thousands euros she had salted away in her Escort Agency bank, as a result of her shrewd business acumen, she would have considered herself to be a poor woman.

Further information handed to her by a very sympathetic Alfonso Torres revealed that Klaus had gambled and lost incredible amounts of money in the stock market for years. *'Oh, why, why Klaus did you not confide in me,'* she mused. *'I would have understood and come to your rescue--just as you had done so often for me over the years.'*

Having digested her former husband's lapses of judgement Angela Di Silva was more determined to put a new spin on the importance to her future of her prosperous escort agency business.

Astutely, in the unexpected revelation that her husband Klaus Di Silva's fortune was founded on quicksand, Angela was aware that she had to tighten up the escort agency's *modus operandi*. Whereas in the past she felt she had her husband's considerable financial clout to back her up now she realised that the escort agency would have to stand its own corner and deal with any problems from the organisation's own resources.

She needed to replace the father-figure of Klaus with a shrewd assistant capable of sharing the responsibility with her. She sat down at the desk in what was formerly her husband's study to work out a strategy. Was there a person already within her organisation capable, strong and wise enough to cut the mustard as her number two?

Former university student Richard Martin, she felt was too young to fill such an important role. Bernardo Sanchez, the 55-year-old tonsorial artiste, was already heavily involved in running his own successful hairdressing salon. Jose Eugenio Moralés, the celebrity former bullfighter, already had enough on his plate keeping his bar running smoothly and making a profit to augment his fees as one of her escorts.

After much serious consideration she came to a firm conviction that the candidate who ticked all the boxes for the vacancy as her 'top honcho' was the imposing 6ft6in Ethopian Jew, Kote Rabtana.

One of the hundreds of *Falashas,* black Jews, who migrated from a persecuted existence in Ethopia, to the country of their religion Israel where they faced a cool reception from the Israelis who paradoxically were mainly children and grandchildren of victims of the holocaust during the Second World War.

Highly intelligent, a truthful, honourable man, Kote was a qualified psychiatrist after gaining his degree in the USA.

* * *

'*That's the deal Kote,*' Angela told him the next morning. '*You will man the office during the day helping me to run both my escort agencies for men and women. I will pay you an extra €500 a week and you will still be able to do your escort duties in the evening so all-in-all you will have a sizeable take home pay each weekend.*'

Kote Rabtana agreed to the new arrangement and pledged: '*Thank you for having faith in me Donna Di Silva. I promise my full loyalty to you and the agency. You can absolutely rely on me.*'

So *Adorable Angela's Escort Agency* was back on the rails and the organisation's two principals were set to lead the organisation to further success.

The promotion of Kote to office manager, manning the phones for eight hours each day freed Angela Di Silva to recruit four new escorts to her male team in Barcelona, and six more women escorts. The next month was hectic as she set up a branch in the capital, Madrid. Her chain of escort agencies was national with a truly international clientele servicing lonely, disturbed and unfortunate men and women from across the European borders and, in a few instances, from the USA, Australia and other far flung regions of the globe.

The coffers of *Adorable Angela's Escort Agency* signified what a sizeable business Angela was building up. The pain and trauma of her husband's gruesome murder was easing but she would never forget Klaus who had been so kind and generous to her throughout their marriage. Yet, at the back of her mind, there was resentment that Klaus had not confided in her and deprived her of the opportunity to help him out of his financial problems.

But as so often had happened to this stoic business woman, who had risen from the gutter as a street prostitute, always there seemed to be hiding round the corner something to kick her in the teeth.

In the eventful life of this courageous business women, who had fought her way up the social ladder from the depths of street prostitution, there always seemed to be something lurking around the corner and threatening to send her back to the streets.

37

Bitchy Maria Torres, the hard-nosed magazine gossip writer, used all her skills at covert manoeuvring, with the help of a neatly folded €50 bill surreptitiously slipped into the grasping claw of the *maitre de hôtel* , to arrange that she was seated next to Angela Di Silva at the weekly meeting of the Ladies Bridge Club.

'*Oh this is a marvellous coincidence,*' the 43-year-old investigative journalist crooned with melodious mendacity. '*I intended to seek you out if you were here today. I was delighted with the assignation you arranged for me with that sexy hairdresser, Bernardo Sanchez.*'

Angela Di Silva, returned the greeting warmly Spanish style, a kiss on each cheek and a vigorous *abrazar.*

'*It is lovely to meet you again, Maria.*' the vibrant escort agency boss said. '*I try hard to select compatible escorts for our clients.*'

Maria Torres responded enthusiastically, saying: '*You certainly did that when you matched me with Bernardo Sanchez. I must be honest. Initially I had reservations when I realised you had set me up with a man 12 years my senior. Bernardo is a sex bomb. He was fantastic in bed. I have never had a more unbridled lover of any age,*'

Angela responded warmly to the compliments of a satisfied customer.

'*Well, we do aim to please,*' she said. '*Would you like me to arrange another liaison for you? But I must warn you that, as much you revelled in the companionship and sex with the handsome Bernardo Sanchez, it is not my policy to pair up the same escort and client on a regular basis. It would not be good for either of them, or indeed in the best interest of the agency if personal bonding replaced what should be nothing more than a pleasurable business arrangement. We are an escort agency and not marriage brokers!'*

Maria Torres smiled at Angela's warning and assured her: *'No, no Angela that is not what I had in mind. It is true that one day I would very much like another tryst with sex-pot Bernardo, I am hoping to widen my experience. Although Bernardo's age of 54 was neither off-putting or showed any signs of an ageing libido I would like to try something different. I have heard you have a young stud on your books who is quite remarkable.*

'If you could arrange a night with this super-boy I have heard so much about I would be absolutely delighted.'

A klaxon sounded in Angela's mind. Where in the world had Maria Torres heard about her young protégé? Who had been gossiping about her escort agency's affairs? Was Maria Torres' curiosity that of a journalist or the natural urgings of yet another agency client yearning for companionship from a man plus sexual satisfaction?

It was a shrewd strain of thought and one that Angela would recall bitterly in the future. But with a shrug of her shoulder she valiantly cast aside her doubts and figured that Maria Torres had listened to the tittle-tattle amongst some of her other clients in the ladies powder room at the bridge club.

'I assume Maria that you are talking about young Richard Martin who was the first escort I signed up when I started the new escort agency for women clients,' said the astute business-woman.

'He was fresh out of the University of Valencia, where he had been sent down for some misdemeanour and was on his uppers. Broke and facing disaster. I spotted his potential as an escort. Good looking, well built, attractive personality. I had him groomed and he has been a success with every client I have placed him with.

'He is still in his very early twenties so Maria you mustn't expect the sophistication you experienced from Bernardo Sanchez. From Richard Martin you will get the enthusiasm of youth delighting in their early exciting steps into the world of sex.

'I will say no more Maria. But if I arrange an assignation with Richard for you I promise you an experience you will never forget.'

Maria Torres, felt smug following Angela's homily, after all she had used all her cunning ingenuity to manipulate the escort agency into pairing her with the youngest escort in her stable, the gorgeous mind-bending gargantuan gigolo, Richard Martin.

'Thank you Angela,' she said gratefully. 'I never fail to be impressed with the efficient way you run your business.'

38

Angela Di Silva could not pin down why she felt uneasy about the magazine gossip columnist Maria Torres.

It was the kind of restive problem she would have discussed with her husband at the end of a working day knowing that he would come up with a calmly thought-out solution. How ironic it was that his death revealed that Klaus, her tower of strength, was haunted by his own personal weaknesses that she had never been aware of.

Casting aside her doubts Angela, anxious as always to please a client, set about convening a tryst between Maria and Richard Martin.

'*Richard this client Senora Torres has specially asked to meet you,*' Angela explained to the young escort she still considered to be her protégé. '*She is a cultured, well educated lady, who has spent quite a lot of her career as a journalist in America. You have done well in pleasing all the clients I have matched you with up to now. I am sure you will not disappoint this lady.*

'Your social skills will need to be at their best to hold the interest and amuse such a worldly-wise woman. As far as your performance between the sheets is concerned you will, forgive the pun, need to rise to the occasion if you are really going to pleasure Doña Maria Torres.'

* * *

Calling on her past propensity to utilise an open-ended expenses account Maria Torres showed no inclination to spare the considerable coffers of her boss the owner-editor of the lurid gossip magazine "Chismografia".

She told Angela that she would meet Richard in the elegant cocktail bar at the five star Hotel Majestic where she would reserve a suite for the night. Towering above the art galleries and the renowned cultural attractions of the Passeig de Gracia, the most modern district in Barcelona, the Hotel Majestic had reigned supreme in the city for nearly 90 years.

The meeting was set for 7.30 pm but Maria Torres had checked into the suite she had booked just after midday. She spent the afternoon secretively setting up a number of miniature cameras and tape recorders, above and around the jumbo-sized bed where she planned Richard Martin would be the star of the night.

Richard's curiosity received a slight jerk at the fusillade of questions that Maria Torres fired at him with the persistent staccato of an expert jazz band drummer. But the English lad dismissed any reservations in his belief that Torres was just a talkative dame.

'How did you manage to get into the escort business, darling?' she lured him into a session of unguarded gossip.

He could see nothing wrong in being up front with his reply. 'I had just left the University of Valencia when I met Angela Di Silva,' he explained.

Sra Torres was quick to demand an immediate response to a secondary query. 'But didn't you want to cash in on your university degree? After all with such a qualification here in Spain you could have carved out a good business career or in one of the professions. '

He replied, almost sheepishly: 'Oh! I didn't get my degree. I was caught by the University officials with a 17-year-old Spanish girl student in my bed. I was barely 19 years of age when I was expelled from the University five days later. I could

185

have gone back to England in disgrace. My father, a Church of England priest, is a kindly man and would have stood by me although he would have been very disappointed. So I decided to dog it out and eke out a living in Spain. But I was almost at the end of my tether when Angela picked me up in Barcelona's Bario Chino and gave me a job in her new escort agency serving women.

'I have enjoyed working for Angela for the past few years or so and it has put me on my feet financially. But I regret getting sacked by the University of Valencia because I was studying at their third campus, Tarongers, which houses the School of Law, Economics, Business and Social Sciences.

'My aim was to qualify as an abogado, a lawyer, and I was doing well until I made that silly mistake with that Spanish girl.'

* * *

39

Angela Di Silva had done well to recover from the violent and ghastly murder of her husband, the news following his death that he had dissipated the major part of the considerable fortune he accumulated as a wholesale jeweler, and the gory atrocity perpetuated against her beloved white gelding, Zephyr, which meant the horse had to be put down by the vet.

After recovering from her own trauma thanks to the care and kindness of the *Sisters of Charity* who ran the nursing home, and the skill of her doctor, she had poured her heart and soul into once again running *Adorable Angela's Escort Agency*--for both men and women.

But without the wisdom and guidance of her late husband, Klaus, she had placed an enormous extra load of responsibility on her own shoulders. Excusably she was occasionally vulnerable to taking her eye off the ball and making a wrong decision. Although appointing the towering Ethopian Jew, Kote Rabtana, as her assistant had lifted some of the load, as always in a vibrant business, the 'buck' always stops with the boss.

* * *

Angela was stunned at the elegance of the well-toned body, the high-cheekbones set strikingly in a glowing ebony visage attributes accompanying the soft lilt of the French language slightly burred by an accent honed in her native West Africa.

She said her name was Sagu Bayam and came from Senegal which was a colony in the now dissipated French empire. She was in her prime at 28 years of age, having spent the past two years, first as a street girl then in a Montmarte brothel. She had fled from France with her handsome Argentinian-born pimp-who, true to his ignominious trade, had dumped her in Barcelona when he had wheedled the 900 euros she had brought with her.

Now, at the end of her tether, Sagu was hoping that there was niche somewhere for her in Barcelona's bustling vice trade enabling her to pick herself up again.

'My 80-year-old mother in Dakar needs my support to stay alive,' she told Angela. *'You see Senegal is a poor country dependant almost entirely on agriculture and the money sent home by young Sengalese working and living abroad.'* Angela Di Silva had no reason to disbelieve a word this attractive African girl had told her.

The girl's face was not so coarse as the average Sengalese. The nose not so squat. The eyes slightly and attractively slanted above well chiselled high cheek bones. The ebony hair more disciplined and not requiring the braiding required by most African ladies to keep their coiffure under disciplined array.

Sagu Bayam had inherited her symmetry and svelte silhouette from her Egyptian mother who had taken a Sengalese sailor as her partner.

'Yes, this girl will be a sensation as an escort,' thought Angela and immediately placed Sagu on the payroll before sending her out on a trial assignation with her male-escort protégé, Richard Martin.

*   *   *

During their long preamble over coffee and liquers Maria Torres continued to ply Richard Martin with questions about the way Angela di Silva ran her two escort agencies. She was particularly interested what he had to say about Angela's newest escort, Sagu Mayam.

She had landed in Spain 18 months earlier when she was rescued with ten other illegal African migrants in a half-deflated rib boat in the Alboran Sea between Spain and Morocco. They were the only survivors that had left the African coast with twenty migrants squashed into the overloaded inflatable.

It was rated as one of the worst tragedies caused by the notorious criminal people-smugglers ever to happen on Spain's vulnerable coastline in years. Red Cross and members of Spain's Guardia Civil were appalled when the survivors claimed they were forced to throw the bodies of their unfortunate fellow passengers overboard as they died from hypothermia and exhaustion.

Sagu Bayam and her ten fellow survivors were rescued near Alboran Island by a Spanish ferry boat and taken to the port of Malaga where they received medical treatment.

Maria Torres' mental database was being crowded by the growing amount of information she was gleaning about *Adorable Angela's Escort Agencies*.

...and there was more to come, much more, during a respite in her night of wild and unfettered passion with Richard Martin, the well endowed escort, unceremoniously dubbed as the *Gargantuan Gigolo*. A compliment indeed from an icon of the sex for sale industry!

40

There was the alluring aroma of percolating coffee wafting from the office machine as Kote Rabtana prepared for his morning conference with his boss Angela Di Silva.

'All our branch agencies across the Spanish Peninsular have reported good business,' reported Kote. *'Our manager in Madrid told me on the phone half an hour ago that everyone of his escorts, men and women, were booked up last night despite the gloomy news in the media of a world recession.'*

Angela, delighted with Kote's report, said: *'The same applied in Barcelona I am pleased to say with all our escorts out on duty last night. Talking of the media I paired our tame journalist Maria Torres with Richard Martin last night. I hope the assignation went well. I feel sure she would have been impressed with what Richard had to offer. I am not sure about Maria however, there is something about her that makes me feel uneasy. However, I cannot pin down my reservations about Maria except I find her a bit self-opiniated.'*

Kote considered what the boss had said and commented: *'I feel sure she is just another client. I know she is a brash journalist but how can she harm us? We run our business properly. Pay our taxes. We do not allow pornography or deal in drugs. So what is the problem?'*

Angela considered what her assistant had just said and commented: *'Wise words Kote. In other words you're saying don't worry unless there is something to worry about. Meanwhile I am quite pleased with the new Sengalese girl, Sagu Bayam, I have just signed up as an escort for my female agency here in Barcelona.*

'She is sensationally beautiful, speaks perfect French,

Spanish, English as well as her native Sengalese tongue, Wolof. She worked as a street girl and later in a brothel in Paris after a treacherous journey in a flimsy inflatable boat from Africa. I sent her out for a trial night with Richard Martin last week just to indoctrinate her into the way Adorable Angela's Escort Agency works. Once I put her to work she will be very much in demand by the agency's male clients.

'We should be very pleased that our business is doing so well and I am very grateful to you Kote stepping in to act as my assistant after the loss of Klaus my beloved husband and mentor.'

Kote Rabtana, a modest man, graciously accepted the gratitude that Angela Di Silva had bestowed on him. *'I enjoy the work connected with this escort agency,'* he assured Angela.

'Both the administrative work here in the office and the hands-on experience with the clients which you have so generously arranged for me in the past few years. Strangely working for you as an escort during that time has added to my experience as someone who won a University degree in psychiatry and one day hopes to practise in that field.

'It has also put me on my feet financially. In fact I have been in touch with the Nacional de la Seguridad Social, who run the country's excellent National Health Service, who say that as there is a shortage of skilled medical specialists in Spain that, subject to me taking a test, in addition to my USA degree in psychiatry, they would welcome an application from me applying for registration as a psychiatrist here in Barcelona or anywhere else in the country.

'Of course Angela I will not leave you or the Agency in the lurch and would give you a satisfactory term of notice before making such a move.'

Kote's news came as yet another shock to Angela nevertheless she sincerely wished him well.

'*I will be terribly sorry to lose you Kote,*' she said sadly. '*But you can count on me for any help you might need to set yourself up as a psychiatrist. You have always been loyal and honest with me and I will always look upon you as a good friend. Having said that I will always miss you and your wise counselling. Good luck in the future I am sure you will be a wonderful and understanding psychiatrist.*'

41

Angela Di Silva was a little sad to learn that she might soon be losing the services of her assistant Kote Rabtana but she was sincere when she had wished him the best of luck in his quest to set himself up as a practising psychiatrist under the umbrella of Spain's efficient national health service.

Kote had stepped into the breach and helped her to run her nationwide escort agency business after the trauma of her husband's death. It was partly because of his assistance that she had been able to pull herself together and keep the agency running smoothly particularly as her husband Klaus, she had discovered after his murder, had squandered a large portion of his fortune in wanton stock market wagers.

She left her office and set off across the city in her new BMW convertible which she had part-exchanged in place of the Porsche that Klauas had bought her. As she sat in the chair at the high class hairdressing salon of Bernardo Sanchez, half an hour later the thoughtful Angela was completely relaxed as she assessed the way her life had progressed.

'If my business continues to thrive I will soon fill in the black hole in my finances left by the stupid indiscreet gambling sprees that led Klaus into difficulties,' she mused. *'Nevertheless he had been a generous husband and paradoxically a good business partner.'*

As Bernardo Sanchez busied himself re-styling her hair Angela reflected that her only regret was, that because of business pressures, she had never spared enough time to bond firmly with the baby son she had handed to Klaus less than 12 months after they were married.

A love child that had been denied the marvel of undying

parental love by a mother and father just too busy to spare quality time with their offspring. Yet they were parents that spared no expense to see that young Tobajas Di Silva had the best education, the most expensive toys, and elegant clothes that money could buy.

Yet Angela and Klaus had seen so little of Tobajas. From birth to the age of four he was cared for on a day to day basis by a loving nurse. He spent less than a hour in the evenings with his parents when they returned from business. Angela recalled that with Klaus she had called an expert in education to discuss the best schooling for their child after he passed his third birthday when many Spanish kids were enrolled in pre-school.

Sara Rodriquez, was a 50-year-old teacher, former school head, and was currently a highly rated executive officer in Spain's Ministry of Education and Science.

'*Your little son, , will be the ideal age to start pre-school when he reaches his fourth birthday,*' opined the stately Senora Rodriquez. '*The Research Department of the University College, London found from an intensive study that children who learn a second language have a significantly higher proportion of grey matter (the area of the brain which processes information) than those who had only learned their home language.*

'*The human brain acts like a sponge during those formative years and the capacity for learning is highest as the child approaches their fourth year. I recommend that you send Tobajas to a Catholic private school. As a boarder preferably as both you and your husband are heavily committed in business.*

'*There Tobajas, like his schoolmates, will absorb English alongside the compulsory Spanish and Catalan languages. At four he will learn his extra languages quickly in fact you and your husband will find when he returns home on a visit he will teach you and your husband to speak better English. At five years of age Tomas will already be multi-lingual.*

'Compulsory education in Spain begins at six years of age when I suggest Tobajas be moved to a private primary boarding school for the following six years before the next move up the education ladder to a private secondary boarding school. After four years Tobajas, if he has done his school work well, should qualify at 12 years of age for "Graduado en Educación Secundaria' certificate.

'At this stage the world of education will be Tobajas' oyster with possible placements open to him in Spain's 56 state-run and 19 private universities run either by private enterprise or by the Catholic Church.'

Angela and Klaus used Sra Rodriquez's shrewd advice as a blue-print for the education of their son and immediately enrolled him in an 8.000€ a year pre-school as a boarder. It was the start of a wondrous educative journey during which he excelled at every stage. Finally winning a Science Degree with Honours at the University of Seville.

Only 12 months back, just before the tragic murder of his father, Tobajas di Silva opted to join the Spanish Air Force with a view to becoming a fighter-pilot. As a trainee-officer he attended his father's funeral in his cadet uniform.

Now, 18 months later, in the next move in his climb up the Air Force promotion ladder, as a member of one of the armed services of the 26 nations which comprise NATO, he had been seconded to the RAF College Cranwell where he was receiving initial training to the highest standard to be an officer and fighter pilot. He would emerge after his studies at the distinguished Cranwell College as a Lieutenant in the Spanish Air Force proudly wearing his pilot's wings.

As Bernardo Sanchez applied the final titivating touches to her new coiffure Angela thought how proud she was of her son Tobajas and vowed that she would work hard to raise enough funds to leave him a sizeable legacy and set him up in life.

The kind of dream that every loving mother fantasizes about...

42

Although, honing into his own irreverent thoughts, Richard Martin was *'truly pissed off'* with the non-stop fusilade of questions fired at him by Maria Torres during their tryst at the five star Majestic Hotel he had to admit later that she *'could be an awesome lay'.*

He dismissed the irritation at her persistent curiosity about Angela Di Silva's escort agency as the nosiness of a middle-aged woman.

But when he got her to her suite and into the jumbo-sized satin-sheeted bed it was a different matter. It was his first experience of a nymphomaniac who kept him on the nest almost non-stop all night.

Tired out, sore in his private parts from his efforts, he almost said a fervent prayer of thanks when the first light of dawn streamed through the silken drapes wafting in the gentle breeze that drifted from the gentle waters of the harbour. The world-famous statue of Christopher Columbus significantly pointed westwards towards America, across the stately *Passeig de Gracia* providing natural air conditioning to cool the passions that had driven Maria Torres and Richard Martin throughout the torrid night.

He was curious why Maria called him to the centre of the room to almost ceremoniously present him with a 500€ banknote thanking him for his strenuous overnight services explaining: *'I know Angela Di Silva prefers that I pay her your propina by cheque with your fee but I wanted to thank you very personally for the wonderful night you have given me. It is a little extra to the tip I will give Angela to pass on to you.'*

There was no way that Richard Martin could have known

that the malevolent Maria had deliberately presented him with that tell-tale 500€ bank note immediately underneath the hotel bedroom chandelier.

Just where she had secreted a miniature camera earlier in the day.

43

The shit hit the fan on the 12th May, the date 450 years, earlier that the ill-fated Armada set sail from Lisbon to receive a bloody nose from Sir Francis Drake. Just as 1558 the day would be as shattering to Angela Di Silva as it had been for the floundering yester-year Spanish sea-dogs.

When Kote Rabtana 'phoned her at 8-30am that morning, asking her anxiously if she had seen that day's copy of the sleazy magazine "Chismografia", Angela wiping the sleep from her eyes answered waspishly: ' *I never waste my money buying, or my time reading, that muck raking rag. What's up?*'

Kote gulped before replying knowing this was not going to be easy. He explained: *'The front page headline of the magazine reads;*

"barca escort agency madam recruits students and illegal immigrants to prostitution"

'The byeline at the top of the article is that of our client, Maria Torres. Your instinct to distrust Maria was absolutely correct. She is a two-timing, lieing cow of the first order. She describes how you led a young university student, Richard Martin, into prostitution. She also falsely claims that you paid money to evil people-smugglers to provide you with female illegal immigrants from Africa, such as your latest escort girl, Sagu Bayam, the beautiful Sengalese girl and groom them into prositution.

'The whole article will not go down well with the City of Barcelona authorities although, Angela, you and I know there is hardly a grain of truth in it. I am sorry to say Angela that you have well and truly been turned over by this evil bitch of a journalist.'

Angela Di Lisa turned her face towards the pillow and wept for the best part of quarter of an hour. *'Oh, Klaus,'* she sobbed to herself. *'If only you were still alive. You would have known just what I have to do. I have worked so bloody hard to build my business up since you died. But I don't deserve this kind of personal attack!*

'My first reaction is to find that evil witch Torres and cut her fucking throat!'

44

The following day was Friday the 13th a truly unlucky one for the beleagured Angela Di Silva.

Although Angela's empire had taken a vicious hit she was inundated again twenty four hours later with a deluge of printed excrement directed at her by the most important daily papers published in Madrid. Neither were the two main Barcelona newspapers, *La Vanguardia* and *El Periódico de Catalunya* , to be denied their share of the most sensational sex story to hit Spain since the nation experienced a sex-revolution in the 1980's--little more than five years after the death of General Franco.

The Spaniards called this period *'desmadre'* , literally meaning 'chaos' in English. Vending machines sold condoms in nearly every restaurant or bar loo. Prostitutes advertised lurid menus offering their special services in the classified section of the popular *'periodicos'.* Homosexuals and lesbians openly proclaimed their inclinations. Despite the increased availability of condoms abortion rates soared to a ratio of one in every two births. All astonishing trends in a nation that only a decade earlier even prudishly banned holidaying women from baring their shoulders in the dining rooms of their package holiday hotels.

The newspapers that sent Angela into shock unselfishly gave the sleazy magazine "Chismografia" credit for breaking the story, most mentioned the name Maria Torres as the journalist responsible. Many of the national press, including the Madrid based *El Pais, ABC,* and *El Mundo* sent their own reporters to investigate the sensational yarn in the next few days. Some reported that they had found reasons to doubt the veracity of the sleazy magazine's reporting.

But it was too late. The damage to Angela Di Silva's integrity and to her business was irreparable. She was ruined and was quite aware that a serious fall-out of the sensational media hoo-ha would be aimed at her sooner or later.

In fact she only had two hours to wait for the flak to reach her when a call came from a top executive of the Barcelona City authority. '*Senora Di Silva*,' said the city hall official, '*sadly it is my duty to inform you that the Ayuntamiento of Barcelona have decided to suspend the license of your escort agency until the allegations being made against you in the media have been disproved.*

'*As you may be aware that although our attitude towards the sex trade are more liberal than in many countries.*

'*We license brothels and other establishments connected to the vice trade providing they maintain a low profile and do not flaunt their business in a way to offend practising Christians be they Catholic or Protestant. Because we are a tolerant authority, that also applies to our Jewish, Muslim and citizens of other religious persuasions.*

'*You must cease your business forthwith until if and when this ban is rescinded.*'

That distressing phone call came shortly after Angela had spent a horrible early morning poring over the huge bundle of newspapers that Kote Rabtana had brought to her home almost at the crack of dawn.

Kote and Angela's sombre conference was interrupted by similar messages via, fax and internet from local authorities in Madrid, Seville & Valencia withdrawing the licenses of *Adorable Angela's Escort Agency*.

'*I am finished*,'she sobbed. '*Ruined by that evil scribe, Maria Torres. It will be no good trying to fight the bans. Like the Barcelona official explained that as a region they depend largely on the tourist trade and try to keep prostitution and the allied sex trade under cover. I am really upset not only because I don't deserve this but also for the people, like yourself, who have worked so hard for me to build up the business.*'

45

Kote Rabtana and his boss Angela Di Silva continued to read how the bundle of daily Spanish newspapers had dealt with the wildly exaggerated story that the treacherous journalist Maria Torres had written in her sordid magazine.

'There is even a photograph taken in a hotel bedroom of our escort Richard Martin accepting a fee of 500 euros obviously for his sexual performance,' said Kote, unable to hide his disgust at the treachery. *'You have always insisted to all of us escorts not to directly accept money from clients and for the agency to handle all money involved in an assignation between escort and client. '*

Angela, equally irate at the way she had been set-up, nevertheless was eager to put the record straight.

'Richard is in the clear Kote,' she said. *'He came to me the morning after his night with Maria and handed over the five hundred euros she has pressed on him. He didn't want to take her money but she wouldn't accept it back. Quite obviously she had secretly installed a camera in the bathroom. God only knows what other pictures are in that camera! Torres is just a double-dyed shit.*

'Oh come on Kote we've had enough for one day. Let's have a drink and and try and forget our troubles.'

Angela went to the kitchen and returned with a bottle of *Moet Chandon* champagne from the frig.

'Will you be kind enough to do the honours, Kote, love?' she said handing him the bottle before fetching a full ice bucket and two fluted champagne glasses.

They spent an hour consuming two bottles of bubbly before Angela asked to be excused as she felt shattered and in need of returning to her bed because she had hardly slept a wink that night.

Kote was starting to worry about Angela. Summing up she had suffered a series of shocks in a short period of time. The cruel mutilation that had been perpetrated against her lovely horse Zephyr by what she knew now were enemies of her husband. Probably the same monster that murdered and decapitated him, the terrible shock that he had dissipated much of their huge fortune by reckless gambling and now the vicious, unfair, and false attack on the escort agency that she had so painstakingly and successfully built up by hard work over the years, could have made her vulnerable to a serious mental break down.

Drawing on the knowledge he had acquired when he studied psychiatry in the USA Kote noted that Angela was becoming susceptible to trembling hands, neck twitching, hesitant speech and small, seemingly unimportant memory lapses. All signs, he diagnosed, that she was suffering from delayed stress anxiety and, perhaps. needed treatment.

'*Look Angela you need a long deep sleep,*' Kote told her. '*Trust me. You know, having qualified as a psychiatrist, I had to pass my medical exams. I have some tablets in my car and I'll go and get them. They will help to blank your mind so that your sleep will be untroubled.*'

Kote hurried to fetch the tablets when he returned he could see Angela's head was already drooping as she tried to fight off her agonising weariness.

He helped her upstairs and into bed and gave her a tumbler of water to wash down the two tablets. He kissed her gently on the cheek and said: '*Sleep tight Angela. I'll be back in the*

*morning to see how you are. Don't forget I'll be here to help in
your hour of trouble!'*

46

Angela slept, like the proverbial log, until 2 am the next morning. The tablet that Kote Rabtana had given her the previous morning prompted a deep slumber undisturbed by worries, nightmares or dreams.

But once awake she lay turning this way and that in her dishevelled bed agonising about the fate that threatened to rob her of the escort agency business she had built so assiduously with her own effort and acumen.

'*Now,*' she pondered passionately. '*I am going to lose it all because of that lieing cow of a journalist. But I am not going to let her get away without letting her know just what a fucking twisting bitch she is. It's not going to help me because she has already done me irreparable damage but at least I will be able to be at ease with my conscience for the rest of my life knowing I had let the malignant Maria Torres know what a total shit house she is!*

'That will be my mission today to let that sick sorceress know just how low I rate her.'

Kote Rabtana arrived at 10-30am the next morning anxious to see if the sleeping tablet he had given Angela the previous morning had worked. To his surprise he found that the escort agency boss's royal blue BMW convertible had left the car park.

Thinking she may have awakened early and travelled to the office by taxi to begin tidying things up he was amazed when he found she wasn't there either.

Angela pointed the nose of the sleek BMW towards Bernardo Sanchez's plush hairdressing salon where she spent an hour luxuriating in the process of a shampoo and set.

Like an ancient gladiator waiting to enter the arena she was girding herself for battle in the only way she knew with her colours flying proudly on crimson lips, blush pink cheeks and scarlet manicured fingernails. She had dressed carefully before leaving home earlier wearing a silver grey two piece suit with a pink blouse of sheer silk and matching handbag and shoes.

Despite the heaviness in her heart she set off enthusiastically for her destination, the four star Laietana Palace Hotel in Barcelona's Gothic Quarter only a walking distance from the Port and Cathedral.

It was there she felt sure she would encounter the recreant Maria Torres at the monthly meeting of the Barcelona Ladies 'Pro-Bus Club', an organisation that embraced one woman of each professional or business sector. Maria Torres had been admitted as the only journalist who had applied for membership of the prestigious club.

Although Angela Di Silva had herself been for several years a member of the Pro-Bus Club, as the representative of the leisure industry, there was an eerie silence when she entered the overcrowded reception bar. Her fellow members had obviously read the original article in the sleazy Chismografia magazine and the follow-ups in the Spanish daily press over the last two days. She knew it would all be a nine day wonder but she was a little hurt that women who she had classified as friends turned their backs on her as she sipped her Campari and Schweppes tonic water.

After ten minutes or so she spotted Maria Torres enter the foyer of the hotel and head towards the cocktail bar. Boldy she confronted the perfidious press woman.

'I hope you are proud of yourself you two-timing bitch,' rasped Angela. *'You are a lieing turd. You will get your come uppance one-day. You are a fornicating witch--I just wanted you to know that's what I think of you.'*

Like many people who dish out the dirt Maria Torres was not so happy to be on the receiving end of criticism. She was furious that Angela had tackled her in this crowded bar amongst her fellow Pro-Bus Club members in front of whom she didn't want to lose face.

Torres lost her temper and, with claw-like talons she lashed out and inflicted a searing gash from ear to chin that oozed blood down Angela's face.

'Who do you think you are calling me filthy names?' she snapped waspishly. *'You are nothing more than a whore. A procurer of other harlots. A female pimp. A madam who lives off the earnings of other sluts.'*

Despite the fact that she had instigated the confrontation with the malicious Maria the amazed Angela was caught unawares with the physical attack from the journalist. She staggered back against the bar and grasped the nearest weapon at hand to defend herself.

In almost a throwback to her days as a street-walker she called on a ploy that prostitutes often used in their gory battles over territory--an empty wine bottle.

The warm blood trickling down her cheek leaving a sickly taste in her mouth incited her to an even more violent level. She cracked the top off the bottle on the brass ferrule that surrounded the counter to the astonishment of the cocktail bar tender who was either afraid or too shocked to intervene in this battle of she-cats.

With the jagged circle of bottle glass she advanced on Maria Torres plunging her vicious weapon into the left breast and sadistically twisting it until a scarlet torrent poured down the considerable cleavage of the deceitful reporter.

Within minutes Angela was surrounded by burly hotel porters and detained in the Chief Concierge's office awaiting the arrival of the police to arrest her and an ambulance to take the squealing Torres to hospital.

There was certainly no way back for the beleagured Angela di Silva now.

47

Angela Di Silva spent the next 72 hours on remand in a National Police cell prior to appearing on charges of attempted murder and violence on another person using a deadly weapon.

Kote Rabtana, accompanied by Angela's *abogado*, Ana Bonet, an experienced defence lawyer, visited her every day discussing the tactics they would use in court against those serious charges.

They agreed that she would plead guilty to the lesser charge whereupon under the bargain-plea system the prosecution *abogado* agreed to drop the attempted murder charge.

The *Judiciary of Spain* combines the nation's Courts and Tribunals and in a practical sense is operated by strictly professional judges and magistrates. There is a third tier comprising less important Justices of the Peace. Angela Di Lisa was arraigned to appear before a Magistrate

'You have pleaded guilty to a very serious charge but even though Senora your abogado has pleaded on your behalf that you retaliated to a verbal and violent attack from Senora Maria Torres you deliberately used a broken bottle to retaliate and seriously injure her,' said stipendiary magistrate Alfonso Delgado. *'In mitigation you have saved the State Judiciary time and money by your plea of 'guilty'. Otherwise I would have referred you to appear before a Judge. Nevertheless I have to administer the maximum sentence allowed by this court for this offence of three years in prison.'*

The tearful Angela Di Silva was handcuffed and hustled between two burly officers to an armoured police van for transportation to Barcelona's Brieva (Avila) Women's Prison where she would serve out her sentence. She was allowed a 15 minute visit from Kote and her *abogado* Ana Bonet, before the police van left. Just enough time to ask Kote: '*Come and see me as soon as the prison authorities allow me to have visitors? I want to give you instructions how to dispose of my property. Three years is a long time even though I could serve only two years if I get time off for good behaviour.*'

As she rocked with the movement inside the tiny cell fitted in the police van Angela finally allowed herself to shed a tear. Her early years as a street walker however had instilled in her the basic mental toughness of a seasoned *guerrero*.

* * *

Angela's only previous experience of prison was when, at the age of 15, in her native Paraquay, she had served three months at a juvenile institution after being apprehended soliciting for the purpose of prostitution in the streets of the capital city Asuncion. She knew the problem that faced every newcomer in prison was to defend themselves against the old lags, the long-serving jailbirds who bullied, sexually abused and extorted money and belongings from the new prisoners. It did not take long for Angela to encounter the evil godmother of Brieveavil Women's Prison 'Big Mo'Molinas the Galicia born former trader in illegal horse flesh at Barcelona's famous *La Boqeria* food market just off the Ramblas. A perverted lesbian the 20 stone Molinas was serving a 15 year sentence after chopping off her lesbian lover's right hand in a jealous rage. As a *Gallegan* she was a native of the most hated region in Spain, hated that is by those born in Spain's other regions who, ridiculously, perceived all those from Galicia to be liars, thieves and murderers.

Everyone in *Briveavil Prison,* using the vernacular of the jail, was '*shit-scared*' of the obese Mo Molinas, the bearded ogress with the voluminous boobs. She ran the prison's black

211

market in illicit cigarette, drugs and alcohol sales. She took her pick of the younger inmates when they were inducted as prisoners and sexually, often pornographically, abused them. She would then discard them like an old boot when she picked a new partner.

Even the women guards were frightened of her and carried scars from the beatings she dished out even to them. Officially she never fell foul of the prison authorities because under the criminal code of *'omertá'* - the vow of silence, handed down from criminal to criminal by the mafia, informers were the lowest form of life in the underworld.

'Oh, Oh! Here comes trouble,' Angela thought as 'Big Mo' deliberately parked herself in the next seat at supper on her third night in the prison.

'Hello dearie,' thundered Mo in Angela's ear, the stench of the garlic sausage she had just consumed for supper nauseating Angela. *'You are the slag who ran that posh escort agency ain't you luv? Well you are going to be my next wife'y. I want to see what you teach me about the sex game. It had better be good or I'll push my butcher's knife up your fanny and cut out your clitoris.'*

Angela had been expecting the verbal onslaught having been warned by other inmates what to expect from the sadistic tobacco and drugs baroness of Briveavil Prison.

'Don't tangle with Big Mo,' friends had warned Angela. *'Don't tangle with her if you upset her she'll have your guts for garters and don't expect any protection from the guards they are too scared of Big Mo to go after that cruel cow.'*

In the four years she had been incarcerated in the prison nobody be it prisoner or guard had ever opposed or informed against 'Big Mo' who was totally shell-shocked to hear Angela

Di Silva's angry response.

'Look Big Mo I know what a real bastard you are,' Angela snarled. *'Who doesn't in this God forsaken hell? I am not frightened of your butchers' knife. If you fuck with me I am quite capable of dealing with a big lump of shit like you having been trained and a holder of a judo black belt. I'll take that butchers' knife off you, ram it up your arse and tickle your tonsils through the tradesmen's entrance.*

' You think you're tough Big Mo? I have met and liked girls on the streets and in the brothels that would gobble you up and spit you out.

'You'd best not forget my warning...don't fuck with me!'

Big Mo left the trestled supper table trembling with temper at the temerity of the attractive former *puta* and escort agency madam in standing up to her. It was the first time in her four years in *Briveavil* that anyone, inmate or prison official had opposed her. She just could not believe it had happened.

'Right you stuck up cow,' she snapped. *'You've got yours coming to you. I 'll make sure you don't enjoy lickin' my pussy!'*

Angela had drawn the battle-lines and, calling on her experience of nearly two decades in the vice trade, she knew she had scored first in making Big Mo lose her temper.

All that Angela had to do now was to draw up an action-plan to deal with Big Mo and secure her place and peace of mind in this dreadful place for the next three years.

48

Supper over, following the spiteful and threatening altercation with 'Big Mo', Angela climbed up three flights of metal staircase where her cell-mate Sofia Gonzales was waiting for her.

Despite the fearsome bulk and reputation of Mo Molinas, the 5ft 6inch Sofia was reputedly the toughest inmate at Briveavil Prison with bulging biceps that would not have disgraced Mike Tyson. She worked on the anvil at the prison's forge where a team of four prisoners supervised by a guard made railings and other metallic fittings for Civil Service sites throughout the Spanish Peninsular.

Sofia was serving a six year sentence for helping two Spanish men and one Algerian in an armed robbery on a petrol station. The caper went pear-shaped.

She was no stranger to the hard physical work she was called on to do at the prison forge. For she was born in a pueblo a few kilometres from Seville. As she had no brothers, being the only child of the village blacksmith Pedro Gonzales, she was put to work at the age of seven working the bellows pump which, amongst other objects, churned out an endless assembly line of shoes that were fitted to the working horses and mules of the village.

By the time she was 16 she had progressed to wearing the split leather apron of a skilled blacksmith and over the glowing forge could hammer a set of horseshoes for a heavyweight plough mule in quicker time than her father.

Blacksmith Pedro was not best pleased when Sofia decamped at the age of 18 with her handsome Algerian lover, Sam Bosche a convicted bank robber. In typical Bonnie &

Clyde style they managed to stay on the run without capture for the next five years until, alongside two Spanish crooks, they were caught in a trap laid by the Guardia Civil aiming to quell a spate of filling station thefts.

Angela, who in a few days had bonded to the refreshingly honest Gonzales, greeted her cell-mate with a smile: 'Sofia you are *just the girl I am looking for. I need a favour, a big favour.'* Then delving into her bedside locker she produced a notepad and ballpoint pen. She deftly produced a sketch of what she wanted and said: *'A blacksmith as skilled as you will have no trouble knocking up two of those for me.'* She handed the roughly drawn sketch to Sofia.

Gonzalez grabbed the piece of paper, examined the drawing and smiled as she said: *'Looks as if you are about to start a full scale war and I know who your enemy is going to be. I heard you had a run-in at supper with that gorrila Big Mo.*

'Let me give you a word of warning--that woman is bad business. She doesn't take prisoners and she has abused , maimed, deflowered and in one case partially blinded several young inmates. The way you talked to her, I heard, you are likely to finish up in a wheelchair for the rest of your life if she gets the better of you.

'You would be advised to avoid her. You have already caused her to lose face and she will want to confirm her superiority before the rest of the prison population. Oddly enough, I am not talking from my own experience she has always steered clear of me-thank God.'

Angela could see the logic in her cell-mate's words of caution.

'You are right of course, Sofia,' argued Angela. *'But I want to serve my time here peacefully so that when the time comes*

for my discharge I can return to a normal life on the outside. So I would consider it as a personal favour.'

Sofia Conzalez nodded her head to indicate that she had already decided to accede to Angela's request.

'I knew I would not be able to persuade you to run,' said the muscular blacksmith. *'I will have made the two items that you have asked me for inside three days. Don't forget I have somehow got to scavenge the metal required from the forge's metal store. But don't forget what I told you Big Mo is a fucking dangerous cow. She wouldn't stop at murder if she thought it necessary.*

'The evil bitch will be well aware that Spain abolished capital punishment in 1978 to fall in line with the rest of Europe!'

Angela Di Silva slept soundly on a cell bunk that night in the knowledge that she was preparing a sound defence against the malice that the prison bully Big Mo was building up against her.

'It will be shit or bust one way or another,' mused Angela. *'At least that is a better option than surrendering to a depraved Gallegan monster!'*

49

Angela Di Silva, or to give her the new identity number 'X113 allocated to her, the next day received her first visitor since she had been admitted to Briveavil Women's Prison.

She was not surprised that it was the towering figure of Kote Rabtana who was ushered into the crowded Visitors' Hall at 4-30pm. They sat opposite each other and kept their arms and hands resting on the wooden table in view of an eagle-eyed guard watching every move.

He was quite surprised how well she looked in her blue and white striped prison shirt and skirt, even without make-up and her face scrubbed rosy clean with prison issue carbolic soap.

'Hello Kote, thank you for coming,' said Angela. *'Don't think me rude but as we are only allowed a 15 minute visit I'll talk business straight away. I want you to wind up "Adorable Angela's Escort Agency" including all our branch organisations across Spain. Also put my house, including all the furniture, and my BMW car and other assets up for sale. From the proceeds, provide you raise enough funds, I want you to see every person on my payroll receives the redundancy money they are entitled to under the labour laws of Spain--that of course includes yourself.*

'Now my aim is to serve out my time here as tranquilly as possible and worry about what the future holds when my discharge day comes.'

There was not a lot of time for the loyal Kote to say much to his former boss but he managed to scramble out that he was pleased the way she was looking and was apparently settling down to a long prison term.

'I will follow your instructions to the letter, of course I will Angela,' he said. 'But I have to say, considering the unfortunate circumstances you have found yourself in that you are being extremely generous to those of us who have worked for you. I'll come and see you again soon.'

As Kote left the senior guard who was in charge of the Visitors' Hall walked across to Angela and said: '*Prisoner X133 your abogado has just arrived at the prison and has permission from the Governor to see you. As you are a new fish at Brieavil you may not know there is a special private room set aside for prisoners to talk to their lawyers. I will take you there now. There will be a guard on duty outside the door of the room so you will have complete privacy.*'

Ana Bonet rose from her chair in the room reserved for lawyers to interview their clients privately.

'*Hola, Angela,*' she said warmly. '*I hope you are settling down here without too many problems. The reason I have called is to inform you that I have looked into the possibility of successfully making an appeal against your sentence.*

'*I have sought the advice of a colleague of mine who is one of Spain's leading advocats. That is a lawyer who works in court, mainly for the defense. It his opinion, having looked at the evidence in your case, that even if he could persuade the magistrate that you were reacting to the false and spiteful article that Senora Torres wrote about you, and the blow she struck you with, that the court could not overlook the dangerous violence you used against her with a broken bottle.*

'*It is my opinion that you would probably lose your appeal and it is also possible that the magistrates might refer you to a higher court presided by a judge who would, if he so decided, could even increase your sentence to a possible maximum of five years! I am sorry Angela but that is the position.*'

Angel Di Silva immediately put her *abogado* at ease and assured her: '*Thank you for your efforts Ana but I have decided in any case not to proceed with an appeal and to serve out my sentence quietly and hopefully earn a full remission so that I can return to a full life after I am discharged!*'

Lawyer and client said their fond farewells with an affectionate embrace and wished each other well for the future.

Angela Di Silva had made a positive step towards her future. The only barrier to her welfare was the menace of the gruesome *Gallegan*, prison bully Big Mo. She knew that a violent confrontation between them was imminent.

'*I'll be ready for that fuckin' bitch when she comes after me,*' inmate X113 vowed to herself.

50

Sofia Gonzales was waiting for Angela Di Silva when she was returned to her cell escorted by a guard who unlocked the door and locked it again after she entered.

'Hi, Angela,' said her cheerful cell-mate. *'I hope everything went well with your visitors. I have managed to make the two metal objects you asked me for ..and here they are.'*

Sofia who worked as a blacksmith in the prison forge produced a weighty package covered in wax-paper and handed them over for approval.

Angela carefully examined the contents of the package closely and was delighted with what she saw. She told Sofia: *'They are beautifully made my love. I could almost say they are a work of art. But the point of asking you to make them for me is to neutralise the threat of Big Mo who, I know, will be coming at me sooner or later. I don't really want to flaunt rules but if I don't square up to Big Mo's bullying my life here in Brieavil Women's Prison for the next three years will not be worth a céntimo.'*

Sofia Gonzales was pleased with her cell-mate's approval, and said: *'My thoughts will be with you when you stand up to that evil ogress. It will be good for the rest of us inmates if you can tame her. We have all lived in fear of her and to be honest the guards have been so frightened of her that they had turned a blind eye to her bullying.'*

*   *   *

The anticipated confrontation between Angela and Big Mo came in the prison shower room, before breakfast, at 6-30am.

Angela had just stepped out of the *ducha,* towelled herself and pulled the striped rough calico prison-issue *bata* around her shoulders when a pair of hairy muscular biceps, slipped under her arm pits, from the rear. A stubby steel like claw squeezed Angela's nipples until she yelled like a stuck pig.

Angela wheeled agonisingly away from the searing pain in her breasts. She thrust her two hands inside the patch pockets of the tatty prison dressing gown and slipped over her hands the two metal knuckledusters that her cellmate Sofia Gonzales had so skilfully fashioned.

Big Mo retreated backwards, totally shell-shocked that she had stirred a hornets' nest and found fellow inmate with the courage to challenge her. She advanced on Angela growling with the resonance of a rampant grizzly bear.

Angela, drawing on skills learned at the Barcelona Women's Judo and Pilates Club that had earned her a coveted black belt, feinted and drew Big Mo to her left. With the sting of a bee, like Muhammad Ali at his best, she threw a knuckle-dustered, right jab that opened a gory gash down Big Mo's face from cheek-bone to jaw.

The prison bully enraged at the flow of blood coursing down her face charged again with all the ferocity of a Spanish fighting bull in the ring. Angela changed her tactics to suit. Bending low she slid under Big Mo's flailing arms and with all her weight behind her planted a vicious left hook plumb on to the Galicia-born *valentón's* navel.'

The red mist had taken over Big Mo's rationale and, in wild abandon, she spat at Angela and yelled: *'You fucking whore--I am going to put you in hospital for a long time to come.'*

Angela's calm and measured response sent Big Mo into an even greater frenzy.

221

'...*I'd rather be a whore than a Gallegan*.' she hissed at her awesome rival. It was contemptuous reference to the Galicia region which had spawned Big Mo--an insult that only a Spaniard with particular allegiance to their *pueblo*, town or province would react to.

It was time, thought Angela, to bring this violent maul to a close. Again she circled the enflamed Mo. Ducking and weaving looking for an opening to finish off an opponent seriously handicapped by the deluge of blood cascading down her face.

Angela swerved skilfully and with judgement mercilessly put all her weight behind a superbly timed right uppercut to the point of her rival's crimson covered jaw. The lights went out in Big Mo's eyes as she sunk into blissful oblivion. Her days as the prison bully were over. She was reduced to a shivering jelly for the remaining years of her incarceration.

It was a battle of personalities that went down as a legend in the annals of Brieval Women's Prison.

51

Although Angela Di Silva was quite pleased with the decisive way she had dealt with the sadistic prison bully she was aware that she had broken prison rules and could face charges of physically assaulting a fellow convict, and also draw an extra sentence to the three years which she was now serving.

But it all depended on whether or not the victim of her attack with knuckle dusters , Big Mo Molinas, would honour the criminal code of silence known as *omertà*. It is commonly thought that the Sicilian Mafia instituted *omertà*. But the code of silence was adopted by Sicilians before the birth of the *Cosa Nostra* as a way of opposing their Spanish rulers around 1504.

The oppressed Sicilians used a proverb which, in their own language, stated: '*Cu è surdu*, orbu e *taci, campa cent' anni 'mpaci'*--"He who is deaf, blind and silent will live a hundred years in peace"

Angela's worries eased a little when her cell-mate Sofia Gonzales, who always had a good link with the prison grapevine, told her: *'They took Big Mo to the prison sick bay for treatment. But she told the doctor and the nurses that she had fallen down the iron stair case. Whether the prison or authorities believe that story is another matter. But if she sticks to that story my guess is that it leaves you in the clear of further charges. But all the other inmates look on you as their hero and you made a lot of friends in what you did this morning.'*

But Angela had to sweat it out for another 24 hours to discover whether the prison officials were going to let her off the hook or not.

At nine o'clock the next morning one of the most popular guards on the staff, Monica Fabrizo, collected her from the cell with the dreaded instruction: *'Come on Angela the Governor has asked to see you immediately.'*

On the long trek to the Governor's office, down three flights of iron stairway, through an endless ribbon of corridors, Guard Fabrizo, who was known to be *muy simpático* towards the inmates stopped Angela in a quiet corner and whispered in her ear: *'Don't worry Prisoner X133 you will think you are on the mat facing serious disciplinary charges but you will find the Governor is a very wise and understanding and fair person if she is convinced you are being honest with her.'*

A few minutes later they arrived at the outer room where the Governor's secretary sat at a desk fitted with internal and external phones plus a computer.

'Prisoner X133 to see the Governor,' said Guard Fabrizo to the 26-year-old secretary Miranda Zappola .

'Take a seat,' ordered the secretary. *'The Governor is on the phone at the moment but she has said she will see the prisoner the moment she has finished her call.'*

A few minutes later prisoner and guard were called in to the Governor's large and well furnished office.

The Governor, *Doña Carmen Perelló,* a 34-year-old *madrileño* had been well trained for the important job she now held. Having won a law degree with honours at the University of Madrid, she practised as an *abogado,* specialising as a court defender in criminal cases. After four years she applied to take the Prison Service entrance examination before spending the two years as Assistant Governor at the notorious women's prison in Madrid.

The position at Brieval Prison was her first senior post in the service, a job she had held for only six months.

'*Thank you Guard Fabrizo*,' Governor Perelló, looked up from her desk. '*Please wait in the outer office while I interview the prisoner. Ask my secretary to give you a cup of coffee while you are waiting and send a pot of coffee for two in this office immediately.*'

As the Guard left the inner office Doña Carmen looked across her desk at Angela and said: '*I would not normally ask a prisoner to sit down when I invite them to my office. But this is a strictly private meeting. An interview I have no intention of recording officially. I intend what I have to say to you in an advisory capacity rather than remonstrative.*

'*The subject of this off-the- record chat is the injuries that prisoner Mo Molinas sustained in the bath house yesterday morning. Now I have absolutely no evidence to say that you were responsible for those injuries. In fact everyone I have spoken with upholds the explanation Mo Molinas has consistently stuck to, despite the severity of her injuries, that she fell down the iron staircase.*

'*Now I am quite conversant with omertá, the code of silence, practised by the underworld so have no choice but to abide by that. But the physical damage sustained by Mo Molinas may prove of great help towards the discipline I am trying to maintain in this prison where I am trying to eliminate bullying, drug running, tobacco smuggling and illegal lesbian activities enforced on weaker prisoners by stronger inmates bullying them into submission.*

'*My advice to you Prisoner X133 is, from now on, do your time in this institution the easy way. Qualify for the maximum remission by good behaviour and I will be very happy. After all, you will well recall, we were fellow members of the*

225

Barcelona Women's Bridge Club before you found yourself in this unfortunate position.

'Having said that I must warn you that if you are found guilty of any violent, criminal or illegal behaviour during the rest of your time here I will throw the book at you. I think you have a good chance of redeeming yourself . You will still be relatively young when you are discharged.

'Finally, I will call you Angela on this occasion although to me you will be prisoner X133 for the rest of your time here. I feel sure, as an intelligent woman, you will take heed of my advice. Talking to you this way I am expressing my gratitude that you just may have done more to end the insidious practise of bullying in this prison than any punitive action I might take as Governor.

'I am sure Big Mo Molinas has been given a painful lesson. Good luck.'

Prisoner X133 expelled a huge sigh of relief as she left the Governor's office chastened but heartened at the kindest treatment she had received in a long time.

52

Bearing in mind the understanding, tolerance and advice gratuitously given to her by Governor Carmen Perelló the meditative Angela accepted, without complaint, any job that the institutional authorities had scheduled against her name.

Some days she would be instructed to police the *servicio* and *duchas* area--the toilet and shower room area where she had so forcefully ended Big Mo's sadistic career as the prison bully--vigorously swinging a disinfectant impregnated long-handle mop.

Another day she would be deputed to collect the *basura* bins sited on each of the buildings three landings and bounce them to the yard before loading the trash on to a waiting flat-bed lorry. A sickening, smelly chore.

Another alternative was a morning stint in the prison *cocina* where she would spend four finger-blistering hours wielding a rusty *pelapata* removing the skin and mud from a pile of potatoes.

After a month of completing these back-breaking chores Angela was ordered, to report to the Governor's office again. This time she was told to proceed to the meeting without an attendant Guard.

'*Oh dear, oh dear?*' she queried herself before announcing herself to the Governor's secretary, Miranda Zappola.

'*The Governor is expecting you Angela,*' said Miranda, reaching for the internal phone. '*In fact you can go straight in.*'

Doña Carmen Perelló smiled as she looked up from her jumbo-sized mahogany table that served as a desk and said: *'I have received nothing but good reports the way you have knuckled down to your work since we last met. You have served your time on the stinking jobs and it is appropriate we give you something worthy of your talents as a successful business-woman over a number of years. Without entering the debate about the sex-trade you were a good leader and some people might think your organisation helped to provide a necessary service for lonely sex-starved men and women.*

'Far be it be for me to pass my views about the sex-industry, one way or another. But you have won your spurs here in the way you have settled down worked hard and promise to be a model prisoner.

'So you deserve encouragement. You may not know this but María Ruiz, the long standing prisoner who has managed the prison library for the past three years, is being released next week. We shall miss María and she has been very popular with both staff and inmates.

'Angela, I would like you to take over from María. That is if you accept my offer.'

The former escort agency boss did not need much time to think over the *propuesta* of a more interesting job, and said: *'Thank you Governor, thank you very much. It is very kind of you. I didn't fancy spending the next three years peeling patatas.'*

Dona Perelló, smiling at Angela's quip, rejoined: *'Well that's settled then. Report to Maria at the prison library tomorrow morning at 8-30am and she will show you the ropes. It will give you a week to learn the complexity of your new job. Good luck!'*

* * *

After lunch of *arroz con albóndigas*, Angela was informed by a Guard that she would be receiving a visitor at four o'clock that afternoon.

She was delighted when she arrived in the Visitors' Hall to discover that her visitor was Kote Rabtana.

'*Hi there Angela,*' Kote greeted her. '*You are looking fabulous. Prison life must be suiting you.*'

She grinned as she replied: '*Well it is a healthy life if you like cleaning out the shit-house, lumping the trash down metal staircases, and peeling a mountain of rotting potatoes for four hours. But the good news is that the Governor called me in to her office this morning and I have been promoted to manager of the prison library from next week. That is one of the cleanest and certainly one of the nicest, if not the very best, jobs in the institution. Considering the position I am in I couldn't be happier.*

'*But what have you got to tell me Kote, darling?*'

Kote Rabtana assured his former boss that having been given her power of attorney he had fulfilled all her instructions to the letter. '*All the trappings, fittings, furnishings and property belonging to the escort agency have been sold,*' he explained.

'*Your house is also up for sale with all its contents and the mortgage that your husband, Klaus, had incurred paid off. Also the properties you owned in other parts of Spain have been sold and all debts paid.*

'*In accordance with your wishes every one of your former employees have been given the correct amount of severance pay as prescribed by Spanish law. In short Angela you owe no*

229

one anything not even a brass céntimo.

'Now for the downside. All that is left from the disaster that has overtaken you in the past year, I am sorry to say, is the relatively small amount of five thousand five hundred euros--not a lot to set you up when you are discharged from this prison.'

Angela faced the news that the loyal Kote had given her stoically. *'Well so be it Kote darling,'* she stated. *'I have to accept it is the price I must pay for the attack I made on Maria Torres which I don't regret--not for a moment. That two timing cow deserved everything I did to her and I can live with my conscience about that.'*

Kote Rabtana broke into her passionate dream of revenge against the treacherous Maria Torres.

'I was clearing out your office at the escort agency yesterday when your son Tobajas came on the phone from England where, as you know, he is serving a 12 month secondment from the Spanish Airforce as a NATO sponsored student in England at the RAF College Cranwell,' Kote informed. *'I hadn't seen Tobajas since your husband's funeral when we got on well together. He is returning to Spain on a two week break and will report to the Spanish Air Force unit he has been ordered to join when he leaves Cranwell in 18 months time.*

'That move speaks wonders about how brilliantly he has done in his studies and flying skill training in England. He has been selected to train with the distinguished "Patrullah Aquila', Spain's version of the RAF's world famous display team the Red Arrows. I could sense that you have not told him about where you are, what you have done to be incarcerated here in Brieval Women's Prison. On my advice he has agreed not to come to visit you at the moment. As much for his sake as yours. Because, as I explained, it would not look good for

an aspiring young Air Force officer to admit that his mother was in prison. Tobajas said that he would like to visit you straight away when I explained what had happened to you. But I got him to realise that you would need his help more when you are discharged from prison.

'He could see my point that in a couple of years he would have inevitably climbed up the ranks in the pecking order of the Spanish Air Force and better equipped to assist your return to a proper life again. He has agreed to keep in touch with me and wants me to let him know when I think it adviseable to visit you. Meanwhile he has asked me to tell you that he loves you very much.'

As Angela was led to cell after Kote had left the Visitors' Hall she sobbed, dabbing the tears that rolled down her cheeks.

Angela Di Silva reported to Maria Ruiz, the prisoner who she was to succeed as manager of the prison library a week later, at 8-30 the following morning.

'Welcome Angela I hope you enjoy the work here,' Maria said warmly. *'Strangely enough, although it will mean that I will return to the outside world next week for the first time after eight years in the prison, I will seriously miss the work here in the library. I hope that you will enjoy the job as much as I have. When I think of it my work here has in some ways prepared me for a return to normal life again. But I have one regret about my imminent discharge from Brieveavil Women's Prison next week. That is I have been unable to make badly needed improvements to the library. I will look back for the rest of my life and feel that I failed miserably in that respect.'*

The observant Angela spotted the hurt, the sense of inadequacy, the feel of not hitting the target that the conscientious Maria Ruiz was suffering as she prepared to

231

end her time as a felon and return to life as a free woman.

*'I am sure you are being too hard on yourself,'*said Angela sympathetically. *'You come across to me as very sincere person and I would be sure you don't deserve to leave this prison accused of failure in the responsible job of library manager which you were allotted. Can you explain, Maria, why you are torturing yourself with self-depreciation?'*

Maria asked Angela to wait a few minutes while she made them both a cup coffee before they settled down for a long talk. The break was as long as it took a tiny kettle to come to the bubble and Maria to pour the boiling water over the spoonful of *Nescafé* she had deposited into two prison mugs.

'Let me explain Angela,' Maria said after sipping the weak instant coffee and nibbling one of the *galletas dulce* she had offered Angela from a battered tin. *'More and more women are committing crime and the female prison population of Spain has trebled since the death of General Franco in 1975. Of the 250 prisoners here in Briveavil more than half of them are serving sentences for drug related offences compared with 22% for male prisoners.*

'Serving them we have less than 60 books here in the library. Most of them are tatty, dog-eared novels, many of them with their fly-leaves ripped out to use as letter paper or, worse, to make reefer rollups or cigarettes.

'Of course the Prison Service bans us from stocking crime books, topics dealing with drugs, prostitution or pornography. Even so we could do with double the quantity of books to give an adequate service for 250 inmates. But our slender budget prevents us spending more money to fill our half-empty book shelves.

'For instance you will meet a 37 year old prisoner called

Jenny Barclay who has spent 25 years of her turbulent life in and out of prison. As a child a she was sexually abused by her father. At 17-years she became addicted to crack with a mind-bending thousand euro a day habit. She was sentenced originally for fraudulent use of stolen credit cards. The first of a long string of offences and prison committals. But now she is trying to go straight and is training here to be a welder. It would help her studies if I could have got her some technical books but they are expensive and we just don't have the money.

'It has broken my heart not being able to help such people. I made a silly mistake when I was young and know just how women like Jenny Barclay feel.'

It was a very thoughtful Angela Di Silva who lay on the bunk of her cell that evening vowing that she would try to take up the torch of the campaign Maria Ruiz would have to abandon when she was discharged from Brieavil Womens' Prison the following week.

53

Angela Di Silva felt the pain of her three year sentence and the withdrawal symptoms of the loss of her entrepreneurial powers as an escort agency boss evaporate as she directed her mental prowess into making a success of her new job as manager of the prison library.

First she categorised the sorry collection of 60 books she had inherited from her disappointed predecessor, Maria Ruiz, and felt it necessary to wash her hands after handling the grubby vandalised tomes with their missing fly leaves, cigarette burns and food stains.

'That pile of pulp deserves to be impaled on rusty nails in the fucking prison loo,' was the verdict she gave. *'No wonder my fellow jailbirds think the only use they have for books is to make cannabis reefers from the tatty pages. The prison population not only deserves better reading matter but they need educating in how to enjoy and how to care for books. If I have anything to do with it the inmates of Brieval Womens' Prison are about to be introduced to the wondrous world of literature.'*

Angela made a list of the categories of the books she wanted to introduce to the library.

Fiction-of womens' interest. Romance, marriage and parenthood

Technical books- dealing with training inmates to take up a new trade, business or activity after they would be released

Biographies-of famous people, particularly women

History-dealing with women who became legends in their own lifetime such as Cleopatra, Joan of Arc, Florence Nightingale.

As a former successful business-woman Angela was quite aware that the big problem was to find the money to stock the library with new and suitable books. She knew she could not expect any funding from the Prison Service which from the days of General Franco had barely veered from the policy of punishing rather than educating men and women who had fallen foul of the law.

On the other hand Angela sensed that Doña Carmen Perelló, the Governor of the Brieavil Womens' Prison was a deeply humane person and, within the bounds of her mandate from the Prison Service, would do her utmost to improve the lot of the inmates. To recruit Doña Perelló's support Angela knew she would have to design a positive presentation to persuade the Governor to support her ideas. After much thought Angela came up with the idea of a project, designed to please not only the sympathetic Governor but also grab the interest of all the cell-mates.

She would call it: *Famoso Mujers Española*--Famous Spanish women. It would feature autobiographies, biographies, non-fiction articles and books, film, videos and audio tapes of celebrated women.

Women like Penélope Cruz Sánchez, a Golden Globe and Academy Award nominated actress born in 1974. One of the most famous Spanish women on the planet Sánchez, after starting her career as a dancer, moved on to Spanish television, and appeared in many Spanish, English, French, Italian and Portugese language films.

Then there was the notorious historical Spanish queen Isabella I (April 1451 - November 1504) who was Queen of

Castile and Leon. She and her husband Ferdinand II of Aragon laid the basis for the political union of Spain under their grandson, Charles V, Holy Roman Emperor. Isabella and Ferdinand deported Jewish people from Spain and made the Inquisition into a powerful body whose main victims were Catholics or people of Jewish or Moorish lineage. However paradoxically, like many noble Iberians, Isabella had some Jewish ancestry , three of her great-great-grandparents had Hebraic roots.

Having settled her plan of action Angela was now ready to face the genial Governor Perelló for the third time.

In her beautiful copper-plate handwriting Angela sent her courteous request for an interview via the Governor's adept secretary, Miranda Zappola.

Just 48 hours later Angela, or as Miranda addressed the *sobre; 'Prisoner X133';* saying the Governor would be pleased to see her the following day at 10-30am.

54

Angela Di Silva, during the first month of her incarceration in the Brieavil Prison, wondered if her former friends and employees, both men and women, at *Adorable Angela's Escort Agency* had already forgotten her.

Only the faithful Kote Rabtana had visited her during that highly traumatic period in any first-time convict's life. A phase when the cell door was slammed for the evening lock-up; when the almost sleepless nights on a hard bunk seemed interminable; when the nightmares began after blessed slumber finally came before the sadistic dawn awakening by a loud voiced guard; when the prison stench of overnight urine, sour sweat and dirty work denims joined the rancid aroma of old cooking oils from the kitchen amalgamated with the acrid stink of carbolic disinfectant wafting from the revolting ritual of slopping out the overnight piss-pots each morning.

All this a nauseous accompaniment to the soggy grey mess the prison *cocineras* called *gachas* which would make any Scottish housewife puke in her own porridge pan!

As she tossed and turned on her prison blanket thinking of her previous life Angela found it hard to stem the tears and stifle the sobs. The emotive memories of her kindly husband Klaus, despite his failures, the misery when, guiltily, she thought about their beloved son Tobajas and the sloppy kisses her beloved gelding Zephyr used to bestow on her, were so vivid that they prompted thoughts of suicide. But Angela was a tough cookie. A street-fighter whose resilient spirit had been honed in the tough career that she had chosen.

The catalyst that began to restore Angela's faith in human nature was her appointment as the new manager of the Brieavil

Prison library. It presented her with a challenge. A chance to organise and lead. Both qualities that she possessed in abundance. Strangely it coincided with a coterie of visits by friends from her past life anxious to let Angela know they indeed had not forgotten her. Although the visitors arrived within the first month of her reign as library manager Angela did not begrudge a minute of the quarter-hour slots she spent in the Visitors' Hall with such old pals as hairdresser Bernardo Sanchez, Jose Eugenio Moralés the former bullfighter, with weightlifter champion and gymnasium owner Louis Sammuels and Monica Kepler, who like Angela, began life as a back-alley hooker.

They each arrived at the prison's Visitors' Hall bearing a *regalo*. A gift of their own choice carefully selected to show the former escort agency boss how much they appreciated what she had done for them and, in particular, their gratitude for the way she insisted they all received the full amount of severance pay they were entitled to under Spanish labour laws.

'*Hurry up and get yourself out of this terrible dump,*' said the cheery *pelequero*, Bernardo Sanchez, who had brought with him a large parcel containing her favourite hair colouring. '*Three years is not all that long and my guess is you have got the guts and nous to behave yourself in prison and earn the maximum remission in your sentence. When you are released come to me and I'll guarantee you a free hair-do every week for the rest of your life. You are a wonderful woman Angela Di Silva.*'

Louis Sammuels, the former weightlifter champion, presented her with a silky *Nike* tracksuit, and said: '*I know the rules allow you to wear your own lesiure wear, and feel like a real woman again, during the relaxation hour each evening. This will help you to put aside your prison uniform*

238

for a while. There is another thing Angela, which you must keep to yourself for the moment, but Doña Carmen Perelló, the prison Governor, has asked me to fit up a room here as a gym, to provide all the equipment, and to arrange a fitness coach to conduct a training class two evenings a week. It is in line with the Prison Service campaign to increase fitness amongst the inmates and, hopefully, reduce the drugs problem which is rife amongst the female prison population across Spain. Hopefully I will see you at those classes. It is important you keep yourself fit while you are here. So that, when you are eventually discharged, you will be strong to face life on the outside again.'

Jose Eugenio Moralés, the former torero, bounced into the Visitors' Hall arrogantly acknowledging the ripple of applause from the female inmates seated with their guests at the rows of tables. Many of them from the poorer areas of Spain's major cities and rationally *afficionados* of the *corrida*, which in their opinion was the highest manifestation of manly *valor.* He handed over a parcel, as required by prison rules, to an eagle-eyed Guard, who after scrutinising the contents showed approval by passing it on to Angela.

It contained, two books, the autobiographies of *Belmonte* and *Manolete* two of the greatest stars of the ancient *bravo fiesta.* They would be excellent additions to the prison library which Angela was so anxious to update and upgrade in a style suitable for the 21st century.

'How are you Angela querida?' he asked anxiously. *'I must say you look wonderful as usual. As I expected Angela you will not let the hijos de putas get you down.'*

Angela did not disguise her pleasure at the exuberant greeting from the former bullfighter.

'It was hard at first, Jose, but now I have settled down,'

Angela smiled. *'The Governor has given me a proper job as manager of the prison library I have a challenge to face up to. My first task will be to find a way to fill the shelves of the library with suitable books. Your two autobiographies will be a start. A small start but you have to begin somewhere. The problem is finance. The Prison Service have not been overly enthusiastic about funding the restocking of prison libraries throughout the country.*

'They are more intent on making a term of imprisonment a period of painful punishment. Yet the right of kind of reading could be a therapeutic tool in rehabilitating inmates who have served their time.'

Jose Eugenio Moralés thought carefully about what Angela had told him and responded in a typically upbeat manner.

'Many of the regular customers in my bar are in the Barcelona book publishing trade. I will put out some feelers on your behalf and try get them to donate some books free of charge to your library,' he promised.

Angela was delighted. It was an offer near to her heart at that particular point of time.

* * *

The following day Angela Di Silva received an important and the saddest in the recent string of visits from her friends.

55

Kote Rabtana strode into the Visitor's Hall in cheery mood, immediately moving towards the Security Guard to let him examine the contents of a huge plastic supermarket bag.

The Guard closely scanned and probed the jumbo-sized box of Belgian chocolates, nodded his approval, and waved Kote towards Angela already seated at a table waiting for him.

'They look delicious, ' the Guard smiled as Kote headed away for his half hour visit. *'Tell Angela I'll call at her cell later to taste one of those lovely chocolates.'*

The former escort agency chief was delighted to see her former assistant. *'Hi there Kote,'*she greeted him. *'You are look ing good. What have you been up to?'*

Kote responded: *'Tidying up your affairs primarily Angela as you know. I know your abogada has told you the good news that we have found another twenty thousand euros to go into your funds it was a rebate from the Spanish Inland Revenue Department for over paid taxes in the last three years. Which means you have thirty thousand, five hundred euros in the bank.'*

Angela intervened: *'Yes Kote my thanks for that. My abogada Ana Bonet told me you had asked her to write and inform me of this extra money which will solve a problem that has been bugging me since I first arrived in prison. I have some instructions how to dispose of that. I want a cheque made payable to my son Tobajas Di Silva in the sum of 30.000,00€ . If Abogada Bonet brings me the necessary documents and cheque book I will sign the authorisation for that transaction.'*
Kote immediately remonstrated with Angela, albeit in her own

241

interest.

'But Angela do you think that is prudent?' he queried. 'Forgive me. I appreciate that money is yours to do what you want with. But that handsome gift to your son will leave you with only five hundred euros to rehabilitate yourself when you are discharged from Brieavil Prison.

'A perilous position for you when you will be looking for a way to earn a living. Of course you will still have the proceeds of your Villa Jacaranda and contents to come when they are eventually sold.'

Angela held up her hand to stop Kote's impassioned dissertation in full flight.

'Hold on Kote, hold on,' she said.

'There is no need for you to apologise my dear. I know you are trying to protect me and I'll never forget you for that. But this is a matter of principle. A matter of clearing my own conscience.

'When my husband Klaus was murdered and because of his wild addiction to gambling it was a shock to find there was hardly any money left in the kitty.

'Which meant that my son Tobajas was robbed of the legacy he might have expected from his father. I want to correct that unlucky anomaly for my son's sake. I want Tobajas to believe the thirty thousand euros is a bequest from his father.

'I appreciate your concern but I will be able to live with my conscience in the knowledge that I have done the right thing by my son.'

Kote was his usual kindly, understanding personality.

'Put like that I appreciate where you are coming from,' he

said. *'You are a good woman Angela and I pray that everything will go well for you in the future. Now I have some news for you. I have heard from the Spanish national health service that they are now prepared to recognise my accreditation to practise as psychiatrist providing I take a booster course at a Madrid medical college and pass a final exam. I plan to leave Barcelona for Madrid at the end of the month.*

'Another piece of news is that I am to be married. Angela you will recall Margaret Maitland, the divorcee you paired me up with after you enrolled me as an escort? Well we have decided to wed in Barcelona next week.

'Margaret will join me in Madrid for six months while I complete my training. She will keep her four bedroom villa in the fishing village of Mongat and we will live there when I start to practise as a psychiatrist in Barcelona.'

Angela felt a touch of sadness amongst her good will for Kote. She liked him enormously and would forever be grateful for what he had done for her over the years. She would miss him badly. She loved him for his benevolence. She felt a tinge of jealousy for the happiness she felt he would give to Margaret Maitland.

Yet throughout the time she had known him, when he worked for her as an escort and later as her assistant, Angela had never fancied him romantically.

Angela Di Silva was reasonably satisfied that she had put aside her past as she prepared the presentation of her plan to improve the library for the approval of Doña Carmen Perelló the Governor of Brieavil Women's Prison.

She had written to several Spanish book publishers for slides and publicity material featuring *Famos Mujers Española*--Famous Spanish women. It featured Oscar nominated actress Penélope Cruz Sánchez and the historical Queen Isabella I of Spain.

She assured the Governor that she would be able to persuade Spain's book-publishing industry to donate some of their books to restock the prison library. She would take extra care that the fiction titles would be suitable reading for inmates.

She would also, she felt sure, be able to beg free of charge non-fiction teaching books featuring languages, skills in cooking, needle work, plumbing, painting and decorating which would help her fellow inmates to make a new life for themselves when they were discharged from prison.

Doña Perelló was fascinated and promised Angela she would do her best to persuade the top brass of the Prison Service that improving the library and educational facilities would help to reduce crime in Spain in contrast to the policy they had employed for more than a hundred years of emphasising punishment rather than education for female criminals.

The Governor told Angela to go ahead with re-stocking the library and asked her to be sure she checked every new book for suitability with her office.

'Congratulations Angela for the thought you have already put into this project,' said Doña Perelló. *'If you can make a success of your plan to modernise our library you may have struck the biggest blow ever in history for the well-being of women jail birds in Spain. Good Luck in what you are trying to achieve! Please count on me using all my influence to help you in this important work!'*

The green light from the Governor was all the assurance Angela needed to put all her skills as a business-woman into transforming Brieavil Womens' Prison library.

56

Angela Di Silva worked as hard bringing the tatty library at Barcelona's Brieavil Prison for Women up to standard as she had done many years earlier founding and building up her nationwide Escort Agency.

Organisation, leadership, inspiration these were her strengths . The very qualities that were needed in her new job as library manager.

She spent her first three months planning, writing, correcting and editing a coloured brochure which she mailed to every publishing company in Spain appealing for donations of complimentary copies of their books, fiction, non-fiction, technical and educational. Their incentive would be the knowledge that, hopefully, they would be helping the inmates to rehabilitate and adapt to a crime-free life when they were released from prison.

It was a complete reversal in Spain of the old way of treating criminals of both sexes. Before the Civil War in the late 1930's and during General Franco's long *reinado severo* the nation's prison population were incarcerated on stringent, almost brutal, conditions. The ultimate punishment in *Espana* for murder and treachery was a gruesome execution by the ghastly garotte machine. A policy that had brought Spain in conflict with the more humane policies on capital punishment employed by other members of the European Economic Community.

Spain finally abolished capital punishment in 1978 but even then the rest of their punitive attitude towards the unfortunate crooks in their lock-ups did not quite match the more liberal ideas of the rest of the EEC.

Spain's publishing world reacted with admirable and merciful support for Angela's appeal. Parcels of gratuitous books, sometimes as many as a dozen newly printed tomes, poured into the mail-room of the Brieavil Prison to be put through a rigorous security check before being handed over to Angela's care.

Inside the next 12 weeks the new library manager found she had more than 250 fiction and non-fiction, books to label and categorize before the back-breaking job of hoisting them onto the now heavily laden shelves. Although the avalanche of literary treasures had eased still one or two new books arrived with the daily prison mail-delivery.

Summing up she concluded, with immense satisfaction, that there were now a better than an available average of four books for each inmate at Brieavil. What is more the average was getting better every day.

She now sought permission of Doña Carmen Perelló, the Prison Governor, to build a bonfire in the Brieavil courtyard. She needed to commit to the flames filthy, dog-eared, excrement- stained and, probably, germ-infested, pages that had been spared by addicted inmates from the hell-bent task of rolling cannabis reefers.

Angela, under the scrutiny of a grinning Guard, Angela applied the match to the paraffin drenched disgusting mass of rotting novels and hard-backs the following day.

A new era in the literary life of the women prisoners at Briavil Prison had began.

*   *   *

But there was no let-up for the eager Angela who now sought another concession from the supportive Governor Perelló.

'It would be wonderful if we could paint and clean-up the room before we open the new library to the inmates,' was Angel's passionate plea. 'If we can get them to take a pride in the new books on display and in the reading room it would go a long way to increasing the use of the new library and, hopefully, prepare them for a more useful, crime-free, life when they are released.'

Once again Doña Carmen Perelló approved saying: 'What a wonderful idea Angela. I totally agree with your theory. We will supply the paint and materials. It will be up to you to find volunteers among the prisoners to do the work. The refurbishment is all for their benefit and it is appropriate that they should help. You have carte blanche to get all the work done, providing it conforms to prison rules and regulations.'

The team of of volunteer prisoners began the new project five days later working during the leisure hour each day except Sundays.

It took two weeks for the refurbishment to be completed. Angela was bursting with new ideas as this work progressed and she asked her cell-mate Sofia Gonzales , who worked in the prison blacksmith's department, for help with another fresh idea .

'I need your help Sofia,' Angela pleaded as they sipped a night-cap of hot chocolate before lights-out, one evening.

Sofia Gonzales laughed loudly as she quipped: 'No, no Angela not another pair of knuckledusters? You are not going to start another war.'

Angela was equally in good humour as she returned the banter: 'Not at all you silly bitch. I want you to use your skills at making something for my new library. I'll make a sketch of what I have in mind and show it you in a few minutes and see *what you think.'*

Sofia replied: *'OK, Angela do a drawing and I'll see what I can do!'*

In the next ten minutes Angela using a ball-point pen produced a sketch for Sofia's approval.

'What's this Angela ?' giggled Sofia after closely examining the drawing. *'It looks like a fuckin' tea trolley?'*

Angela was pleased that she had baffled her cell mate with her sketch.

'No Sofia it is a four wheel, three shelf, trolly to be rolled round the block every evening during the leisure hour from which our fellow prisoners can return their old library books , borrow fresh ones or order other books which are not on the trolly.'

As Angela anticipated her friend Sofia Gonzales agreed to help and, jokingly holding her hand out, asked her cell mate: *'Alright Angela, I'll do it. What's in it for me?'*

Angela thought the question hilarious: *'I'll give you one of my chocolates you mercenary bitch! I'll get the OK for you to do the job and for the materials needed to make the trolley from the Guard who is in charge of the carpentry and blacksmiths' workshop. The Governor has already given me the all-clear to get such things made to get the new library up and running quickly.'*

So, as the new library project zoomed towards completion, Angela oozed energy and ideas with all the impetus which had made her one of the leading business-women in Spain before her unfortunate and, in someway self-inflicted, fall from grace.

57

Angela di Silva had never worked harder during the next 12 months when she frequently felt there were not enough hours in each working day to organise the best, most efficient library in the Spanish prison service at Brieavil.

Every one of the 60 inmates, plus the prison guards, including the Governor and office staff, were issued with a borrowers' ticket for the new library accompanied by a letter asking everyone to respect the books they were lent. The letter announced:

"If you deliberately damage a book you are hurting every one of your fellow inmates. The books in your new library belong collectively to everyone in the prison. Remember by borrowing the right technical books you can begin to study a new trade to set you up when you are released from Brieavil Prison. If you cannot see the book, on our shelves, about the work you would like to do in the future, after discharge, tell manager Angela who will try to get it for you. Angela will try to organise instructors and classes in the particular trades that you want to learn. All depending, of course, that there are enough inmates to form a study group."

Angela recalled a conversation she had with her predecessor as library manager, Maria Ruiz, about an habitual criminal and drug addict who desperately wanted to learn to be a welder so that she could go straight for the first time in her life when she was eventually discharged from Brieavil.

The story touched the heart of the kind-hearted Angela who sent a message through the prison grapevine asking the 37-year-old Jenny Barclay, who had spent 15 years of her life behind bars, a to come and see her at the library.

'*Every time I have been released from prison over the years I have found it impossible to get accepted for a straight job, because of my record,*' explained Jenny Barclay.

'*I was only 17 years of age when I became addicted to crack cocaine and was on the road to disaster . I was first imprisoned after fraudulently using stolen credit cards to feed my habit. I am not afraid of hard work and would really like to become a welder like my brother who works in the Barcelona shipyard.*'

Angela, hardened by years of experience in the world's oldest profession, was not an easy touch for a sob story immediately took to Jenny Barclay. Here was a person anxiously trying to put her appalling background aside and set along the road of respectability with honest work. She deserved help and with that in mind Angela contacted the welders' union for advice on what books would further Jenny's ambition to be a welder, and what training qualifications she would need to earn a living in the trade.

Welding became the best subscribed learning subject in the prison. By pointing out to Governor Perelló that it would be in the interest of the prison if a number of trained welders were part of the inmates. Text books on welding were shipped in and a course of twenty prisoners, with expert instructors, was organised twice a week . After six months there were eight qualified welders ready to step up for jobs in Spain's railway system as soon as they were discharged from Brieavil.

Painting and decorating was the next most popular subject for prisoners anxious to take up an honest trade when they were released.

The take-up of books from the ever-increasing library was remarkable and the discussions at the weekly literature club were vibrant, constructive and appreciative.

The new library was a remarkable success and Governor Perelló proudly invited top brass from the nation's prison service to bear witness to the triumph. It let to a more instructive policy of trying to educate hardened criminals during their incarceration. It didn't always succeed but successes far outweighed the failures.

As the second anniversary of Angela's prison sentence drew near it was recognised that she was the architect of a remarkable achievement in the battle to rehabilitate women who previously were considered to be unredeemable old lags.

Angela would look back and conclude that this was the greatest achievement in her colourful life. Greater than building the biggest multi-euro escort agency in Spain.

58

Angela Di Silva had been so engrossed in her job as library manager that , genuinely, she had not given a thought to the fact that she was now eligible for parole under the conditions laid down by the *Ministero en Libertad Condicional.*

Spain's national Probation Department decreed that any prisoner having served more than two thirds of their sentence was entitled to be considered for immediate release, under the parole regulations. In fact it came as a complete shock to Angela when Governor Doña Carmen Perelló summoned her to the office and said: *'If I am completely honest the last thing I want is for you to be released. What you have done for the prison in transforming the prison library and offering a new life within the law for your fellow inmates has been remarkable.*

'But I have to be fair to you Angela, with all the gratitude in my heart for what you have done for all of us at Brieavil, I have recommended that you appear before the local Parole Board when they sit here next week.

'You will face them with my strongest support for the way you have served your time here. Nevertheless I will personally be sad to see you leave the prison.'

* * *

So it was six days later that Angela was escorted into the interview room where the local Parole Board, comprising one male and two female members sat at a table alongside Governor Perelló.

The presiding chairman, Humberto Estherado, addressed Angela in officious tones: *'We have had only glowing reports*

*about your conduct as an inmate and your excellent work
as library manager during your 24 months here at Briavil.
That is why this Board, backed by the recommendation of
the Governor, have decided that you be released on parole in
seven days time. The regulations of parole will apply during
the remaining twelve months of your sentence when you will
be required to report to your local parole officer every week.
We advise you not to get involved again in criminal violence
otherwise the consequences for you will be serious. Good
luck Prisoner X133.'*

The days flew by as steadily as the countdown at a NASA
space launch. The evening before she was due to be released
Angela was totally surprised to be called to the dining hall
where Doña Perelló was waiting to make a presentation.

*'Your fellow prisoners at Briavel have asked me to make
this presentation on their behalf in gratitude for all you have
done in organising the very best library in the entire Spanish
prison service,'* said the Governor unveiling an ornate carved
cabinet. *'They have all contributed from their pocket money
to pay for the special timber that went into this book cabinet
which was designed specially for you and made up by inmates
in the prison carpentry workshop. I hand it over to you Angela
with our thanks and best wishes for your future.'*

* * *

It was an emotional Angela Di Silva who slipped out of the
iron-studded back door of Brieavil Prison for Women at the
crack of dawn the next morning lugging her new cabinet and
a brown paper parcel of personal belongings.

Resisting the temptation to call a taxi, realising that her
dwindling funds would have to last until she found a job,
Angela waited for a bus to take her to the Bario Chino where
she would look for a cheap room to rent.

253

Wiping the tears that rolled down her cheeks she gave herself a stern lecture: *'Look here Senora Di Silva you have just got to stop feeling sorry for yourself. Like it or lump it you are back in the real world. The sooner I get a job and some money coming in the better.'*

*   *   *

After three weeks following her release Angela was starting to feel desperate after being turned down for job after job. She was turned down for humble jobs ranging from washing hair in a local peluquería, kitchen portering in a café and chamber maid in a tourist hotel obviously because of her prison record.

Her need was now urgent. She had less than forty euros left in her kitty and the rent for her cockroach infested room in the Bario Chino was seven euros a week. She had reported to her local parole officer once a week as instructed. But she was now in a panic wondering how she could explain to the parole officer if she was evicted from her room for not being able to pay her rent-small as it was. Proudly she refused to even consider appealing to old friends like Bernardo Sanchez, Jose Eugenio Moralés and Louis Samuels for a loan.

She had to be decisive, a quality that had served her well throughout her working life. She had to earn money-and quickly. Basically, she knew only one way. As the girls on the game always said: *'Once a whore, always a whore!'*

That evening she washed her hair and ironed the one fairly decent dress she had salvaged from what was once one of the finest ladies'wardrobes in Barcelona and stuffed cardboard into the holes appearing in the soles of her red high-heel shoes.

After scraping the remnants from the bottom of her now

exhausted make-up pots she strode off across the bustling Bario Chino towards a familiar corner near the ferry terminal at the end of the Rambla. She thought what a silly sentimental cow she was turning out to be as her eyes misted and smeared her mascara while she began to intone the hooker's time-honoured sales pitch. The lithe figure of a man moved in on her.

'Fancy a good time dearie?' she whispered with the urgency of a predatory bird of prey.

She was shaken out of her maudlin meandering as a familiar voice, a voice from the past, reacted to her plaintive begging-bowl plea

'Now Angela that is not necessary,' he said in a cultured English accent. 'I am not allowing you to go down that road again. Come on Angela we'll take a cab--you are coming home with me.'

She was flabbergasted and could only mutter: 'Richard? Richard Martin is it really you? Oh my God, my star prodigy! The original Senor Gargantuan. When the fuck did you jump out of the woodwork?'

He hailed a passing taxi, and helping her into the back of the cab placed a strong arm around a waist trimmed to pencil slenderness after three poverty stricken weeks of near-starvation diet while she had pounded the cobbles of the Bario Chino searching for honest work.

59

Angela Di Silva trembled from the shock of her totally unexpected meeting with her former protégé, Richard Martin, at the very spot on the Ramblas where she had picked him up soliciting seven years previously and she enrolled him as the first male escort in her new agency.

As the taxi rolled sedately through the traffic across the picturesque city of Barcelona she nervously fired a barrage of questions at the man who she once lewdly pinned the soubriquet "Gargantuan".

'How did you find me?

'Where have you been during the past two years since I have been in prison?

'Are you still working in the sex trade?

'Where are you taking me now Senor Gargantuan?'

The young Englishman laughed loudly: 'Whoa, whoa, there Angela. There will be plenty of time to talk later. But first because the prison authorities only reluctantly give out details of when and what time inmates are released. So I was taken by surprise when I learned you had been discharged just over three weeks ago. Kote Rabtana told me you would be short, very short, of money. So I knew it was important that I found you quickly. During that three weeks I must have trudged over every inch of the Bario Chino and the entire length of the Rambla looking for you.

'It seemed to me that you would find it difficult to find any kind of a job with your prison record. Knowing that you weren't a quitter it was obvious that sooner or later you would *turn to hooking, the business you know so well, to get you out of trouble.*

'But where could I begin my search for you on the streets? So I remembered where you found me soliciting all those years ago. There you were trying to hook a "trick" by the same bollard outside the Lladro ceramic shop in the square near the Balearic Islands Ferry Terminal. Bingo!

'As they say in our trade: Dust to dust, once a whore always a whore, if the 'flu don't get you then the syphilis must.'

Less than 15 minutes later as the taxi rolled into a long driveway, Angela felt the hairs at the back of her neck rising as she recognised the terrain.

When the driver pulled up in front of a massive rise of stone steps, flanked by a pair of sculpted lions, she cried: *'But this is Villa Jacaranda, Richard. This used to be my home!'*

Once again the young Englishman grinned at the practical joke he had just perpetrated. He firmly took her arm and steered her up those twenty stone steps to the imposing carved door where he said, with contagious simplicity and humour: *'All will be revealed later, Angela, darling, as the actress said to the Bishop.'*

60

It was to be a day full of surprises for an emotional Angela Di Silva as she revelled in the familiar surroundings of her once beloved Villa Jacaranda where she had spent an idyllically happy marriage with Klaus before fate had so cruelly intervened in her eventful life.

Richard sat her in her a huge armchair after tugging on a braided bell-pull to signal that he wanted the coffee he had ordered to be served immediately.

A few minutes later Angela reacted enthusiastically when a homely woman arrived wheeling a tea trolley carrying coffee pots, sugar bowl, cream jug, cups, saucers and small plates along with a large platter of chocolate cookies.

'*Carmella, Carmella darling--is it really you?*' was the joyous cry from Angela as she leapt from the cosy confines of her luxury armchair.

'*Yes. Doña Angela it is me,*' said the plump servant giving her former boss an enthusiastic *abrazo*. '*Senor Martin found me in my small apartment near the port and gave me back my old job as housekeeper. It has been lovely working here again in a villa which I always loved, and still do. *'

Angela recovered enough to react, as Richard employing the anglicised cliché of '*Will you be mother?*' invited her to pour the coffee.

As they sipped the steaming beverage and nibbled the biscuits Richard: '*Look Angela I know you are bursting to ask me a lot of questions on how I came to buy your old home. But it is a long story and we have a lot to discuss. I suggest that Carmella takes you up to your old room, which still contains* many of your old dresses and outfits. Have a nice hot bath to relax after the anxiety of being released from prison. Have a refreshing nap on the bed for half an hour. Put on one of your pretty dresses and meet me downstairs for lunch at three o'clock.

'Meanwhile I have got to go into town. Tell me the address of the room you were living in at the Bario Chino. I'll settle up any rent you owe and bring any of your bits and pieces back here.

'After lunch I'll spend the afternoon telling you the whole story. OK Angela?'

61

After one and half hours solid sleep Angela Di Silva awakened feeling fresh and then hurried to the ensuite bathroom for a scalding hot shower.

Housekeeper Carmella brought her in a stone pitcher of ice cold *zumo de naranja* as she helped the former mistress of the house to sort out one or two nice dresses from the over-laden wardrobes that she had last seen two years earlier before she was sent to prison.

Shoes, nearly 100 pairs, some brand new, nearly all hardly worn, were the next to be viewed and selected.

To Angela's delight the vast stock of her favourite cosmetics and perfumes was almost untouched or pristine new in their original pots and jars.

An hour later she descended the villa's winding staircase with the serenity, beauty and regal bearing of Queen Sofia of Spain.

Carmella had prepared a simple but delicious lunch for two. Serano ham cut paper thin topped by wedges of honey-dew melon. Followed by poached wild salmon, thinly sliced Dutch cucumber and tiny baby potatoes from the neighbouring island of Mallorca. It was accompanied by a bottle of fine red Rioja *Gran Reserva*.

*'We will talk in the library,'*said Richard immediately. *'It is a long and weird tale I have to tell you.'*

* * *

'Angela, you will recall that when you first picked me up while I was soliciting in the Rambla I told you that I had

been kicked out of the University of Valencia after the faculty officials found me in bed with a 17-year-old Spanish girl, a fellow student,' Richard began his explanation.

'I desperately didn't want my family in England to know of my disgrace. Not that my father, a vicar, a charitable priest in the Church of England would have refused to stand by me but I definitely did not want to hurt them. You see, without being pompous, I came from a well-bred, almost aristocratic, family of which I learned fragmentally from my parents' conversations in front of me during my childhood.

'It seems my father could trace his family back to the 14th Century and was believed to have descended from Hervey de Stanton, who was Chancellor of the Exchequer for England during the reign of King Edward II. Religion was always forefront in the family for Hervey was the son of Sir William de Staunton, or Stanton, of Staunton , Nottinghamshire.

'Sir William married Athelina, daughter and co-heiress of John de Masters of Bosingham, Lincolnshire. William held the living of Soham, Norfolk, as early as 1289 in the reign of

King Edward I (Longshanks) and afterwards the livings of Thurston and Werbeton, and about 1306 was ordained priest receiving the living of East Derham. In 1300 there was mention of William visiting the Court of Rome.

'There was a trace of noble lineage through my father's family tree for the next eight centuries. But my father the Reverend Oswald Staunton Martin was a humble member of the Church who never boasted of his illustrious ancestors. Father also never bragged about the money that had passed down to him from his past relatives, who included several knights of the realm and a couple of peers. Nor did he flaunt his wealth but it is on record he made several large personal donations towards restoring his own church, St Phillips.

'My mother also brought money into the marriage when they wed in the 1950's for she was the only daughter of Sir Aubrey Cleevewod KC a famous lawyer who defended several notorious murderers, fraudsters and, in a couple of cases, traitors.

'I had to return to England hurriedly two years ago just about the time your escort agency collapsed and I heard the disturbing news that you had been sent to prison. My mother was ill and died eight months later while I stayed to help my father who was also desperately ill.

'Mother left nearly five million pounds in her estate from property she herself had inherited and stocks and shares. I knew my father, who was suffering from pancreatic cancer, would not last long after my mother. They were devoted to each other.

'In fact Dad died 18 months ago and after probate I found that, including the five million pounds my mother passed down to him, that as his only child I had inherited more than

£15 million in property, including the 400 year old vicarage, several antique cars which he collected as a hobby, and a number of extremely valued oil paintings which I had all sold at auction.

'Meanwhile Kote Rabtana, kept me informed how you were doing. Did you know Angela that Kote married one of our clients, Margaret Maitland, and has now passed his final exams to qualify as a psychiatrist in the Spanish health service? He plans to practise in Barcelona.'

Angela acknowledged with a nod of her head that she was aware of Kote's marriage and that she had wished him well him both for that and his intended career in psychiatry.

Richard continued his explanation with a revelation that

took Angela completely by surprise and provided her with fruit for thought.

'So much for where I got the wherewithal to buy this villa,' said Richard. 'Now comes the hardest part for me to explain why I went out and bought your former home lock, stock and barrel.

'Angela I have to confess here and now that very first day when you picked me up in the Rambla years ago I have had the hots for you. But you firmly put me in my place that day when I assumed you had picked me up because you fancied me.

'You made it clear that day that not only were you happily married but that your only interest in me was business and you saw me only as a prospective escort in your agency. I will always be eternally grateful that you paid for me to be groomed as an escort.

'I have to say that all the clients you paired me with added to my experience and were pleasant interludes in the life I was developing. But through the years Angela you were always the woman I hankered for yet while your husband Klaus was alive you were tantalising unattainable.

An unrequited dream.

'When Klaus was so brutally murdered, although it was terrible for you, it opened up the possibility that dreams do sometimes come true. But then you were sent to prison and you must have thought I had forgotten all about you. However, after what I have explained, you understand why it was impossible for me to visit you in prison because I was away in England clearing up my affairs after the deaths of my parents.

'As soon as the probate of my father's will was cleared I

headed back to Barcelona and was delighted when Kote Rabtana told me this villa was up for sale with all its contents.

'I apologise for being presumptuous Angela but I bought this villa in the hope that one day you might move back here one day--as my wife.

'I do not want to hold a pistol to your head Angela. If after careful thought you cannot agree to my proposition I will give you this villa as a gift after your term in prison, and then walk away from you forever. Well there you are Angela I have bared my soul and now its up to you. But I pray you decide to stay as my wife. If so I will give you one million euros, which is half of the money I paid for it. In that case we will be joint owners as a husband and wife should be.'

Angela sat back in her chair eyes closed as she tried to quell the emotion that was surging through her. After several minutes she opened her misty eys and turning towards him said: *'Oh Richard that is the most romantic proposal any man has made to me. You were quite correct while Klaus was alive I would never have been unfaithful to him--and I never was! But ever since I met you in my mind I was always attracted to you. Particularly your body which is why I hung that descriptive epithet of "Gargantuan Gigolo" around your neck. But hold your horses boy. We don't have to rush anything. Let's find out about each other first before we take decisive steps. Enough to say that I am attracted to you and your impressive equipment --what woman wouldn't be?*

'Let's go to bed buster and see what happens.'

Richard Martin' s merriment at Angela's jocular tones was uncontrollable as he asked: *'A good idea . Your room or mine?'*

62

The master bedroom in the imposing Villa Jacaranda on the outskirts of Barcelona is situated at the rear of the building and featured an elegantly tiled terrace, with two luxurious recliners for sun bathing purposes adjoining the elegant *en suite* sleeping unit.

At midnight a full moon glided at funeral pace over the nearby Tibidabo Mountain its reflection creating a shimmering *salchica* shape in the lapping Mediterranean below where tiny gaudily painted fishing boats, illuminated by powerful arc lights mounted on their stern, were chugging off on their nocturnal search for succulent sardines.

Richard Martin and Angela Di Silva did not switch on their terrace lights. Clasping hands as they stretched out naked on adjoining recliners they were absolutely content with the darkness and their own company. Totally absorbed by the wonders of the warm and romantic night around them and despite their vast experience they felt the magic of love beginning to engulf them.

The fourteen year difference between them neither bothered them or even engendered one single negative thought.

As it was they were simply a man and woman on their first date.

When Angela turned towards him the minty flavour of her breath and unbridled passion in her kiss took his breath away. He responded. Their tongues frantically searched each other's mouth with a sensuous urgency.

Without a word hand-in-hand they left the moonlit terrace for the subdued up-lighting of the bedroom and the voluptuous caress of the lilac coloured, and scented, silk sheets. The throbbing in Richard's well muscled groins increased to an almost unsustainable ache. As for Angela she was transported, as if on a magical Arabian carpet, to a period of her life when she was a 16-year-old virgin experiencing first love with a devastatingly *'guapo'* Paraquayan boy called Jimi. A period before life threw her into a world where sex was transformed from undying love to a commodity to be sold on street corners and tinsel -decorated brothels.

Richard'sprobing fingers searched her body eagerly curious to find the secret places. Angela's skin, he was intrigued to discover, was like satin. He had to control his juices in order not to precipitate the supreme pleasure ahead.

Tenderly, oh so gently, he pushed her down on the plump pillows. He eased his body between her wide open legs. In true *caballero* style he took the weight on his elbows so she could barely feel him on top of her. He kissed her again.

A long lingering kiss.

Her cool hands clasped his cheeks reaching rapaciously for more kisses. Her professional knowledge of the mating game came to the fore. She guided his searching mouth towards her hardening nipples. They both had reservoirs of pent-up emotions to deploy.

He moved a thigh, the quad muscles toned by tiring sessions in the *Gimnasio Campeóns,* and eased himself between her legs. She brought her own thighs together moaning with the pleasure that was overcoming her. She arced her back as he thrust into her. She groaned with ecstasy. Even when he came she refused to release him and got her reward again until the storm subsided.

Both of them knew there was an entire night ahead of

them.

'*In fact a whole life,*' she thought decisively.

Spent for the time being, Richard turned over to satiate the need for a recuperative sleep.

But, unashamedly selfish, Angela wound her arms around his waist. Her right hand grasped the wondrous cudgel that she had tagged years before as gargantuan.

She whispered in his ear: '*I think I can fall in love with you Richard Martin!*'

Then, roused from his cat nap, feeling his barbarous baton respond to her groping fingers, Richard smiled like a cat who licked the cream as he heard Angela whisper: '*Don't forget from now on that is all mine*'

Dutifully, like a soldier called to arms, the rampant Gargantuan Gigolo turned towards her again with all the enthusiasm of a sniper with the enemy locked in his rifle sights. That is exactly the way it was. The way it was always going to be for the rest of their lives.

63

The following day Richard Martin hurried to the *Registro Civil* situated in the Plaça Duc Medinaceli to register the wedding which was staged, as Spanish marriage laws required, giving 15 days notice, at the imperious church of *La Sagrada Familia* the unfinished masterpiece by renowned architect Antoni Gaudi.

It was a huge affair with 200 guests. Tobajas Martin gave his mother away. He wore the dress uniform of an officer in the Spanish Air Force. Angela looked stunning in a gorgeous silver gown and matching tiara. Kote Rabtana was Richard's Best Man. Many of Angela di Silva's former escorts were in the congregation, male and female.

It was 20 October 2008. A day when the whole world was quaking with fear about what the effects would be of the global recession which was causing banks on both sides of the Atlantic to collapse.

It was also the day that leading Spanish newspaper, *El Pais,* headline roared:

SEX FOR SALE HIT BY CREDIT CRUNCH

The text underneath read:

"Women working in the world's oldest profession are being hit by the global financial problems.

"Prostitutes in Spain are reporting a drop in trade of up to 40% as the economic downturn affects many parts of the country. It is estimated that 300,000 women work as prostitutes in Spain.

"According to ANELA, the country's National Association

of Brothel Owners, Spaniards spend around 50 million euros a day on prostitutes."

ANELA's Secretary General, lawyer, José Luis Roberto told *El Pais* that he was concerned about the effect on prostitutes' income and added: *'When a brothel whose earnings come from room rentals and drinks had 40% decrease in income , it means that the number of clients has decreased. The girls' income has decreased at the same level and face a crisis.'*

During the speech at her wedding reception Angela made a surprise announcement.

'Now I am once again a married woman my first duty will obviously be to my new husband,' she disclosed. *'But I can tell you now that I have accepted an offer to work as Director for a newly launched Benevolent Fund For Ailing and Ageing Prostitutes who have fell on hard times.'*

The applause that resounded round the room was spontaneous and broke out again when bridegroom Richard jumped to his feet and said: *'I support my wife in everything she is going to do and I am donating 250 thousand euros to her new project. Angela is her name and she is an angel who is proving that she has always had her fellow human beings in her heart.'*

The bride leaned towards her new husband and holding her napkin to her crimson mouth, so as not to be overheard, whispered: *'Thank you my darling Gargantuan cabellero!'*

GLOSSARY SPANISH-ENGLISH

Abogado   lawyer, solicitor

Abrazo   embrace

Aficionados   bullfight supporters

Amadas   female loved ones

Apartmento   apartment

Apartmentos di amor love nests

Arroz con albóndigas rice with meat balls

Azul celeste   sky blue

Banderilla   barbed dart used in bullfight

Banderillo   bullfighter who throws banderilla

Bario Chino   Chinese Quarter

Basura   rubbish, trash

Bata   dressing gown

Besar   to kiss

Beso   a kiss

Buenos Dias   Good Day

Burdels   brothels

Cabelleros   gentlemen

Café con leche   coffee with milk

Camerero   restaurant waiter

Camerero di vino wine waiter

Cava   Champagne style bubbly wine

Chuletas cordero lechal chops from a sucling lamb

Cocina   kitchen

Cocineras   cooks (female) cocnieros (male)

Contables   accountants

Comida   midday meal

Compañero companion

Con ajo   with garlic

Conversación   conversation, talk

Cornada   wound from a bull's horn

Corrida   bull fight

Cosa Nostra   Mafia, Sicillian, Italian, International

Cucarachas   cockroaches

Depósitos de Cádaveres mortuary, morgue

Desayuno   breakfast

Desmadre   chaos

Don   Spanish polite title prefix to men's name

Doña   as above apllied to women

Ducha   shower (as in bathroom)

Ensaladas langoustes lobster salads

Esposa   wives (esposo =husband)

Fábrica   factory

Finca   large house, usually in the country

Gachas   porridge

Gallego   someone born or lives in Galicia

Galletas   biscuits (dulces-sweet or queso-cheese)

Gracias   thank you

Guapo   handsome, good looking

Guerrero   warrior

Hielo   ice, cubes of, for drinks

Hijo de puta   Son of prostitute (insult)

Hola   hello (greeting)

Hornillos   stove or oven

Hombre   man

Huevos Beneidict   Eggs Benedict (muffin, ham, poached eggs & Hollandaise Sauce)

Infamia   disgrace-as applies to an informer

Jefe   chief or head of an organisation

Jerez   sherry, fortified wine made in Jerez de la Frontera

La Huerta   market garden

Lengua   tongue

Lenguado   sole (fish)

Limon mantequilla lemon butter

Los Caracoles   The Snails (world famous restaurant in Barcelona)

Madrileño   native of Madrid [female Madrileña)

Mafioso   member of the Mafia (international)

Medio hecho   medium done (as in ordering steak)

Mi casa es tu casa   my house is your house (polite welcome to a guest)

Móvil   portable appliance as in mobile cell phone

Mozo   youth, young man

Muchacho   boy, lad

Naranja   orange

Océano Pacifico   Pacific Ocean

Omerta   Code of silence adopted by crooks (international)

Para mi   for me

Parrillas   culinary grill

Padre   father

Patrulla Aquila   Spain's air display team similar top RAF's Red Arrows

Patrón   boss, employer

Pelapata   potato peeler

Peluquería   hairdressing salon

Peluquero   male hairdresser/stylist

Perfecto   perfect

Periodistas   journalists

Plaza De Toros   Bullring

Propina   gratuity, tip

Propuesto   proposition

Putas   whores, prostitutes

Querido   dear, darling (term of affection)

Regalo   present, gift

Religosa   nun/monk

Reinado Severo   strict regime (as under General Franco)

Salchica   pork sausage

Segur   follow

Sobre   envelope [as in mail]

Tablao   Flamenco show

Tarde   afternoon

Tauromino   bullfight enthusiasts

Titular   headline (as in newspaper)

Toreros   bullfighters

Tortilla   omelette

Tumbet   cooked mixed vegetables

Usted, Ustedes   "you" polite term singular and plural

Valentón   bull

Valor   courage

Vaso   glass (for drinking)

Zumo de naranja (limon orange juice, lemon juice